The Mennonite Queen

Patrick E. Craig

PUBLISHING

Cover by Cora Graphics Cora Bignardi—www.coragraphics.it

Author photo by William Craig—Craigprographica

This is a work of fiction. Names, characters, places, and incidents are products of the author's imagination or are used fictitiously. Any resemblance to actual persons, living or dead, is entirely coincidental.

The Mennonite Queen

Copyright © 2019 by Patrick E. Craig

Published by P&J Publishing

P.O. Box 73

Huston, Idaho 83630

Library of Congress Cataloging-in-publications Data

Craig, Patrick E., 1947-

The Mennonite Queen / Patrick E. Craig

ISBN 978-1-7323224-0-0 (pbk.)

ISBN 978-1-7323224-7-9 (eBook)

Printed in the United States of America

CONTENTS

DEDICATION

The Mennonite Queen is dedicated to my grandchildren: may you learn from the stories of your family, may you cling to the thread that runs from the known past into an unknown future...

ACKNOWLEDGMENTS

To my wife, Judy, for her tireless proofing and editing work on this book, and her prayers on its behalf.

To Becky Carey Lyles, for the excellent and challenging editing job she did on The Mennonite Queen.

To Jenny Springer Hershberger, who has risen out of the pages of my first six books and taken her place in my heart forever.

A NOTE FROM PATRICK E. CRAIG

THOSE OF YOU WHO FOLLOWED *The Apple Creek Dreams* series and the first two books of *The Paradise Chronicles* know Jenny Hershberger. Throughout both series I used a literary device where Jenny was the "author," thus many of my readers assumed Jenny was a real person who wrote the stories. Jenny, an Amish woman whose church frowned upon adherents gaining notoriety in the secular world, gave me the manuscripts to rewrite and publish under my name.

To a large degree, the device worked. A friend of mine told her mother, who read *Jenny's Choice* I would be interested in knowing what she thought of the novel. "Why?" her mother asked. "He didn't write it."

By the time I finished *The Amish Princess*, Jenny had assumed a life of her own, and she became as real to readers as she is to me. So now, in *The Mennonite Queen*, I have Jenny take us back to the Hershberger family's early European roots. I surrounded the fictional characters of this tale with real people and places from the 1500s—people like Isabella Jagiellon, the Hungarian queen who issued the first religious tolerance edict.

In this fictional account, she is the matriarch of the Hershberger family. Franz von Waldeck, the historical Bishop of Münster, Germany, and Jan Bockelson, the self-proclaimed king who led the Anabaptist rebels into a terrible defeat at Münster, also play a central part in *The Mennonite Queen*.

We fiction writers take a lot of liberty with our stories. Though this narrative uses real characters to relate a fictional tale who knows? The events may have happened as written... but you must ask Jenny—she knows.

PART I
ISABELLA—THE PRINCESS

ISABELLA JAGIELLON OF POLAND was born in 1519. She married John Zápolya, king of Hungary, in 1539. But before that marriage, three years are missing from most history books: the years when Isabella and Johan Hirschberg, one of the first Hershbergers, lived together as man and wife. This book tells that story.

When he was an old man, Johan's son, Abel, with the help of his brother, John Sigismund Zápolya, chronicled the events, and their manuscript passed from generation to generation in my family for four hundred years. More recently, my mother's grandmother, Hannah, gave the book to my mother, Jerusha, and I received it from her. Although the document was brittle and worn, and in some places nearly illegible, I used it to research and write the story of The Mennonite Queen, our family's matriarch.

"Isabella"
From The Journals of Jenny Hershberger

PROLOGUE

1559— SIC FATA VOLUNT, THE WILL OF FATE

*T*he woman groaned and turned on the couch, awakened by a patter of rain rattling the windows. Outside, dark heralds of the unseasonal storm hid the moon. Distant lightning illuminated the room. An unearthly light touched her face momentarily and then faded as the gray predawn took victory over the indigo night. A long roll of thunder shook the window again, and she pulled her shawl tighter, a frown furrowing her brow.

I must tell him... before I go...

Queen Isabella of Hungary focused her eyes on the candle sputtering in the persistent draft that plagued the building. The flickering light illuminated Filippo Lippi's painting above the fireplace, *Madonna and Child Enthroned.*

Mary held the Christ-child, the love in her eyes captured perfectly by the artist. Jesus's tiny hands clutched his mother's robe, but he was not happy, nor was he comforted. Isabella could imagine his little mouth quivering—as though someone unseen was preparing to tear him from his mother's arms.

Isabella blinked back tears.

Ah, my Abel, my son... where are you tonight?

3

The fire in the small stone fireplace had burned down, and the still-flickering coals cast dancing shadows. The mantle's lone occupant, a golden crucifix, glowed in the flickering light from the embers—like the flames on Münster's tower the night they escaped...

She sighed and turned away. The edict lay on the floor where it had fallen when she fell asleep. She reached down to retrieve it and a sharp pain shot through her arm. She groaned and picked up the document.

The door creaked open and her personal servant, Angyalka, entered the room. The diminutive young girl carried a tray with a cup, a small biscuit, butter, and a teapot. She set the food on the desk and hurried to the queen's side

"Your Majesty, you did not go to bed last night. I looked in your bedchamber, but you were not there."

"No, dear." She sighed. "I was reading the edict of toleration, and I fell asleep. I remember wondering if it has done any good toward dispelling the antagonism between religions and then the storm woke me and I was still on the couch."

"It has done much good. I'm sure of it." Angyalka knelt beside her queen. "You must take better care of yourself, Your Majesty. You need more rest, and you hardly eat anymore. I worry. You are not well."

Isabella brushed a stray lock of blonde hair from Angyalka's cheek. "You dear girl, always with my best interests in your heart." She pulled the girl close.

Angyalka returned the embrace. "It is because you are so kind, Your Majesty."

Isabella kissed the girl's forehead. She rose off the couch and made her way to the desk, the document in hand. Angyalka held her elbow, steadying her.

Isabella did her best to stand tall, but she had to admit the girl was right. Her strength was fading, and she often fell asleep in the midst of a task, so she lowered herself into the chair, the familiar aches and pains making themselves known once more, and spread the document before her. The sharp pain in her arm came again, but she ignored it. Her thoughts were far away.

Ah, so many days since Münster, my dearest Johan...

Angyalka hovered by her side, her hands twisting together. Isabella noticed her maid's distress. "I am fine, dear girl. Do not worry about me." Isabella indicated the tray. "Would you spread my biscuit with a bit of our wonderful Transylvania butter and pour a half cup of tea? That will give me strength for the morning. And if you'll please hand me Menno's book, I will read while I eat my breakfast."

The girl prepared the simple meal and fetched the requested tome from the bookshelf. She handed it to the queen, bowed and withdrew.

Isabella opened the worn copy, found her bookmark and turned to her favorite passage.

And this is the voice of Christ, "Ye have heard it hath been said, An eye for an eye, and a tooth for a tooth. But I say unto you, that ye resist not evil, but whosoever shall smite thee on thy right cheek, turn to him the other."

Staring into the embers, Isabella sipped her tea, seeing Menno Simons as she'd known him so many years earlier. His soft voice and gentle words of peace and nonviolence still echoed in her heart and soothed her soul. She could imagine him teaching the Anabaptists by the light of a different fire, a Frisian fire. She heard again the words that had captivated her heart.

Our weapons are not swords and spears, but patience, silence and hope, and the word of God. With these, we must maintain our cause and defend it. The Apostle Paul wrote, "The weapons of our warfare are not carnal, but mighty through God." With these, we intend and desire to resist the kingdom of the devil; not with swords, spears, cannons, and coats of mail.

The door opened, and Angyalka peeked around it. "Dr. Bian-

5

drata has arrived, Your Majesty. May he come in?" Isabella nodded, and Angyalka opened the door.

Isabella beckoned for the doctor to enter.

His stern face broke into a smile as he approached. "Ah, you look much better today, Your Majesty. The tonics I gave you are working."

"Yes, Giorgio, but they are bitter to the palate. When I am drinking them, I often consider death a better option."

The doctor chuckled. "Still have your sense of humor, I see."

She looked up at her physician and teacher. "I am not afraid to die, Giorgio." She chuckled. "Ah, don't look so shocked, my old friend. I know I am ill, and I know the end is coming soon. But I have my faith... and my memories. And you have taught me much about God and the ways of men, rich treasures locked forever in my heart."

The doctor bowed. "Your Majesty honors me, but my small ideas—"

"And where did I learn to welcome diversity, to tolerate differences of belief?" The queen opened Menno's book. "God has blessed me to sit at the feet of wise men like you, men who taught me the true meaning of our Lord's words." Isabella leaned forward in her chair.

"My life has been filled with religious turmoil. Luther's Protestant Reformation burst upon Europe at the time of my birth. The peasants revolted against religious intolerance in Germany and were brutally suppressed. And then the Catholics wiped out the Anabaptists at Münster—only a few escaped the sword and the flames—when I was sixteen-years-old. Catholics hate Lutherans, Unitarians hate everyone and Anabaptists are burned alive. But I was blind to the hatred and persecution. Men like you taught me to respect an individual's right to decide how best to practice their faith." She fell back and closed her eyes.

"I must rest again, Giorgio."

"Yes, Your Majesty, you must." He took her hand and helped her to the couch. Then he eased toward the door. "I will call again tomorrow."

"You are like an old mother hen, Giorgio, always cackling and safeguarding her chicks. But I do not need protection from death, for it only means I shall be with Him, forever."

ISABELLA TOSSED ON HER BED, in the grip of a dream. Shouts and screams reverberated off the burning buildings that surrounded her. She was running, running from the heat, running from the chaos, terrified of the soldiers, who were everywhere. The gates of the city rose in front of her but before she could get out they swung open, and a fat man in the robes of a Catholic priest rode in, mounted on a white horse. She screamed...

And then Johan was with her. His powerful arms wrapped around her, infusing her with his strength.

"Come, my love," he murmured. "This way."

Together they ran. Isabella was holding a small child whose tiny arms clung to her, and then she saw a small, unguarded door in the wall.

"Through here, my dearest," he whispered.

His strong hands guided her through the gate. Behind them, a hoarse voice shouted, "Find them, find them now! Kill him and bring her to me, alive."

Together they hurried along toward the river. Johan's powerful hands guided her, kept her on her feet and strengthened her, but she could not see the path.

"This way, Isabella. Lift your feet, run like the wind. I am with you, I am always with you..."

Isabella awoke, sobbing and curled in a fetal position, like every time she dreamed of Johan.

PROPPED WITH PILLOWS, Isabella lay in her bed, her breathing shallow, her body wracked with pain. Her dark hair was spread around her head like a halo. Beside the bed, her grim-faced doctor stood watching. Angyalka sat in a small chair next to the bed, weeping.

Isabella's eyes fluttered open. "Ah, my friends... here to bid me farewell?"

She heard Angyalka burst into a fresh paroxysm of weeping.

The doctor leaned down and placed a damp cloth on her forehead.

Isabella reached up and took the doctor's hand. "Has my son, John, returned?"

"A messenger came this morning." He gently returned her hand to her side. "John is hastening home. He is sorry for the delay, but Suleiman..."

"Yes, yes. Suleiman..." She closed her eyes. "I will wait for John."

THE NEXT TIME ISABELLA AWAKENED, a beloved face was bending over her, the eyes sad, the mouth knit in a frown. "Ah, my son." She smiled. "Away so long."

"Only a month, mother. You know how Suleiman is. We must attend to his wishes first. But without him, Ferdinand and the Hapsburgs would take Hungary."

"Sit, John, and listen." Isabella took her son's hand. "I have something important to tell you before I depart this earth."

"You are not going anywhere, mother. You will live and get well."

She lifted an eyebrow. "We never lie to each other, John."

"No, Mother."

"Let's not begin now. I am dying. That is a truth we both know. But before I go, I must tell you the one thing I have held from you." She motioned to him. "Sit here by me."

John sat. "What is it, Mother?"

Isabella pushed higher on the pillows. "John Sigismund Zápolya, son of the king of Hungary and protector of Transylvania, you are my only heir." She closed her eyes and then slowly opened them. "But you are not my only son."

"Not your only son?" John's eyes widened. "But, Mother, how can that be?"

I name "My first son, your older brother, is named Abel. I have not seen him since I was a seventeen-year-old. He was the son of my first husband, Johan Hirschberg."

John stared at his mother, mouth agape. "But, how... when?"

Isabella smiled. "If you will bear it, I will tell you the story..." She stopped for a moment, smiling at the sweet memory. "Long ago, when I was a young girl living at Wawel Castle in Poland..."

CHAPTER 1: WEBS OF POWER

1519

*H*igh on the ancient ramparts of Wawel Castle, red banners adorned with white eagles snapped in the crisp March breeze. The massing gray clouds veiled the winter sun, and the biting wind heralded another rainstorm. King Sigismund I of Poland surveyed the magnificent building around him. The massive stone walls spoke a silent reminder that his ancestors had lived on this hill for centuries. From his vantage point on the colonnaded balcony, the city of Krakow spread like a jeweled necklace across both banks of the Vistula River. In the courtyard below, men from all over Europe worked at renovating the ancient stronghold.

In the distance, someone was swearing loudly in Italian.

Sigismund made his way down the ornate stairway and through the bustling crowds of workmen to where his chapel was taking shape. The workers bowed, but he passed by without acknowledging them. The smell of pine logs freshly cut in the forests above Niepolomice mixed with the stinging odor of hot tar bubbling in pots assailed the king's nostrils. A cacophony of sounds—hammering, shouting, and the creaking of hoists—filled the air, but it was all music to Sigismund's ears. At last, he came to the site of his latest project. He stood admiring it, imagining the holy masses that the priests would hold inside and the sweet music of the choir resounding within its beautiful walls.

Ah, my beautiful chapel!

The completed foundation stood, but nothing had been added since Sigismund's last visit. Hands on his hips, the Italian architect, Bartolommeo Berrecci, surveyed the piles of huge stones and thick beams. Workmen leaned on their tools smiling while Berrecci berated a tradesman who argued back in Italian. Berrecci shook his finger at a pile of stone.

"What shall I do with this *giunca*? I can't use these ugly rocks to build the greatest chapel in Europe. Take them back! Take them back!"

The tradesman, his face growing redder each moment, signaled to Berrecci, who turned and saw Sigismund. Both men bowed. The king put his hands on the men's shoulders.

"What is the problem, Master Bartolommeo?" Berrecci, he knew, was an impatient man with a quick temper.

Berrecci moved away and kicked at one of the pieces of stone. The marble broke into two sections. "Your Majesty, this *scemo* tries to pass off this *spazzatura* as decent stone for your chapel." The Italian's hands moved in elegant choreography with his words. "The material is crisscrossed with hairline fractures. It will disintegrate within ten years. I cannot use this, Your Majesty."

"*Scemo*, is it? Why you!" The tradesman stepped toward Bartolommeo, fists raised. "Keep it up, and I'll knock your head off, you little *ratto*."

Laughing, Sigismund stepped between them. He turned to the tradesman. "Why did you deliver inferior stone?"

"It is not my fault, Your Majesty." The man clutched his chest. "I received this delivery and tried to tell Berrecci that it was not up to his standard. But he was in such a hurry, he ordered me to bring it. Another delivery is coming next month

—perfect stone cut from the heart of the mountains, but this one, he is so *impaziente*! He demanded the stone, and now we are in this *conflitto*."

"Return the stone." The king lifted a finger. "I will make sure they pay you for hauling it. And, Master Berrecci..." He put his arm around the Italian's shoulder. "You can do something else until the new stone arrives."

Berrecci blew out a long breath. "Yes, Your Majesty. I must finish the galleries. I will wait."

Sigismund whispered in Berecci's ear. "Before he leaves, perhaps you should tell him exactly what you want once more, just to make sure he understands."

Berrecci turned to the tradesman. "You—I want marble of the highest quality—stone that will stand for a thousand years."

The tradesman bowed low. "Yes, Master Berrecci, I swear it will be the finest stone you have ever seen."

"Good, you may go."

Sigismund smiled again as Berrecci dismissed the tradesman with a lifted hand.

"And you!" Berrecci said, addressing the workmen who had been watching the interchange, "Get back to work."

The tradesman called his helpers, and they reloaded the carts while the other workmen hurried about their tasks.

Walking with Berrecci among the materials stacked below the high wall to which the chapel foundation was attached, King Sigismund said, "Tell me again, Master Berrecci, of your plan."

Berrecci led the king to the spot where the excavation had begun. "I will build a square base of heavy stone on this spot and set the panels in the stone. Among them will be the mighty crowned eagle of Poland. On top will be a golden dome with eight windows set in deep bays. Although I will design much of the interior, I have commissioned Sebastian Tauerbach and Hans the woodcarver to build the wooden ceilings and decorate the walls with friezes and royal portraits. This," Berrecci said, beaming with pride, "will be the finest chapel in all Christendom, Your Majesty."

At that moment Sigismund heard someone call from across the courtyard. He turned to see a page running toward him. The boy bowed and dropped to one knee before the king. "Your Majesty, Queen Bona requests you come as soon as you can. The French envoys have arrived a day earlier than expected."

Sigismund nodded. "I must go, Signor Berrecci. Matters of state call me. I am gratified by the brilliant work you have accomplished so far, and I await my chapel's completion with great expectancy."

Berrecci bowed. "Your Majesty honors me. I will use every bit of the God-given talent the Creator has given me in this work, to the glory of God... and Poland."

WHEN SIGISMUND ENTERED the envoy room, he found his young wife, Bona Sforza talking with the French ambassador and his companion. She was pointing out features of the elaborate frieze decorating the wall. At his arrival, the two men turned and bowed.

"A magnificent frieze, Your Majesty," said the older of the two.

Sigismund nodded. "Yes, it is called 'The story of human life' and is an illustration of the Greek text *Tabula Cebetis*." He pointed to the ceiling coffer. "Above us are the sculptures that Sebastian Tauerbach just completed."

The younger man nodded his head. "Marvelous, Your Majesty, wonderful."

"Ah, Monsieur de Lengeac," Sigismund smiled at the youthful man with the white wig. "I am honored King Francis sends an envoy of such stature—one so young yet so skilled in the arts of diplomacy that your king trusts you with this mission."

"God's gifts have brought me this post, Your Majesty." Lengeac ducked his head.

"But, Monsieur, you are so young..."

Lengeac drew to his full height. "I am twenty-three, Your Majesty." He turned to the dignified man standing beside him. "May I introduce Chevalier Pierre Du Terrail Bayard, one of our finest soldiers and a hero of France. He has been my protector and guided me throughout the difficult journey from Paris."

The chevalier bowed.

Sigismund glanced from one man to the other. "Your reputation precedes you, Chevalier. As I understand it, you served in the Italian Expedition of Louis XII 1499. Then you distinguished yourself in the combat of French and Spanish knights at Barletta 1503, were wounded at the siege of Brescia, and taken prisoner at the Battle of Spurs. A valiant and distinguished career."

The knight's eyes widened with surprise. "Your Majesty honors me. I am but a simple soldier." He bowed again.

"No, Chevalier, we know your reputation even here in Krakow, and it honors us that King Francis sent two such men as envoys. I can see he considers this mission of great importance." Sigismund nodded to a servant standing against the wall. "Show these men and their party to the quarters we have prepared for them."

He took Lengeac by the hand. "You must rest from your long journey. We were expecting you tomorrow and have already eaten. I will have my servants deliver food and drink to your quarters. Tomorrow, we will discuss the matter of Isabella over breakfast, and then we wish to honor you with a state banquet in the evening."

The two men bowed and left. Sigismund turned to his wife. "Ah, my dear, Francis is eager to win our support for his election as Holy Roman Emperor. He will offer his son as a match for our little Isabella. But you know I set my mind on Charles of Spain to be the emperor. These men will need to be very skillful negotiators to convince me otherwise."

"You must let them convince you, Sigismund." Bona shook her head. "You know one day I hope to install Isabella and her husband as the rulers of the Duchy of Milan, my home and my inheritance. A lesser son of the French king would be the perfect ruler as long as there was a Sforza at his side."

"Yes, Bona, Milan and your family's role there is always in your thoughts. But in the great scheme of things..."

Bona's eyes flashed. "A marriage alliance with France will bring our family back to power. We must do everything we can to see my country returned to greatness."

"But, my dear, in your concern for the tiny Duchy of Milan, you do not grasp the totality of the problems that confront Poland. That heretic, Luther, challenges the Catholic Church daily. The masses are rising, and the Catholic nations tremble in the face of this so-called reformation. Poland must remain Catholic, and to do that she must be aligned with other powerful Catholics such as the Hapsburgs or the Spanish king."

"But France is Catholic..."

A glance from Sigismund silenced Bona. "France is a minor player in the affairs of middle Europe. Our daughter came at a propitious time. Around us, great political turmoil rattles all of Europe. Nations are changing, rulers are rising and falling, heretics challenge our great religion. As the rulers of Poland, our divine mission is to guarantee that Poland remains free and strong and Catholic forever. Our daughter may play a role in that preservation. She is a trump card we cannot waste on the Duchy of Milan."

"But, Sigismund, she is only a baby. Surely she cannot be that important to your plans for Poland? Especially when Milan is at stake..."

Now Sigismund's eyes flashed. "Enough of Milan! Isabella is a baby, yes, but as you see by the men Francis has sent to negotiate on his son's behalf, she is a baby who may hold the future of nations in her tiny hands. We cannot use her unwisely."

LATE THAT NIGHT, the storm that had been threatening all day broke above the castle walls. The wind howled, rain poured from the leaden sky and lightning lit the frothing river. Thunder crashed ominously amid the roiling heavens. Alerted by a tiny voice crying in the night, a nurse scurried toward the royal nursery, a solitary candle in her hand. Grieved by the child's frightened visage, the nurse bent to take the baby in her comforting arms.

"Ah, my little Bella, not happy with the storm?"

The baby's tiny hands clutched at the nurse, and her frightened cries soon subsided into soft cooing.

"You will have storms in your life, my little one," the nurse whispered. "And I will not be able to protect you. You must grow strong in your spirit and learn to bear what comes.

CHAPTER 2: A QUEEN IN WAITING

1529

*I*sabella rifled through her wardrobe, searching for suitable clothes for the journey. She listened impatiently while her maid chided her. "Be sure to take your hunting clothes, Isabella. You will be in the woods often while you are at Niepolomice."

Outside her apartment, Isabella could hear the angry shouting of her younger sister Anna, who was pitching another of her temper tantrums.

She turned to the servant hovering behind her. "Maria, why is Anna always grouchy?"

Maria, a comely girl of eighteen, shrugged her shoulders. "You are your mother's favorite. She does not care for your three sisters. I do not understand why. You go with Queen Bona on her trips, and she leaves the others behind."

"But why me, Maria?"

"You are the oldest child. Despite what your father wants, your mother has always hoped that someday you will be the ruler of Milan, and her family will return to power. So she is looking for a suitable match for you. When you were only five years old, she went behind your father's back and promised you to Henry, the son of King Francis of France. Your father was furious when he found out and canceled those plans in no uncertain terms."

"I don't want to be a queen of anything. My mother may dwell on our high station in life, but I wish my life were simpler."

"Isabella, you should not talk that way. Maybe you prefer to be a peasant, eking out a living on an impoverished farm with an ignorant sweaty husband and a passel of children who are always hungry. No, Isabella, life destines you for greatness. You will be a queen. Now, hurry and finish choosing your clothes. You will be late for your lessons. Now I must see to your trunks."

Maria finished folding clothes Isabella had already chosen and then hurried from the room.

Isabella sighed and went to the window. *Maria makes it sound so terrible, but I don't see what is wrong with a simple life, to marry a farmer or a tradesman. Then I'd never have to learn Latin.*

Across the busy courtyard stood the finished chapel, her father's most significant contribution to the castle's renovation. The golden dome gleamed in the sunlight.

A knock on the door was followed by, "Isabella, are you there?"

"Yes, *Tata*."

Sigismund entered the room, and Isabella ran to embrace him. Isabella loved her father. He was a kind man. "What is it, *Tata*?"

Sigismund stepped back and looked at his ten-year-old daughter. "I want to talk to you before you leave for Niepolomice."

"Why must I go? We returned from Lithuania only two days ago. I want to be home with you."

"Your mother..." Sigismund shook his head. "She has too

much fire. Bona should have been a man so she could fight duels and command armies. I can never make her sit still."

Isabella tilted her head. "Are you here to discuss my eventual marriage, *Tata?*"

Sigismund's eyes twinkled as he nodded. "Ah, my wise little *córka*. Yes, your marriage."

"But why must I marry? I want to learn more and discover things, well... some things. I hate Latin."

Sigismund laughed and motioned for her to sit on the couch, and then he sat beside her. "It is difficult to be a king in these times, Isabella. To the west is the powerful Hapsburg family; to the east are Suleiman and his Ottoman Turks. They both wish to rule Hungary and Poland. In the meantime, I have your mother to deal with. She tried to marry you to the king of France's son when you were only five years old. She saw the folly of her ways when the Italians captured King Francis of France in war."

Isabella moved closer to her father. "Are you sure you did not have a hand in keeping me from marrying the French prince, Tata?"

Sigismund laughed out loud. "Well, maybe just a little. Your mother sometimes thinks she is my king. I desired a Hapsburg marriage for you to guarantee our security in the changing Europe that is coming. I felt it best to align with those who will someday rule Europe. But I now see they only wish to supplant me, to put a Hapsburg on the throne of Poland."

"So then who am I to marry, Tata? And what about my sisters? They can marry someone too."

Sigismund's face grew serious. "I am negotiating with John Zápolya, the king of Hungary. You would make him a good wife, and it would unite our two countries."

"Wouldn't it also keep the Hapsburgs away?"

Sigismund shook his head. "For someone so young..."

"Mother talks about these things to her servants, and I listen."

"It would not be for a while Isabella, but I wanted to let you know what I am thinking. As for your sisters, well, I have plans for them." He rubbed his forehead. "All these negotiations sometimes make my head hurt. The twists and turns are hard for me to follow."

Isabella snuggled under her father's arm. "That's not true, *Tata*. You see everything that goes on around you."

"That may be true, little one, but so do you. When I tell you of these things, you always understand. Now run along to your classes."

Isabella wiggled closer. "Oh, *Tata,* must I? All Janos talks about is Latin, and Pieter discusses nothing but the end of the world day after day. Can't I stay here? I learn so much more when I am with you."

Isabella gave her father a petulant look. Sigismund stood and shook his head. "You received your blue eyes from me, but you inherited your stubborn nature from your mother. Now, do as I say. You will need your education one day."

"ISABELLA! PAY ATTENTION!"

Isabella pulled her thoughts back to the classroom. "I am sorry, Master Pieter." She felt a flush rising in her face.

"What did I say?"

"When, Master Pieter?"

Pieter shook his head and sighed. "You must remember what I teach, child. As a Christian in a world soon at an end, your responsibility will be to aid God when He ushers in a new era of history."

"Please describe this new era, Master Pieter."

"Now I must give you extra work, Princess. You did not listen today."

"But what do you say about the new era, Master? Will it be good?"

"God will restore the world with the help of true Christians. A new age of mankind will emerge."

"Please, tell me more."

Isabella watched as Pieter placed the Bible that he was holding on the desk. He was frowning. "In this kingdom, people hold everything in common and distribute everything according to need. The common people hold power, and no lords will rule over them."

"You are fortunate that you are my favorite tutor, Master Pieter. For if my father heard you are teaching these things, you might lose your head."

Her tutor turned white and then red. "Ah... I misspoke myself, Princess. Shall we return to our study of mathematics?"

Isabella tried to smile, but his words troubled her heart.

I'd sooner be a commoner. A strong husband, several stout children...

"Isabella! Mathematics book, please."

ON ANOTHER DAY, Isabella was lost in thought when she heard Pieter approaching. She flushed with impatience and quickly opened her reader.

"Too much religion today, Princess, my recalcitrant protégé?" Master Pieter looked over his nose at her.

"No, it's not that." Isabella shook her head. "I am deciding what I will be."

"What do you mean?"

"I mean, am I a Catholic, a Protestant, a Unitarian, or a Muslim? Or should I enter Yeshiva and become a Jew?"

Isabella saw the shocked look on her teacher's face and chuckled.

"But you are a Catholic," he insisted. "You were born a Catholic, you will die a Catholic."

"Isn't that something I should decide?"

"Your parents baptized you into the Catholic Church when you were a baby. Just as the tiger, you can't change your stripes now."

"But that's the problem, Master Pieter. I didn't get to choose. My mother dressed me up in fancy baby clothes and took me to the priest and, voilá, I'm a Catholic. They should have waited for baptism until I could decide for myself."

"Ah! Maybe you will be an Anabaptist."

"What's an Anabaptist?"

"The Anabaptists are a sect that believes infant baptism is wrong. Also, Anabaptists teach that the way back to the church after they excommunicate someone is repentance and rejection of sin."

"You mean just be repentant instead of paying the priest and crawling around the church on your hands and knees in sackcloth and ashes?"

"Correct."

"I am intrigued by these Anabaptists, Master Pieter. What else do they teach?"

"They say the church, although made of many individuals, is the bride of Christ and that she should prepare herself for the Lord's return as a bride prepares herself for her bridegroom."

"Oh, I love that. Tell me, Master Pieter—how is it you understand these Anabaptists so well?"

He waved aside her question. "Forget the Anabaptists. If you want to change your religion, become a Christian humanist."

"What's a Christian humanist?"

"They teach the human side of Jesus and that we can be good speakers and teachers like he was. They want to create people who will engage in the civic life of their communities and guide others in a virtuous and prudent life."

"But Jesus was more than human."

"Isabella," Pieter said, "we are far off the track. I want you to study Christian Humanism, a philosophy that entails the best of human living. The Anabaptists are far outside the teachings of the church and the humanists."

"But doesn't religion include spiritual living? From what you say, it seems the Anabaptists are looking to discover both the practical and the spiritual side."

A flush mounted from the teacher's neck to his face.

"Never mind, Master Pieter." Isabella lowered her head. "I will study what you ask."

But I want to study the Anabaptists.

CHAPTER 3: THE PLAN

1531

*I*sabella stared out the window of her room. Outside, the rising sun painted the clouds a brilliant orange. Shades of rose and purple dissolved into sapphire as morning dawned. The glory of the heavens did nothing to ease Isabella's grouchy mood.

Men only think of war and marriage.

"Isabella!" Her mother marched into the room. "Why are you not ready to be presented to King John's emissary?"

"I am only thirteen-years-old, Mama. I am not old enough to marry anyone."

"You have a place in history, Isabella, a responsibility." Bona Sforza's tone was cold. "The Hapsburgs press us from Austria. Your father thinks they are our friends, but they are not. They want more land and more power. If they have their way, Poland will join Greece and Rome—just another fallen empire. John Zápolya is a strong wall between the Austrians and Poland. Charles and his brother, Archduke Ferdinand, control half of Hungary, and they look to rule Poland next. We must align ourselves with Zápolya."

Isabella crossed her eyes and put her hands over her ears.

"These things make me very irritated, Mama. Kings and kingdoms may occupy your every waking moment, but I couldn't care less." Isabella turned back to the window. "Isabella!" Her mother stomped her foot. "You will follow my wishes. I am your mother and your queen. I will tolerate no resistance in this matter. Now, get dressed!"

Bona stormed out of the room. As Isabella finished getting dressed, she heard the queen in the hallway berating Maria for not having Isabella ready. Isabella put her hands on her hips and stuck out her tongue, her only means of defying her strong-willed mother.

The young maid entered. She stared at Isabella's extended tongue for a moment and then giggled, her hand over her mouth. Isabella giggled, too. Soon, both girls were convulsed with laughter.

"Isabella!" Her mother's voice cut through their laughter. The girls composed themselves, avoiding eye contact lest mirth overtake them again, and set about to make Isabella presentable for the Hungarian ambassador.

∼

"ISABELLA, may I present King John Zápolya's ambassador, Stephen Bathory. He will arrange the wedding between you and the king of Hungary. It is a great honor for he is Vavoldé of Transylvania himself."

Bathory had dressed in a silk jacket adorned with white fur and overlaid by a flowing red robe. A black hat sat atop his head, and black silk trousers stuffed into leather boots completed his outfit.

Bona remained beside Isabella, her hand on Isabella's shoulder. The princess nodded and then stood still, hands at her side, trying to avoid laughing.

He is an altogether ridiculous figure of a man.

"I am honored to meet such a lovely girl." Bathory gave Isabella a mincing bow. "King John is eagerly looking forward to this marriage. An alliance between the great countries of Poland and Free Hungary will be most profitable."

"Your Eminence..." Isabella lifted her chin. "I am not knowledgeable about these things, for I am only thirteen years of age." She felt her mother's hand squeeze her shoulder.

"Hmm..." The ambassador frowned. "I must say a slight age disparity exists. I was not aware of this."

Isabella smiled. "How old is the king, Your Eminence?"

"He is forty-five, Princess."

"Forty-five?" Isabella's nose wrinkled.

Bona's fingers dug into her shoulder, and Isabella managed a smile. "I am glad he is such a renowned personage. He must have accomplished many things in his long life."

The ambassador returned her smile. He looked Isabella over and waved his hand dismissively. "Well, after all, the discrepancy in ages is of little matter. You are a lovely girl, and the two of you will make a handsome couple. John is a great king, a warrior. He has kept the Turks from conquering Europe."

Isabella looked straight into his eyes. "But he is a vassal to Suleiman."

The ambassador's mouth tightened while Bona's fingers dug even deeper into Isabella's shoulder.

"And why are we discussing affairs of state with a thirteen-year-old girl?"

From behind them, Sigismund's hearty laugh broke the sudden chill in the room. "I'm sorry I am late, wife, but I seem to have arrived just in time." He put his hand on Bathory's shoulder. "I warned you, Ambassador. My daughter, Isabella, is not your typical young girl. Her teachers are the greatest in Europe, and she speaks four languages. The king of Hungary will have his hands full." Sigismund grew serious. "A marriage of state between Eastern Hungary and Poland will change everything in Europe." The two men exchanged a knowing glance.

"Come, Your Eminence, let us go to lunch. I must show you the Governor's Parlor." Sigismund took the ambassador's arm, and the two men walked away, deep in conversation.

"Daughter!" Bona spun Isabella around and held her by both shoulders. "You must control your tongue. Your little rejoinder was not diplomatic. You did not endear yourself to the ambassador."

"But, Mother, the king of Hungary is thirty-two years older than I am. He will be more of a grandfather to our children than a father. I do not want this."

"Do you think what you want matters, Isabella?"

"But I want to marry for love. I want..."

"For love?" Bona laughed out loud. "Who taught you that?"

"No one, Mother. Johannes teaches me Latin and cosmology and lets me help him create a map of Hungary. Pieter teaches me of spiritual matters. But they do not teach me of love."

"Who teaches you of such things?"

"My heart, Mother, my heart."

"Your heart? Faugh! You need not love John Zápolya to give him heirs, Isabella. And those heirs will extend the Jagiellon line. Now go and prepare for the state dinner."

Isabella turned to leave.

"And Isabella…"

Isabella turned back to her mother.

"Never let me hear about what your heart wants again."

ISABELLA SAT on the couch in her room. The day had turned gloomy, matching her frame of mind. It reminded her of a morning during her recent stay in Vilnius. She had gone out alone. It was a chilly day, and she followed a path that wandered through the snow blanketing the hills of Lithuania.

As she walked, two young girls had hurried past her. They carried bundles of sticks and laughed as they went along their way. They wore long muslin dresses, warm woolen coats, and they had woven scarves wrapped around their necks. The girls smiled and waved, not recognizing the princess. She waved back. As she did, she realized she envied them their freedom.

Isabella sighed. Others might think her position and privilege were a blessing, but they burdened her. She might be Princess Isabella of Poland, but she did not want to be a pawn in Europe's endless power struggles.

She longed for the uncomplicated life of a commoner and imagined rising every morning with her husband in their cozy thatched-roof hut. They'd eat a simple breakfast of porridge and hot tea and then go out to the small barn behind their house to milk the cows and goats. She pictured a child following her into the barn for a cup of the warm frothy milk. Later, she would churn the rest into butter for the fresh bread she would make every day.

Isabella's cat jumped up on her bed. "Ah, Bacuri. You might enjoy the life of a barn cat—plenty of mice to eat, piles of hay to sleep in and lots of adventures around a farm."

The cat meowed and jumped off the bed.

"Not interested? Well, I am."

Isabella rose and wandered to the bookshelf to find something to read, but not the books on Christian Humanism that Master Pieter had given her to study. She picked up another book, one her mother had given her, one written in Old French, a language Isabella knew well, titled "The Travels of Marco Polo."

Stretched across her bed, she turned the pages, picturing the lands of the Middle East and Central Asia that Marco Polo visited on his way to China. His adventures carried her away to the fantastic court of Kublai Khan, but after a while, she tired even of this.

Closing the book, she fell onto her pillow and cried. This was not the life she would have chosen if she'd had a choice. "Father in heaven," she pleaded, "please help me. I do not want to marry John Zápolya."

Hearing the rattle of cartwheels on the cobblestones in the courtyard below her room, she climbed off the bed and walked to the window. She peered out from behind the drapes and saw the master of the stables speaking to a bearded man in simple clothing.

The stranger was standing in front of a rough cart while tired looking muddy horse stood in the traces with its head down. A young girl sat in the cart beside bundles and a few household goods. Next to the bearded stranger stood a tall young man with long hair and broad shoulders. He had a handsome face, and he looked strong. He appeared to be observing the workmen as they labored at their tasks.

Isabella watched as his gaze followed the line of the balconies. Before she could step back from the window, he caught sight of her. Even from her room, Isabella could see his sky-blue eyes, eyes that contrasted against darkened skin that had seen much time beneath the sun.

Isabella did not know why but she blushed and drew back. She waited a moment and then peeked out again.

The stable master pointed toward the stables, and the bearded man nodded and bowed. He beckoned, and the two men led the cart away. The young man glanced up again at Isabella's window and smiled.

Isabella ducked back. When she looked again, the little group was headed toward the stables. As they left the courtyard, the first supper gong announced dinner and Maria hurried into her room.

"You do not want to make your mother angry again, Princess. We must get you ready for dinner."

Isabella finished changing her clothes. When the second gong sounded, she hurried toward the grand dining hall, but she was not thinking of dinner—only of the travelers, and of the handsome young man, and the bluest eyes she had ever seen. As she walked her heart was racing, and she knew that no matter what her parents said, she did not want to marry King John Zápolya... ever!

PART II
JOHAN—THE COMMONER

Is there anything like the first time you see the one you will love forever? I remember when I met my Jonathan on a fall day in Wooster, Ohio. I was an Amish girl, and he was, well; he was so different from anyone I had ever known. But from the moment I looked into his eyes, I was his, only and forever.

And so it must have been for Isabella the first time she saw Johan. She was a princess—she traveled in the elite circles of the ruling class of Europe. Her father was king of the great country of Poland. Johan was a simple lad dressed in plain clothes who, though matured beyond his years by hard work and difficult circumstances, was still a commoner. But none of that mattered the day Isabella first looked into the eyes that captured her heart.

"Johan"
From The Journals of Jenny Hershberger

CHAPTER 4: DEER MOUNTAIN

1529

*T*wo years before the marriage discussions in Poland, Johan Hirschberg, a young Swiss shepherd, leaned against a solitary tree that rose from the middle of a verdant meadow in the heart of the Alps. Not far from where he sat, the great snow-capped peak of Hirschberg Mountain loomed, a forbidding tower of granite and ice. A small herd of goats grazed nearby while their kids gamboled in the green grass. From his vantage point, he could see the farms around his village clinging to the sides of the high valley that spread like a cobbled blanket toward the town of Basel.

A cool breeze soothed his brow, and the gentle bleats of the goats were a familiar language to him. The smell of the wildflowers that carpeted the meadow was a sweet perfume, and a thrush perched in the tree lifted a sweet song. An unsaddled mare stood near Johan, her bridle trailing in the long grass of the meadow and her long tail sweeping an occasional fly from her back.

Johan often came here to sit in quiet reverence and awe of God's creation. Here he felt as though his soul was sending roots into the heart of the towering peaks of the Swiss Alps. His father, Samuel, had come to this valley fleeing the peasant's revolt in Galacia. He had taken a new name from the mountain and Johan had been the first of his family born a Hirschberg.

He heard a rustle in the brush behind him, and as he turned, a magnificent red stag with wide antlers jumped from the trees and ran straight through the herd of goats, scattering them like leaves in a windstorm. Moments later, his father, crossbow in hand, and their Laufhund hunting dog burst from the same thicket. Both were panting.

"Johan, did you see the stag?" Samuel asked. "Where did it go?"

Johan pointed. "There, Papa." The deer's tail waved like a flag just before it disappeared over a rise.

Between breaths, Samuel said, "I nearly had him. If Adolphus had not barked, I would not have missed my first shot." He glared at the dog. Adolphus whined and cowered at his master's feet.

Samuel relented and leaned over to pet the dog. "*Das, ist, Adolphus, ganz richtig.* I, too, almost shouted, when I saw him. One of these days..."

He took the arrow from his bow and sat in the grass beside his son. "Something on your mind, Johan? You only bring the goats this far up when you are thinking about something."

"Yes, Papa. What David taught at the meeting last night... I have thought much on it today, and I know he is right."

Samuel nodded. "I agree, but it is strange to receive words that, even while they sound harsh in your ears, ring true in your heart." He took off his leather jacket and used the sleeve to wipe the sweat from his brow.

"All these years we have obeyed, without question, the Catholic Church's rules. Our family has faithfully attended Mass, we have prayed for those we assumed were in purgatory, and we paid indulgences to escape our sins. Then Martin Luther..." He shook his head.

"But what we did had nothing to do with Christ, did it, Father? I mean... Christ paid for every sin on the cross. Last night David said Luther teaches that we are justified by faith and faith alone. We need not be the priests' slaves and pay them money for every wrong thing we do, while they live in wealth and comfort. We are free from the moment we place our trust in the Lord."

Samuel looked both ways as if someone might be listening. "Yes, what Luther says is true, but truth does not make the priests happy. Many people are being persecuted for following the German."

"I know, Papa, but must not a man stand firm for the truth, even though it may cost him everything? That's what David said last night. To be a disciple of Jesus, we must bear the same cross our Lord bore, even unto death."

Samuel stared across the valley. At last he spoke. "You are only thirteen but you are wise beyond your years, Johan. The mountain gives you strength and the pure air gives you a strong mind. But never forget the Catholics hate the Lutherans. Much trouble will come as Luther's teaching spreads. It is difficult to understand."

Johan picked at the grass while he thought. At last he spoke. "David said the priests should not baptize infants."

"That is hard, Johan. I can see the wisdom in it, but the church..."

"Should we not wait until we are old enough to understand what following Christ means? I know this is right. But why do they persecute people for accepting such a simple teaching?"

"It is much to ponder." Samuel rubbed his jaw. "I am not yet old, my son, but I am set in my ways. I will need to hear this new truth many times before I understand it."

"Will we go to the meeting again tonight then, Papa?"

"Yes, Johan, though this teaching will bring trouble, for us and for others who accept it. But, as you say, we must stand for the truth. I will listen again. Almost this man persuades me."

"But for now, Johan..." Samuel rose to his feet. "Will you not help me run that stag to earth? He was in the garden again today, eating our cabbages. Your mama will not be quiet until I hang the thief in the tree beside the door."

"Yes, Papa, I will go with you. The goats will find their own way home. Lisle, come."

The horse raised its head and nickered and then came to Johan's side and stood patiently while Johan rose. Samuel smiled and shook his head. "Such a way you have with horses, Johan."

Johan grasped the mare's mane and swung up on her back.

"She is more than a horse, Papa. She is my friend."

JOHAN STOOD at the back of the small barn, listening to the speaker from Basel. Torchlight flickered against the walls as the speaker taught from the Scriptures. After years of Catholic dogma and the priests' insistence that Jesus's work was an incomplete one, this man's teachings blew through his heart like a fresh wind off a glacier. Men and women listened intently. Here and there small children sat quietly or slept in their parent's arms.

"While not worshipping the Bible itself," David was saying, "for that would be idolatry, we accept the Scriptures as the authoritative Word of God. The Word must always guide believers."

Heads nodded in affirmation.

"Those of us who reject infant baptism are called Anabaptists. We derive our understanding of Christ from the Word alone, and we have a deep commitment to follow Jesus's teaching in every part of our lives. Such a view runs counter to notions that the commands of Jesus are too difficult for ordinary believers or that Jesus's significance lies only in providing heavenly salvation."

He lifted his Bible. "God's Word tells us the salvation of the soul is part of a total transformation that begins in this life. When we place our faith in him, our spirits, souls and bodies are forever changed.

"And now," David continued, "I want you to know how Anabaptists differ from other Christians. For many of us, following Christ's command to love one another is not optional. We renounce violence in *all* human relationships. We base this view on Jesus's words when he said 'But I say unto you, love your enemies, bless them that curse you, do good to them that hate you, and pray for them which despitefully use you, and persecute you.' Peace and reconciliation—the way of love—are at the heart of the gospel. God gave his followers this ethic not as a point to ponder, but as a command to obey. The way of love was costly for Jesus, and it will be costly for his followers. The way of peace is a way of life."

Johan folded his arms. The words sounded right, but to apply the teaching—that would be difficult. Priests encouraged secular authorities to use force to control outbreaks of the "heresy" spreading from Germany. Not that long ago, German aristocrats had slaughtered thousands of peaceful peasants for adhering to Protestant beliefs.

No, that would be too hard a way to live.

The door flew open and the man who had been standing guard rushed into the room. "Soldiers are marching up the mountain. I can see their torches. We must all leave and leave now."

The people in the room gathered their children and bolted out the door. In seconds, the only ones left were Johan, his father, and David, the speaker. Samuel took David by the arm. "Our house is up the mountain. You can rest there and tell us more of your teaching." He smiled at the look of doubt on David's face. "The soldiers will not come to our home. It is too far for lowlanders."

Samuel lifted a torch from the wall while Johan doused the other torches in a bucket of water by the door.

"Come quickly now. The soldiers must not find you here, Brother David." Samuel hurried Johan and David from the barn and up the mountain.

LATER THAT NIGHT, the Hirschberg family sat around the kitchen table—Johan, his father, Samuel, his mother, Mareili and his younger sister, Annalisa. David, the teacher from Basel, sat in the place of honor at the head of the table. Outside, the wind had picked up. Johan could hear the first raindrops hit the roof as a summer storm blew in off the peaks.

Samuel smiled. "We thank God for this providential storm. It will drive the soldiers off the mountain. By now, they're on the way back to their warm barracks in Basel."

The Anabaptist teacher smiled and refused another helping of cheese and bread that Johan's mother offered. "I have met your sister, Elspeth, in Basel, Brother Samuel. She was one of the first to agree to our beliefs."

"I received a letter from her about her and Hans's new beliefs." Samuel nodded. "I get the impression she is preaching to everyone who will listen, which worries me. Things are so uncertain now."

Johan looked up from his meal. "I am proud of *Tante* Elspeth. She is not afraid. I want to be like her." He turned to David. "Tell us more, David. I want my mother and sister to hear your words."

"I am happy to speak the truth." David smiled. "One thing we know for certain is that the church, the body of Christ, has only one head. Jesus is lord of his church, and we are his body. We put aside racial, ethnic, and class distinctions and those between men and women because the unity and equality of the body sets them at naught.

"As the Apostle Paul teaches in Romans, we are all equal in Christ Jesus. Whether Jew or Greek, slave or free, male or female, we are one in Christ Jesus."

Johan's mother smiled and shook her head. "This may be the most difficult part of your teaching, Brother David, this part about no difference between men and women. It is freeing for me but will be hard for most men to receive."

AFTER BROTHER DAVID HAD RETIRED, Samuel and Johan remained before the fire. Samuel took out his pipe and lit it. "I am sure what our guest says is true, Johan, and I believe *du leiber Gott* has shown us the way. Tomorrow, I will tell David that I and my house will follow the new way he speaks of."

They sat in silence, watching the fire die to ash. Finally, Samuel rose. "I have much to do tomorrow, my son, as do you. You should take your rest."

"I will come soon, Papa. I want to think on these things a while longer."

Samuel left but Johan remained long into the night, puzzling over the things David had taught. When the gray of first light was creeping into the room, Johan stood and stretched. He slipped out the door and walked down the path and into the small barn behind the house. The mare nickered in the dark as he brought her some grain. She nuzzled against him and he whispered to her. "I am afraid, Lisle. I think our peaceful life is about to change... forever."

CHAPTER 5: FIRE IN THE NIGHT

*J*ohan peered through a crack in the drapes that covered the window of Tante Elspeth's house in Basel. Behind him, his mother and sister huddled in the darkness. Outside, burning houses lit the night with a ghastly glow. Screams accompanied the shouts and curses of armed soldiers as they dragged suspected Anabaptists from their homes. The little church that met in this place was no more—the congregants were in prison or in hiding... or martyred. Johan and his family were the only ones that remained. Now they were waiting for their chance to leave the city.

Annalisa stirred. "When will father return, Johan?"

"He is making arrangements for us to leave, Annalisa. He should be back soon."

"Will the soldiers catch him?"

"I hope not, sister."

~

IT WAS the end of December. The Hirschberg family had been

celebrating Christmas with Tante Elspeth and Onkel Hans in Basel when the riots against the Anabaptists started. They began when clergymen, accompanied by soldiers, went house-to-house ordering suspected heretics to renounce their beliefs or face destruction. They turned into a violent, citywide assault on anyone suspected of being an Anabaptist. When the fat cleric came banging on Tante Elspeth and Onkel Hans's door, Johan's mother and sister hid in the cellar while Elspeth and Hans answered the knock. Johan and his father waited in the kitchen and Johan watched through the crack in the door while the priest waved the Notices of Denunciation in Tante Elspeth's face. "You and your husband are heretics, followers of the cursed Anabaptist heresy. I give you both the opportunity to purge yourself of these foul beliefs and return to the Reformed Church, the one true church. Do you repent?"

Tante Elspeth pushed the papers away. "Those who follow Christ and obey his words belong to the true church. Men who love God love the church and love their enemies. If you were faithful followers of Christ, you would not be murdering us.

The cleric's face flamed red. Spit flew from his mouth as he shouted at Tante Elspeth. "Acting as the local midwife, you have told the mothers of this town not to baptize their children. That is a mortal sin. Do you repent? If you do not, you will burn in the fires of purification!"

Tante smiled at the priest and kept her voice low. "Yes, I repent. I repent for years of misunderstanding God's Word and not listening to the Holy Spirit as he sought to guide me—for trying to buy my way out of hell with indulgences and denying that Christ's work on the cross was complete. I repent for following liars and thieves who made themselves fat on the ignorance of the laity, using fear and deceit as their tools. As for the children, now I have a Bible, and I know it teaches they must wait for baptism until they are old enough to know what they are doing."

"I am warning you," the priest shouted, "you will pay for this!" The soldiers crowded closer, brandishing their pikes.

Onkel Hans did not shrink back but pointed his finger at the men. "You say you have reformed the church," he cried, "but you have not. Protestants still worship Mary as the way to Christ. And you fight bloody battles with the Catholics for control of Swiss cities, even when Christ says all men are brothers. The Bible says Christ is our peace and has broken down every wall between men, women, slave and free. Yet, here you are at our door, threatening fire and death. It is not I who should repent, but you."

By then, the fat man was shaking with rage. He motioned to the soldiers behind him. "Take them to the prison," he screamed, waving his hands like a madman. "They'll sing a different tune as the fires of Christ roast their flesh."

The soldiers grabbed his aunt and uncle and tied their hands behind their backs. Jerked around so that she was facing the door, Tante Elspeth saw Johan peering through the crack between the door and the frame and a sad smile formed on her lips, and then the soldiers led them away. Johan wanted to run after them, but the look in his father's eyes warned Johan not to cry out, and his hand held Johan like a steel trap.

THE DAY after his aunt and uncle's arrest, soldiers marched through the city, stopping at every square to read an announcement. "The authorities shall imprison those who shelter Anabaptists or attend their meetings, using torture when necessary, until they recant. Obstinate heretics shall remain in prison until death. I shall execute those who recant but fall back into Anabaptism. The council has ordered a disputation with the imprisoned heretics to encourage them to return to the church on the twenty-ninth of December and requires all citizens to be in attendance in the main square of the city."

On the appointed day, Johan and his family went to the square that also served as Basel's marketplace. Most of Basel's citizens were there, milling around, talking and laughing. Someone had brought kegs of ale, and many in the crowd were already drunk. Several citizens stood with grim faces talking quietly, but many people laughed and pointed at the prisoners on the platform, as though expecting some entertainment. The soldiers, clerics and government officials who surrounded the prisoners were stone-faced. To Johan, they looked like vultures waiting to tear at a dead carcass. He saw his aunt and uncle on the platform. They wore manacles on their wrists and looked exhausted. He made eye contact with his aunt and offered a tentative wave. Though bruised and haggard she held her head high and returned Johan's smile.

Johannes Oecolampadius, the head of the reformed Protestant Council, stood up from his seat and the crowd quieted. He then read a proclamation. "Anabaptism is self-willed, Pharisaic hypocrisy that pleases itself, condemns true orthodoxy, and leads to disobedience and sedition." He turned to the prisoners. "If any among you will recant of this vile heresy, we will welcome you back into the church with open arms."

Four Anabaptists repented, but four others, including Johan's aunt and uncle, remained silent. Johan could see the anger on the faces of the clerics. They spoke among themselves, hands waving and gesturing, all the while glaring and pointing at the unrepentant ones.

Oecolampadius turned to the prisoners and tried once more. "I will behead Hans Ludi and Jakop Treyer. Hans and Elspeth Semmelweiss, unless you recant of the blasphemy against infant baptism, I will turn you over to the Catholic soldiers, who will burn you at the stake."

A gasp rose from the crowd.

Oecolampadius pointed at the four dissidents and shouted, "Do you recant?"

All four shook their heads. Elspeth stepped forward. "Our Lord said to whom much is given, much is required. If martyrdom is the reward for what he has given me, the exchange is in my favor."

"No!" The cry was torn from Johan's lips, but before he could go on his father silenced him with a stern look.

Onkel Hans and the other Anabaptists stepped up beside Elspeth. Their faces were white, but they nodded their heads as Elspeth spoke. Oecolampadius glared at them for a long while, his face set in anger. He shook his head and nodded to the soldiers, who shoved Elspeth and the others down the steps of the platform. Johan stared after his beloved aunt, his heart pounding and tears starting from his eyes. Many in the crowd cheered, and the drunken ones shouted curses at the condemned ones as the soldiers led them away.

On the morning of the executions, Johan went with his father to visit Elspeth and Hans in prison. Before they entered, Samuel warned Johan, "If we confess we are Anabaptists, we will face the same fate as Elspeth and Hans. If you value my life and the life of your mother and sister, you will remain silent, my son."

"But, Papa! Should we not stand as Tante Elspeth and Onkel Hans did and not retreat from what we believe?"

"The Catholics would burn us at the stake today. Do you want to do that to your mama or your sister?"

Johan lowered his head. "No, Papa."

When they asked at the prison gate to see Elspeth and Hans, the brawny guard sneered at them. "Come to see the heretics before they burn?" He leaned closer, his bushy eyebrows taut above his nose. "Say... are you Anabaptists, too?"

Johan opened his mouth and was about to reply when his father jabbed him in the ribs. He shut his mouth.

"We are here to see my sister and her husband," Samuel said. "Oecolampadius has given permission for relatives to visit the condemned before their execution."

The guard grunted and called for the warden who came and unlocked the door and led them along a rock-walled passageway and down rough-hewn stairs into a dark dungeon. An open sewer ran through the middle of the passageway. Torches that burned and smoked fitfully in the gloom lit the damp walls.

Johan gagged and held his nose, nearly overcome by the smell of human filth combined with that of rotting food. A cat-sized rat scurried out from the first cell they approached. Johan jumped back, but the rodent veered away and disappeared into a wide crack in the wall.

From behind the bars, someone spoke in a grating voice. "Don't hurt Anneli. She is my only friend." The man cackled and fell to muttering under his breath.

The jailer led them past several cells before they came to Elspeth and Hans, who shared a cell. "Five minutes," the man said before he left them.

Elspeth and Hans were sitting quietly on the bench in their cell. Johan marveled at their calm demeanor. "Tante Elspeth, are you not afraid?"

Their faces were dirty, and they looked thin and tired, but there was a light in their eyes that Johan would always remember.

"No, Johan, I am not." Elspeth smiled. "The fires will burn for a short time. No doubt we will suffer, but these men do not know the eternal fire that awaits them because they have rejected Christ and his truth. I weep for them, and I pray for their souls."

"But Tante..."

Johan's father interrupted him. He grasped the hands of Elspeth and Hans through the bars. "What can I do for you?"

Hans pressed against the bars. "In the hearth," he murmured, his words barely discernible, "you will find a loose stone, on the left side beneath the mantle. Beneath it is our life savings. You must take the contents and flee this place, Samuel. Do not go back to your farm, for I have heard the guards talking. Oecolampadius will not rest until he stamps out the Anabaptist belief in this city and in the surrounding cantons. He has sent the soldiers to scour the countryside. They are on the mountain even now, rooting out heretics. If you return to your farm, they will be waiting. You must go to Poland. My cousin works at the king's palace. He can find a place for you. His name is Noah Semmelweis."

"Leave the mountain? Our farm?" Johan blurted.

"Quiet, Johan." Samuel hissed. "You would condemn us with your outbursts." He turned back to Hans. "What will happen to your house?"

"We have no relatives except you. The authorities will confiscate it." Hans shrugged. "More important is the safety of your family. You must go, tonight!"

At the sound of heavy footsteps scuffing across the rough floor, Johan swiveled. The jailer was coming toward them. He whispered to the others, "He's coming!"

The man stopped behind them. His heavy, putrid breath raised the hairs on Johan's neck and sent shivers down his spine. "Enough!" he growled. "You two must leave, now. We have orders to deliver the heretics to the executioners immediately."

The thought of his dear aunt dying such a terrible death turned Johan's stomach. He reached through the bars to grab her hand. "Tante! Tante!"

"Do not fear for me." Elspeth touched his cheek. "I am not afraid to die for my Lord. My Lord gave his life for me. I willingly give mine for him." Elspeth caressed Johan's tear-stained face. "You must not allow our deaths to cause you bitterness. Do not let the seed of hatred enter your heart. This is but a small test for me, Johan. But for you, who have your whole life ahead, it is a turning point. Will you walk in the way of hatred and death, or will you follow Christ on the path of peace? You must decide."

"Tante, Onkle Hans, please, repent, confess! Tell them what they want to hear. I do not want you to die!"

Elspeth shook her head. "Ah, my Johan, I cannot deny the truth. I beg of you, do not let unforgiveness rule your heart. Revenge is not what Christ teaches. Love your enemies and *pray for those who persecute* you. An eye for an eye is not the way of Christ."

Johan felt the hand of the jailer on his arm, pulling at him. "Come on, you."

Johan and Samuel turned to go. Hans spoke once more.

"Do what I told you, Samuel. Remember... Noah Semmelweiss."

Tears burned in Johan's eyes while thoughts of blood and death crowded into his mind.

"I will avenge you, Tante. Anabaptists will not always fear the Catholics and the Reformists."

Johan heard the cell door creak open behind him and the jailer's harsh voice ordering Elspeth and Hans from the cell. He turned his head and saw his aunt stumble on the rough stones. He heard her gasp as the jailer jerked her to her feet. His uncle cried out. "Johan, don't look back."

Then the soldiers led Elspeth and Hans away. Johan never saw them again.

CHAPTER SIX: FLÜG DER ANGST

FLIGHT OF FEAR

From one back street to another, Johan and Samuel zigzagged to Elspeth and Hans's house, checking at each intersection to make sure no one followed them from the prison. From the square, they heard the crowd cheering as the executions took place. In the alley behind the house, they looked both ways to make sure there were no soldiers to see them at the home of heretics. Then they climbed over the fence and crept to the back door. It was locked.

Samuel knocked and whispered, "Mareili, it is us. Open the door." He knocked again. A moment later the lock clicked, and the door cracked open. Annalisa peeked out. She let them in and locked the door behind them.

Johan peeked out the window but saw no one. "Has anyone been here since we left?"

"I was watching for you at the window, and I saw soldiers coming down the street. Mother and I were frightened, and so we locked the door and hid. They were talking and laughing about the executions as they walked by. We thought they might try to come into the house, but they went on down the street."

"It is not safe in Basel." Brow furrowed, Samuel clenched and unclenched his fists. "Mareili, we are leaving Switzerland tonight. We cannot go back to the farm, so we will take only what we brought with us for the visit."

Johan's mother's mouth opened in surprise and then she burst into tears. "Not go back? Why do we have to go, Samuel? All my mother's beautiful things are in our house on the mountain. Can't we be secret believers and stay in our home."

Samuel shook his head. "I would have us stay if I could, Mareili, but I am sure the authorities already know we are Anabaptists too. Elspeth is my sister. We were lucky to even get out of the prison today. Johannes Oecolampadius has determined to stamp out the Anabaptists. The climb up the mountain will no longer keep them from finding us." He paused and wiped his eyes with the back of his sleeve. "They martyred our dear Elspeth and Hans today. I will not see you and my children suffer the same fate."

Mareili's face twisted, and she burst into tears. "But who will care for our animals, for Lisle?" Annalisa threw her arms around her mother and wailed.

Samuel tried to quiet them. "Hush, hush. You will bring the soldiers."

"Why do they hate us so, Father?" Johan slammed his fist against the wall. "What have we ever done to them? Why can't we follow Christ the way our hearts tell us to do?"

"Their hatred is not about our beliefs. It is about money."

"Money?"

Samuel placed his hand on Johan's shoulder. "When parents baptize a baby, the act places the child on the church's and the city's tax rolls. So if Anabaptists refuse to baptize their children, our fat clerics and rich aldermen lose income. If all the people became Anabaptists and refused to pay the baptism tax, those extortionists would have little left since they no longer collect indulgences."

He shook his head. "No, Johan. They will do their best to

destroy every last Anabaptist." He put his hand on his wife's shoulder. "It is too late for us to say we are not Anabaptists, Mareili. By our visit to the prison, they have connected us to Hans and Elspeth. Our neighbor, Wilhelm, is watching the farm. He has always wanted it. I will send word to him, somehow, that I am giving it to him. We cannot stay, we must go."

"But how, Samuel? What will we do?"

"We will slip down to the river after dark. I know a man who travels to Mainz on his barge to sell goods. I have sold my hay to him for many years. He is a good man, and he will help us. I will go now and make arrangements. Have everything readied when I return."

JOHAN OPENED the drapes a tiny crack and looked out. Groups of Reformist soldiers passed up and down the street. After a long day of heretic hunting, most of them were drunk. They laughed and cursed the Anabaptists, and some were singing crude songs. The light from their torches crept through the small opening into the room, illuminating the tapestries and paintings hanging on the whitewashed walls and the simple wooden cross hanging over the mantle. Johan shut the drape and stood in the darkness waiting for his father to return—his mother and sister were asleep on the couch, their simple belongings packed and ready to go.

There was a creaking sound, and then Johan heard the back door of the house open and the sound of a step in the kitchen. "Hssst, Johan. It is I." His father came in. He looked tired. "I have made the arrangements. We leave tonight. My friend will give us a good price for our fare to Mainz. Now we must find the money Hans has hidden. Close the drapes tight and then help me."

Johan pulled the drapes and returned to his Father's side.

Samuel took the tinderbox down from the mantle and struck a light to a piece of the char cloth inside. When the cloth was flaming, he lit a candle from it. Then, Johan and his father knelt by the hearth and ran their fingers along the stones, searching for the loose one Hans had mentioned. When one shifted under Johan's hand, he pushed harder. "Papa!" he whispered. "Here it is."

The stone made a scraping sound as it loosened. Johan slid it out, laid it on the floor, and reached into the hole. He pulled a heavy a heavy cloth-wrapped bundle from the hollow and carefully placed it on the hearth.

His father unwrapped it, revealing a beautiful golden crucifix on top of a leather bag. Johan hefted the bag. He handed it to his father, who opened it and took out a few coins.

"Hans has blessed us, the dear man." He returned the coins to the bag. "Enough gold is here to buy a horse and a cart when we get to Mainz and supplies for our journey to Krakow. We will take only the clothes we have. We leave everything else behind." He held up the cross. It gleamed in the small light from the candle. "But we will keep this. It will remind us of my brave, sweet sister and her husband."

Johan felt tears start in his eyes. "I do not want the gold, Papa. I want them."

Samuel put his hand on his son's shoulder. "I know, Johan. It is a hard thing."

They were quiet for a moment, remembering their loved ones. Then they rose.

"How will we travel all the way to Poland, Papa?"

Samuel wrapped the cloth around the bag and the crucifix. "Ernst will take us down the Rhine to Mainz, and from there we follow the *Via Regia* to Poland. I've heard the old Roman road is still passable after all these years. With a horse and cart, we should be able to travel fifteen miles a day."

"How long will the trip take us?"

"Barring any unforeseen circumstances..." Samuel rubbed his jaw... "about six days down the Rhine and two months from Mainz to Krakow. We will need to wait in Mainz until the roads are passable. Let us pray for an early spring." He pocketed the coin bag and placed the cross with their bundles. "Come now, Johan. Let us rouse the women and prepare for our trip. We must leave soon."

They started for the stairs, but Johan heard a noise outside and grabbed his father's arm.

The two of them crept to the window. Pushing the drape apart just far enough to see, Johan spied another group of soldiers walking in the street. Their torches cast strange shadows on the walls of the houses across the street.

They stopped at the corner several yards away. Their loud voices carried to the house. One soldier produced a wineskin, and the men passed it around, laughing as they did.

"Quite a day in the square," a soldier said. "One those heretics won't soon forget, I'll wager."

Another man laughed. "A waste of good wood, if you ask me. We should have bound them and thrown them in the river."

"I expected them to scream more." The third soldier took a long pull on the skin. "But they went like lambs to the slaughter. They faced death with courage, you must admit."

The first man spoke again. "Yes, you must..." He was silent for a moment. "The woman never flinched. I've been in battle and seen men screaming before less terror than that, but she..." The soldier took another drink. "I will not soon forget the peaceful look on her face as the flames engulfed her. Her behavior was not what I expected."

Johan stiffened. They were talking about Tante Elspeth! He took a step toward the door, but his father clasped his shoulder with an iron grip.

"Johan!" Samuel hissed. "Do not move."

"But, Papa, they are talking about Tante Elspeth and Onkel

Hans. They burned them, and they're laughing about it. Those men are murderers. I hate them."

"Those men had no choice. They followed orders, and in doing so, they witnessed our Father's peace that passeth all understanding. By his power, Elspeth and Hans stood strong, Johan. And now they are with him in heaven.

Samuel turned Johan toward him. "You must put away your hate as did our Lord Jesus when he asked his Father to forgive those whose torture would soon end his life."

But Johan knew he could never forget… or forgive.

IN THE PRE-GRAY hours before dawn, the Hirschberg family slipped aboard a large barge anchored downstream from the Middle Bridge on the Rhine River. The bargeman was a stout older man who hurried the family to the small cabin at the stern. "Stay in here until I tell you to come out. If the soldiers see you, my life will be forfeit, too."

Seabirds flocked around the barges, their melancholy cries filling Johan's heart with loneliness for their home on the mountain. He gazed back at Basel once more and then followed his mother and sister inside.

Annalisa wrinkled her nose. "What's that smell?"

"That's from people doing their business in the streets." The bargeman pointed to a small ravine on the shore. "The rains wash the sewage into that little gully over there and dumps it into the river." He chuckled. "Don't worry, *leibchen*, we'll soon be well away from the city."

"I thank you, Ernst." Samuel clasped the man's hand. "You are saving our lives."

"You've done plenty of favors for me over the years, and your crops have always been the easiest to sell downriver. Besides that, you are saving me the money I would spend to hire crewmen for this trip. Now keep out of sight until I call you on deck."

THAT AFTERNOON JOHAN and Annalisa sat in the bow, seeing a world they'd only read about for the first time. They marveled at the ancient castles built on both shores of the Rhine and watched bargemen rowing or poling boats and barges upstream toward Basel or down toward Mainz. Vineyards and fields on the bank slipped by. After a long silence, Annalisa turned to her brother. "Do you think we will ever return to our mountain?"

A great emptiness welled up inside Johan. "No, sister." He shook his head. "I do not think we will ever see Switzerland again."

A DAY after they left Basel the Hirschbergs crossed the Swiss border and floated downstream on the Rhine between France and Germany. As they passed a large city, Johan saw an enormous spire that rose high above the crowded houses and public buildings. He pointed and asked, "What place is this, Herr Ernst?"

"This is the city of Strasbourg, and that is the great cathedral, Notre Dame de Strasbourg. Some say it is the tallest building in the world. I have yet to see taller. The Catholics owned it." Ernst spit into the river. "But the city gave it to the Protestants five-years ago, which angered the papists, who then tried to burn it down." He smirked. "But the brave Protestant lads drove them off."

"That's good to hear. I hope they killed all the Catholic pigs…" He turned and walked away. Hand on the rail, he stared at the Rhine's blue waters sliding beneath the bow.

"What is wrong with me?" he murmured. "I used to think I should respect others, but now I want to kill all the Catholics and Reformists because they murdered Tante Elspeth and Onkel Hans."

"Yes, Johan, what you are feeling is wrong."

Johan jerked around.

Brow furrowed, Mareili came and stood by her son. "You have changed, Johan, and not for the better. You've grown bitter. I have never seen that in you."

"Tante Elspeth loved people, Mama. She and Hans lived the way Jesus taught, and what did it gain them? Persecuted by Reformists and burned to death by Catholics who believed they were saving the church. I hate them! I will always hate them." He pounded the railing with his fist.

"You are wrong to hate, Johan." Mareili shook her head. "Jesus said if someone strikes us on the face, we should turn the other cheek. Brother David taught us..."

Johan stiffened. "Did Brother David teach us how to escape the Reformists and the Catholics? Did Brother David tell us how to save Tante Elspeth and Onkel Hans? Where was Brother David when they came for the Anabaptists? I did not see him at the trial. Where was he hiding?"

"Johan..."

"Always it is the same, Mama. The leaders go free, and the followers pay the price." He turned his back on his mother. "Yes, I have changed. I am sick of being a passive sheep waiting for slaughter. One day the Anabaptists will rise and kill their oppressors, and when they do, I will be with them."

CHAPTER 7: VIA DOLOROSA

*O*n the morning of the third day of their journey, great purplish clouds formed along the horizon. In mere minutes, the towering bank swept out of the northern sky. The front of the mass turned black, and the storm became a swollen, burgeoning, monstrous beast. Called on deck to help pole the boat, Johan felt as if Satan's breath pushed and piled the clouds until they roiled in an ungovernable mass of destruction.

A bright explosion in the storm's heart tore through the clouds and flickered out. From the black depths burst a violent concussion, a crushing boom that rolled on and on. Another flash rent the darkness, and then the rains came, blowing straight at them in cold sheets that took Johan's breath away. Huge waves broke over the bow.

Ernst pointed to the shore and shouted over the wind's roar. "We must get to shore before the boat swamps!"

Ernst turned the boat toward the bank, and they all poled as hard as they could until they grounded on a sandy beach. Johan and his father grabbed a coil of rope, jumped over the rail into the shallow water, and waded ashore. They wrapped the line round and round a huge tree and made the boat fast. The rain poured down, and Johan and Samuel climbed back on board and joined the others crowded into the small cabin. Soaked to the skin, they huddled together, shivering like tree leaves in the wind. A strange smell filled the air as the lightning bolts ripped through the heavens.

The wind howled and moaned. The boat stuck fast in the sand, but Johan could feel it rocking and jolting from the force of the wind. Above the noise of the storm, a loud cracking sound followed a thunderous boom that shook the barge. Ernst, Samuel, and Johan ran outside. It surprised them to find tree branches blocking their way. The wind had blown over a towering oak. It missed hitting the boat, but its branches covered the deck. Johan clung to the rail as Ernst surveyed the damage.

Johan heard voices and peered between the branches. Through the rain, he could see soldiers, their heads bent against the downpour, struggling to keep their footing on the slick muddy path. "Papa!" He grabbed his father's arm. "Soldiers!"

"Get down," Samuel hissed.

Without even one of them looking their direction, the soldiers passed. Apparently, they did not see the barge hidden among the branches of the fallen tree.

"Phew!" Ernst grinned. "The angels were guarding us, for sure. Had the soldiers seen us, they would have questioned us. That tree fell at just the right time."

An hour later, the storm moved on. Although rain continued to pour down, the men cut the limbs and shoved them off the boat. As dusk settled, the sky cleared. Ernst and Samuel looked the boat over, but aside from a few broken pieces in the deck railing, there was no damage. Johan went ashore and looked around for the soldiers but could not find them. Ernst and his father brought food and built a small fire to cook their meal, and Mareili and Annalisa joined them.

Glad to be onshore for a change, Johan climbed the bank to

get away from the fire so he could watch the stars come out one by one. The night air was crisp after the rain.

He'd stretched out on a large boulder when Annalisa plunked down beside him.

"I miss our house." She was silent for a moment, and then she moved closer and snuggled against her brother for warmth. "You said we would never go home and I think you are right Johan."

He sat up and put his arm around his sister's shoulder. "No, Annalisa. You must forget Switzerland and our valley. There is no room there for Anabaptists."

THREE DAYS later Johan was on deck with Ernst when they floated past the mouth of a large river. Boat after boat was moving from it into the main current. "That is the Main River," Ernst said, "the largest tributary to the Rhine. Those boats come from the eastern part of the German empire, and some of them carry goods from as far away as Belorussia. And that," he said, pointing, "is Mainz."

Crossing the current, he aimed his barge toward the left bank. Hundreds of boats lined a long promenade where goods were being unloaded, vendors were hawking their wares, and people were bustling here and there. Beyond the promenade, the city of Mainz rose in spires and steeples to the top of a hill dominated by a huge cathedral.

When they reached the far shore, they poled the boat to a mooring spot between two larger barges tied up along the promenade. Ernst helped them carry their goods ashore and up the bank, and they stood there together.

Samuel reached into his pocket and brought out coins, but Ernst covered them with his hand and shook his head. "No, my friend. You do not owe me. I have saved the cost of hiring a crew, and besides, you will need all your money to get to Krakow. Go with God." He pointed them to a nearby inn, and they said goodbye to him there.

Mareili and Annalisa waited with their things at the inn while Samuel and Johan walked into town to find a horse and a cart. As they walked, the smell of freshly baked bread wafted out of a shop along the way and the shouts of carters and draymen filled the air. Samuel stopped and bought a loaf and some fruit. He inquired of the shop owner for a stable and they went back out on the street.

Samuel swept his hand over the bustling panorama. "Somewhere in Mainz is the shop where Gutenberg invented the printing press, Johan."

"Yes, Papa. I knew that. If it weren't for him, Martin Luther would have disappeared into history without a trace, for we would not have his teachings in printed form, nor would we have Bibles of our own."

Samuel smiled. "So, my son, you have an interest in history?"

"Gutenberg's press gave us the Bible, Papa. That is why I am interested. The priests kept us blind for years. We never knew faith alone saves a person—no prayers to the saints, no indulgences, no buying one's family out of purgatory."

Samuel shook his head. "Sometimes, I think you are too old for your years, Johan."

THEY STAYED at the inn while they waited for better traveling weather. Samuel purchased a sturdy cart and a good horse with the money Hans provided. He also bought tools from a farrier. He built a hiding place for their gold in the cart's bottom, and they only kept enough money in their pockets to buy supplies along the way. Johan and Annalisa visited the cathedral and the shop where Gutenberg had printed the first

Bible. When it was time to leave for Krakow, the innkeeper gave them warning.

"The old Via Regia is still there," the man said, "but the emperor's soldiers haven't guarded it for a hundred years. It has fallen into great disrepair in places, from a great highway to a simple path. Brigands and highwaymen are always on the lookout for merchants and other wealthy travelers to ambush.

"Slap a bunch of mud on your horse to make him look bedraggled and add a few tatters to the cloth that covers the wagon. Don't carry more than a week's worth of supplies. The robbers will think you are poor refugees and will leave you alone."

Two months after they arrived in Mainz, Johan and his family set out for Krakow and the court of Sigismund I to find Hans's cousin. The first few days of their journey along the old Roman highway a few kilometers north of the River Main were without incident. It was March and warming days had replaced the chill of February. Johan enjoyed the feel of the sun on his back and the quaint German villages they passed through, all beginning with the letter "H"—Hocheim, Hattersheim, and Hoechst. They traveled during the day and camped along the road at night. Their gelding was young and strong, and Annalisa named him Traveller. Johan took care of him and soon he had Traveller as well trained as Lisle had been.

After several days, they came to the Frankfurt ford and crossed the shallow river on foot. Traveler pulled the cart through the water with ease. They found a campsite outside of the city where they met a man named Siegfried who was traveling to Leipzig. He was from Speyer, in southern Germany, and was more than happy to give them the latest news as they sat around the fire that night.

"The Catholics held a big meeting," he said. "They called it a Diet and announced they were forming an army to act against the Turks."

"Why the Turks?" Johan asked.

"Don't you know, boy? The Turks have invaded Hungary and are moving toward Vienna in Austria. I think they want to make all of Europe followers of their filthy prophet. But once they dealt with the threat of Suleiman, the Catholic bishops denounced Luther and the Protestants—and tore into the Anabaptists."

Johan sat taller. "What happened?" Samuel asked.

Siegfried looked long and hard at Samuel. "You folks ain't stinking re-baptizers are ya?"

Johan was about to say something, but Samuel interrupted before he could. "No, we are not. We are going to Krakow. I'm a farrier, and I will look for employment in Sigismund's stable."

Siegfried took a bite of the bread he had been eating. "Well, I'm glad you ain't Anabaptists, for the Catholics have declared the death penalty in Switzerland for anyone who gets rebaptized, and they are trying to do the same in Germany. I think it's the right idea. Anabaptists is Satan's spawn."

"What else did the Catholics do at their Diet?" Johan asked.

"They banned Luther's teaching and marked the Zwinglians for destruction, too." He chuckled. "That's a laugh. Me, I'm a Lutheran and I always will be. The Catholics better lie low. And I don't think they got the courage to run Zwingli and Calvin out of Geneva either. Mostly them Catholics is just fat windbags."

Samuel changed the conversation to horses, for Siegfried was a horse trader. But before Johan crawled into his blankets, his father came to him.

"Johan, you must be more careful," he whispered. "You were about to speak out tonight before I stopped you. Don't you realize you could put your mother and sister in great danger?"

Johan stared at his father. A taste of bile rose in his throat.

"Tante Elspeth and Onkle Hans gave their lives for the truth. Why will we not stand for what we believe? And why do we not rid the earth of scum like Siegfried?"

"Elspeth and Hans gave their lives for what they believed, yes, but I am not ready to do so, nor am I interested in taking up the sword." Samuel rubbed his jaw. "I have many questions, and until I know the answers, I will not put your mother and sister at risk. When you are older and have your own family, you may do as you wish regarding their safety. But this is *my* family to protect. While you are in my care, you will do as I ask. Now go to sleep."

"Yes, Papa." Johan turned over and stared into the darkness. The hard ground chilled him through his blankets.

I will never forget how you died for what you believed, Tante, and I will have my revenge. But for now, I will do as Papa asks.

AFTER THEY LEFT FRANKFURT, the weather turned foul, raining every day for two weeks straight. The road became a muddy morass that made travel difficult and slow. By the time they reached Görlitz, Mareili came down with a hacking cough. They found lodgings in the city. But despite a roof over her head and a dry bed, Mareili's illness worsened.

Samuel decided they needed to stay until Mareili improved and found work as a farrier, so they would not deplete their resources. Johan often joined him, but many days he stayed with his mother or sat in the main room of the inn listening to the tales of traveler's coming from the east or going to Poland. It was there that he learned more about how the Catholic Bishops of Germany had forbidden any expansion of Luther's Reformation. Mostly the people of Görlitz laughed and ignored the Catholic edict because the whole region was already Lutheran.

Summer passed, and autumn came on, but Mareili was still not well enough to travel. One day in September, Samuel told Johan and Annalisa, "We must stay until spring. We cannot risk traveling in the winter. We will wait until the roads are dry, maybe March or April, if your mother is able."

But the day before Christmas, as Johan sat beside his mother's bed, listening to her labored breathing, he knew she would not live out the winter. He called Annalisa from the other room. Though pale and weak, Mareili reached out and took their hands.

"You must not grieve long for me, my children. Der liebes Gott plans our lives. My times are in his hands, and I am not afraid. Help your papa, for he will need you. Johan, take care of your sister and keep her safe."

Hot tears ran from Johan's eyes. "Mama, you must get well. Don't go."

He felt her hand on his cheek. "We had a good life on the Hirschberg, Johan. I go now to a place where the grass grows green on the mountainside and the eagle calls from the tall crags. I will miss you, both but I know I will see you again. When he returns today, tell your father I love him. Goodbye, my little ones."

His mother's soft hand slipped away and her eyes closed. Annalisa threw herself on her mother's breast, wailing. Johan stood and stared down at his mother. A serene peace lay on her face but Johan had no peace, only anger and bitterness in his heart.

First Elspeth and Hans, and now they have killed you, Mama. We had a happy home until the clerics came. I will have my revenge.

PART III
DAYS OF DESTINY

JOHAN AND HIS FAMILY buried Mareili and lingered in Görlitz for two more months, waiting for good weather. In March 1531 they started the final stage of their migration to Krakow. And thus it was, a little over a year after they fled Basel, the Hirschberg family came to Krakow and the court of Sigismund I.

On the day they arrived, as Johan stood in the courtyard with his father talking with the stable master, he was being watched from a window above. Had he known what was in store for him and the girl looking down at him, he might have urged his father to find work elsewhere. But the Lord had already intertwined these two lives from far distant places and that intertwining would affect many generations.

"A Love For the Ages"
From The Journals of Jenny Hershberger

CHAPTER 8: LOVE'S ARROWS

$\mathcal{T}$he early April wind cut through Johan's thin shirt, but he suppressed a shiver and ignored the passers-by's stares. With his father and sister, he was waiting in the Wawel Castle courtyard for Hans's cousin, Noah, the stablemaster.

The Hirschberg's clothing was tattered, and their faces bore the grime of a long journey through foul weather. Annalisa huddled on the wagon seat wrapped in a blanket, and Johan stood with his father beside the battered cart. Their horse's once-sleek coat was dull and splattered with mud. His head hung low.

Johan stared at their surroundings, awed by the enormous palace. In front of them was a three-story stone building with bronze-topped towers at each corner. Behind the building stood another with a massive red brick tower. Brilliant red tile covered the roofs.

To the left, a magnificent cathedral reached into the gray sky, its towers crowned by statues and crosses. Against the cathedral's wall stood a magnificent stone building with a gold-domed roof. Scaffolds rose against one end of the courtyard where not yet completed galleries rose three stories into the sky. Workers rushed back and forth like ants preparing for winter amidst piles of materials and lumber and a cacophony of shouts and hammering.

Soon the servant who'd met them at the gate returned with Noah, Onkle Hans's cousin. Noah was not young; his brown beard had white streaks, and lines and crease seamed his face. His eyes were kindly though.

"I am Noah Semmelweiss." His gaze flitted from them to the horse and the cart. "They told me you asked for me. How may I help you?"

Samuel reached out his hand. "I am Samuel Hirschberg, Hans Semmelweiss's brother-in-law."

"Samuel Hirschberg?" Noah stepped closer and grasped Samuel's hand. "What are you doing so far from Basel? And how are Hans and Elspeth?"

Samuel glanced around at the many people filling the court-yard. "We will speak of them later if you don't mind. I am wondering if the king has a need for a good farrier and if you might have a place of rest for my children."

"Ah, yes." Noah smiled. "Hans told me of your work in his letters. Magnificent horses fill the king's stables. Work for a craftsman such as you is always available." He reached for the horse's reins. "Come with me. You can stay at my house while you get established. It will delight my wife, Margot, to have visi-tors from the homeland."

Noah led them and the horse across the courtyard and out through a gate on to a street. After a short walk, they came to a large house. Noah pointed to a gate at the side.

"You can put the cart in there. I have a small stable with a stall for your horse." Noah helped Annalisa out of the cart. "Come, little one. You look tired. Let my Margot make you some of her delicious rabbit stew. After that, you can rest."

~

JOHAN SAT ON A STOOL, watching Noah's wife, Margot, a plump, pleasant middle-aged woman, bustle from one end of the kitchen to the other. She stirred this pot and then another, out of which crept wonderful smells. Between stirrings, she kneaded the dough for Zopf bread.

"My mother made the best Zopf bread in the Canton of Basel-stadt," Johan whispered.

Margot smiled. "Where is your mother?"

Annalisa looked stricken as Johan replied. "We buried her in Görlitz. She died at Christmas."

Annalisa looked at Johan and then put her face in her hands and wept. Margot stopped what she was doing and came to Annalisa. She enfolded her in a great embrace. "There, there, little one. I am so sorry. Do not weep."

Margot's soft lap and soothing voice soon comforted the girl. Johan watched, feeling very detached.

I wish I had someone to comfort me...

Margot asked Annalisa to help her, making room for her at the breadboard where she showed the girl how to plait the dough into woven loaves. With Annalisa occupied, Margot sliced sausage, adding the thick chunks one by one to the stew. She popped a sausage slice into Annalisa's mouth and handed one to Johan. Noah and Samuel came into the kitchen and they all sat at a rough wooden table. Noah prayed before they ate and then turned to Johan's father. "So Samuel, tell me of Hans and Elspeth and why you have come to Krakow."

Samuel lowered his head. "I am sorry to tell you Hans and Elspeth are dead." Margot gasped while Noah stared at Samuel with disbelief written on his face. Johan stared down at his plate.

"Dead? But how, when?"

"The Catholics killed them in the Basel persecutions a year

ago, after the Reformists turned them over for rejecting infant baptism." There was silence, broken only by muffled snuffling from Annalisa. Margot looked away as she wiped tears from her eyes with the corner of her apron.

Samuel went on. "The next day they scoured the city arresting Anabaptists, and we fled that night. Before he died, Hans told me to come and find you. We escaped from Basel with little but our lives. On the way..." He paused... "Mareili became ill..." His voice sunk to a whisper. "She died in Görlitz. We had to wait until the roads were passable to continue our journey, and now... well, here we are."

Annalisa's snuffling turned to open sobs.

Margot lifted Annalisa from her chair and pulled her onto her lap. Holding her close, she rubbed the girl's back, rocking her back and forth. Tears were running down Margot's face.

When Anna's sobs stilled, Margot glanced at Noah, who nodded. She managed a smile as she spoke to Samuel. "We built this big house thinking we would fill it with children, but the Lord had something else for us. Noah's job provides our needs and more. We would love to have you stay in our home."

"Yes." Noah agreed. "It would honor us."

"We have been here ten years," Margot said, "and we miss Switzerland. We wanted to stay, but with the peasants' revolt and the religious turmoil we desired a peaceful place to raise children, so we came here. Then we had no children." Margot sighed. "The Poles are nice people, but we will always be outsiders. They are Catholics, and we are not. However, we do not speak of our faith. As long as the work gets done and Noah takes good care of his horses, Sigismund does not pry into our private lives.

Noah nodded. "Yes, it is good work. But as Margot says, we miss home."

Margot looked at the little girl on her lap. "You have brought Switzerland to us. If you lived with us, we would speak our native language, eat Swiss foods and enjoy our country's music and dances." She kissed Annalisa on the forehead. "And I could have a girl to mother and a strong son to make me proud. Please stay."

Samuel nodded, tears in his eyes. "Your kindness is overwhelming. We will accept your offer, at least until I get on my feet... that is if my children agree."

Annalisa looked at the tender face above her. She climbed down and threw her arms around Samuel's neck. "Oh, yes, Papa. Please!"

"Johan, what say you?"

Johan shrugged. These people were nice, but he missed his mother and aunt and uncle and the mountain. "Whatever you wish, Papa."

Samuel eyed him for a moment. "Fine, then. That settles it. We will stay."

THE HIRSCHBERGS soon settled into a routine in their new city. Samuel worked in the blacksmith shop at the castle, shoeing horses and tending the forge. Noah hired Johan to muck the stalls and feed and care for the many beautiful animals that filled the stables. Johan had a natural love for horses so he didn't mind the work. He developed a good rapport with the others who tended the king's mounts and quickly learned the Polish language. One day, soon after they arrived and just when he thought life in Krakow might be tolerable, he walked around a corner, a full manure bucket in each hand, and crashed into a young girl, knocking her down and splattering her dress. Johan set the buckets down and reached to help her, but she rose on her own, her eyes flashing fire.

"You ignorant stable boy!" She spat the words at him. "Look

what you've done to my dress. Why don't you watch where you are going?"

"I'm very sorry." he ducked his head. "I should have been watching."

The girl's face was red, and she trembled from head to toe. "Do you know who I am?"

"No, I don't." Johan smiled. "I'm new here. I do not know you." Then a memory came to him of a girl watching out a window on the day they arrived.

"Wait! Yes, I know you. You're the peeking girl."

The girl's face turned even redder, and she pulled herself to her full height, chin lifted. She looked to be about thirteen. "I am not 'the peeking girl!' I am Princess Isabella, daughter of the king. You have dared to soil my person with your filth, and then you presumed to touch me. You are a filthy, ignorant, disgusting stable boy, and you will beg my pardon, now."

He stepped back. "I beg Your Majesty's pardon for deigning to touch your most sacred person."

You silly spoiled creature...

"And I have soiled your wonderful dress. For that, I am deeply repentant." He bowed low. "If you cannot forgive me, Your Highness, I don't know how my life will be worth living." He straightened, a smile tugging at his lips.

You are beautiful though...

"Ooh, you, you..." Isabella raised her hand to slap him, but Johan caught her wrist and stared down into her eyes without speaking.

Isabella struggled for a moment and then burst into tears. Wrenching her hand away, she turned and ran back the way she had come.

The unfortunate meeting with the princess concerned Johan, but no one at the stable approached him regarding the matter, and so nothing came of the incident. But Johan remembered the collision with the imperious young woman for two reasons—

the sting of her insults, and her beauty. She was the loveliest girl
he had ever seen.

~

THE NEXT TWO years passed quickly. Johan had many opportu-
nities to show his extraordinary skill with horses and soon
Noah elevated him to second groom. On a bright day in April
1533, Johan, now sixteen, hurried through the stables. Excitement almost crackled in the air as he rounded the corner and
saw Noah standing on a box in the courtyard's center,
instructing all the workers who had gathered around. "Suleiman
the Magnificent has sent a wonderful stallion to Sigismund. We
have made all the preparations, but I want you to go now and
make sure we have overlooked nothing." He pointed to two
workers. "You two, make sure the special stall we had built is
without blemish." He waved his hands with excitement. "The
horse will arrive in an hour. The rest of you must gather in the
courtyard for the presentation."

Noah turned to Johan. "Because of your horse-handling
skills, Johan, I want you beside me. But you must be very careful, for the stallion is young and full of spirit."

When he arrived in the courtyard, it surprised Johan to see
Princess Isabella standing to one side with her father. He had
not seen her since the incident in the stable. A wimple secured
by a pearl tiara covered her long dark hair and she was wearing
a white gown. He whispered to Noah. "I have not seen Princess
Isabella for a long time. Where has she been?"

Noah's gray-flecked eyebrows clumped. "You know the
princess?"

Johan smiled at the memory. "We met once in the stable."

Then the gates to the castle opened and trumpets blared.
The Ottoman ambassador rode through on a mighty white
charger, followed by a retinue of mounted Turkish soldiers.

Behind the ambassador came an ornate closed-in van. From within came a shrill scream and the thud of hooves striking the walls. The ambassador bowed.

The Ottoman ambassador's salutation to Sigismund was long and flattering. Johan shifted from foot to foot, eager to see this beautiful horse.

"As a token of the friendship between the two great kings of eastern Europe, Suleiman the Magnificent wishes to present to Sigismund the Supreme a stallion from his private stables. The horse's name is Al-Buraq in honor of the wonderful magic horse that bore Muhammed from Mecca to Jerusalem in one night. That same blood flows in this young stallion's veins. Behold, Al-Buraq, king of horses." The ambassador swept his arm back and bowed low.

Two dark-skinned slaves dressed all in white livery and wearing golden turbans, lowered the ramp, opened the doors of the van, and stepped inside. Moments later, they emerged leading a black stallion by a rope attached to a jewel-encrusted bridle.

His smooth coat glistened beneath the sunlight. When they led him down the ramp, he stopped, looked at the crowd and reared, his shrill whistle echoing between the courtyard walls.

His nostrils curled, and his eyes were so wide the whites showed. As he came down, he lashed out, knocking the grooms aside. Ears flat against his head, he charged straight toward the king and Isabella, who screamed and covered her eyes. Sigismund grabbed the princess and turned, shielding her with his body.

Johan leaped for the horse. He snatched the whipping rope and pulled the stallion's head downward. The horse stumbled and halted, trembling from head to foot.

"Whoa, boy, whoa," Johan murmured. "Settle down. You will be all right." He raised his hand and the screams from the onlookers quieted.

The stallion tried to lift his head and rear again, but Johan held tight. Talking softly, he let the stallion lift his head high enough to look at him. After a moment, the horse nickered and stretched his nose out to smell Johan.

Johan stroked the black's face, speaking in almost a whisper. After several more minutes, the horse calmed and stood quietly. The two grooms, now back on their feet, edged alongside them, and took the rope from Johan. Noah spoke with the two men who had prepared the stall and together with the slaves they led the stallion away. Johan watched them go. The horse was a beauty.

Someone touched his shoulder, and he turned to look into the king's smiling face. Johan bowed.

Sigismund raised him by his arm. "Wonderful, my boy, wonderful! You saved my daughter's life and mine. How can I repay you?"

Johan glanced at Princess Isabella.

She was staring at him with wide eyes. "You!"

Sigismund looked from Johan to her. "Do you know this boy, Isabella?"

Her face reddened. "We... we met once before in the stable." She turned to Johan. "Thank you for saving our lives..." She paused, awkwardly.

"What is your name?" the king asked.

"Johan, Your Majesty. Johan Hirschberg."

"That is not a Polish name. Where are you from?"

"From Switzerland, Your Majesty. Your stablemaster is my uncle's cousin."

As Johan stood beside the king, Sigismund looked around for his stablemaster. "Noah!"

Noah, who stood not far away, hurried to Johan's side and bowed. "Yes, Your Majesty?"

Sigismund put his arm around Johan's shoulder. "I want this young man to be the one to care for the stallion. And be sure to raise his wages. He is now a first groom." He smiled at Johan. "You have earned my undying gratitude, Johan Hirschberg."

Johan bowed. "That is most kind, Your Majesty, but I only did my duty."

"Nonsense, my boy. I have seen nothing like the way you handled that horse." Releasing Johan, he took Isabella by the arm. "Come, Isabella."

The princess turned, then looked back at him. "Thank you again for what you did." She paused. "I was unkind the last time we met. I apologize."

Johan bowed again. "I have put your words as far from me as the east is from the west, Princess."

Isabella nodded and walked away at her father's side.

Johan stared after them.

Truth be told, I have never forgotten, Princess Isabella.

CHAPTER 9: HARD HEARTS

On a bright morning, a month after Al Buraq's arrival, Johan was working with the stallion in a small paddock next to the stables. The stallion's ears twitched this way and that as horses whistled and called or thumped the walls of their stalls. Around them, the smell of fresh hay, oats, grain, and cut grass blended with that of manure and the potent medicines used to keep the animals free of parasites.

He loved his work, and he enjoyed working with the stallion. The wild and excitable young horse was intelligent and inquisitive. He had responded well to Johan's gentle hand, and the two were becoming fast friends. Johan was brushing out the stallion's black mane when he heard a feminine voice behind him.

"I wish to ride this horse today. Please ready him for me."

Al Buraq shied and backed away, nostrils flared. Brush raised, Johan turned to find Princess Isabella standing behind him in the paddock with two of her male retainers.

He frowned. "What is it you want, Your Highness?"

"I said…" she lifted her chin, "ready the horse, for I will ride him today."

Johan eyed the princess. Her dark hair was pulled away from her face and she held a riding crop in her hand.

He shook his head. "I'm sorry, Your Majesty, but this horse is not ready for anyone to ride. He still needs work. You are too young and small to handle him. As you well know, your father's stables offer many other gentler horses from which you can choose."

Isabella's face reddened, but her voice remained calm. "You forget yourself, and you forget who I am. When I command, you obey. Now, ready the horse."

"I am sorry, but I will not, Your Highness, for that would endanger your life."

Isabella took a step forward and stared up at Johan. A muscle twitched in her jaw. "I have been riding all… my… life. I *can* ride this horse, and you *will* ready Al-Buraq. That is my command." She lowered her voice. "I *will not* tell you again."

Johan laughed. "I am not frightened of you, Princess."

"Fool!" Eyes flashing, she struck him full across the cheek with her crop.

With a great effort of will, he did not grab her arm as he'd done before. He felt something wet where she struck him and his face throbbed, but he did not flinch.

"*Now* will you do as I say?" Eyebrows raised, she cocked her head.

Feeling the wetness trickle down his cheek he reached in his pocket for a rag and wiped his face. The cloth came away red. The place where she lashed him burned like fire, but he ignored the pain and turned to the servants. "This horse is untrained, too dangerous for anyone to ride. If Princess Isabella insists, I am not responsible for the result." He placed a hand on the horse's neck. "I am telling you this so the king will not blame me if the horse injures her. Do you understand?"

The servants looked at each other and then nodded.

"Then I will prepare the horse." While they waited, he

retrieved a mounting box, a small saddle and a bridle from the barn. He saddled the horse and put the bit in its mouth. Al-Buraq tensed and fought the bit, but Johan stroked the horse's neck and whispered to him and Al-Buraq calmed. Johan glanced down and noted the length of Isabella's legs and then adjusted the stirrups.

Three mounted men rode to the paddock's gate.

"I will be ready in a moment," Isabella called to the men. "Open the gate for me."

She turned to Johan. "These men are my guards. I am sure that between my skills and theirs, we will keep Al-Buraq in line."

"I will hold him while you mount. Remember that if you treat him like you treated me, he will never forget."

"What?" She frowned.

"Your Highness," Johan bowed. "Your horse is ready."

Isabella went to the big black stallion, who shied away from her. Johan gently coaxed him back to the box. She stepped up on the box, put her foot in the stirrup and swung into the saddle. Al-Buraq stood as still as a statue, though Johan could see his muscles tense. Still speaking gently, Johan checked the stirrup length. When all was ready, he handed the reins to Isabella.

"Do you see?" Isabella peered down her nose at Johan. "The horse is mine to command—"

"Careful!"

Al-Buraq snorted, gathered his muscles and leaped straight into the air. Isabella screamed as Johan and the two servants leaped aside. When he landed the horse jerked his head, pulling at the reins and then reared up. Striking out with his front feet, he lowered his head and spun. His huge muscular body twisted and writhed.

Isabella clung to the pommel with one hand and with the other, yanked at the reins, but Al Buraq jerked his head from side to side. "Help me, please," she cried.

Johan jumped in close to the horse. Yanking the reins from Isabella's grasp, he pulled Al-Buraq into a sharp turn, rebalancing him. Then he forced the horse forward a few steps, muttering to him.

Al-Buraq quieted and Johan brought him to a stop. Isabella jumped off, stumbled, and fell to her knees, pale and shaking. Johan moved the horse away. Her servants lifted her to her feet, just as the men in her escort ran up.

One who seemed to be the leader stepped forward. "Are you hurt, Your Highness?"

Isabella shook her head, sucking in quick breaths. At last, she spoke. "I am fine. He is right. The horse is too strong for me and needs more work." She turned to Johan. "Once again, you have saved me from harm. I, I thank you."

Johan bowed low. "No need to say anything, Your Majesty. I bear the mark of your consideration." When he straightened, he smiled at her.

Blood rose in her face. "You are infuriating, and insolent."

"No, Your Highness. I may be many things, but I am not insolent. I am a freeborn man from the free country of Switzerland. Everything I did today was for your own good. If you wish to discharge me for preventing you from being harmed or killed, another stable in Krakow may use my talents."

He could see her face pale at his words. She clenched her jaw.

"I cannot override my father's wishes by ordering you to leave. But know this. I dislike you. If you stay out of my way..." she was shaking... "we will avoid future confrontations."

"That might be best, Your Majesty." He nodded, struggling to maintain a solemn expression, so as not to further antagonize her. "When the horse is ready to ride, I will inform Noah, who will inform your father." He bowed again.

Without another word, she turned and stomped away, her

servants trailing along behind. The captain of her guard turned to Johan. "Your face is bleeding. Did the horse hurt you?"

Johan petted Al-Buraq's neck. "This horse would never hurt me."

~

THAT NIGHT, Isabella lay awake for a long time, haunted by Johan's blue eyes and handsome face. Her violence toward him shamed her, for, despite his insolent manner, she knew he had been protecting her. She tried to sleep, but strange things kept happening to her body. First she was burning and then she was freezing.

What in the world is happening?

She rose from her bed and stepped to the window. Drawing the curtains aside, she pushed open the double frames. A large spring moon hung high in the sky, casting shadows from the tall towers onto the walls across from her room. The faint fragrance of plum blossoms and night-blooming jasmine rose to her window.

A black form swept across the courtyard—the owl that lived in the tower was hunting for mice like it did every night. Clouds drifted across the face of the moon and the call of a night bird broke the silence. The night was lovely, but tonight Isabella did not care.

She sighed and crawled back into her bed, but she could not get comfortable. She reached over and rang the little bell on her nightstand.

In a few minutes Maria came into the room. She rubbed the sleep from her eyes and yawned. "What is it, Your Highness?"

"I'm sorry to wake you, Maria, but I... I can't sleep. I had an upsetting experience with a horse in the stable today and my muscles are still sore. Please send someone for a cup of soothing tea."

"Yes, Your Majesty." The girl went out for a moment and then she returned to Isabella. "Now, what upset you, my princess?"

"Oh, nothing…" She hesitated. "Well, this groom… this boy… well, he's a young man… He works in my father's stables. He's arrogant and disrespectful, and he insulted me twice today. Ooh…" She clenched her fists. "I hate him."

Maria sat on the bed and took the girl in her arms. "So it wasn't a horse, was it?" She chuckled. "Is this groom handsome and tall and strong, the one with the deep blue eyes?"

"Yes, and he's so good with horses." Isabella sighed then straightened up in the bed. "I mean… no, he's ugly and rude and a bully. I despise him."

"You sound like someone who doesn't know what to think, Princess."

"What is wrong with me, Maria?" Isabella put her face in her hands. "I can't stop thinking of him. And I am so ashamed. I struck him across the face with my crop. I hurt him, but he did not retaliate or say a word. Instead, he looked at me with a strange expression and smiled. Oh, he exasperated me!"

Maria laughed and pulled her closer. "My princess, there is nothing wrong with you except you are fourteen and becoming a woman."

"But why do I have these feelings? I hate him, I despise him…"

"You have lost your heart to this young stable boy, no?" Maria stroked Isabella's hair.

Isabella looked up and blinked. "Lost my heart? What do you mean?"

"I mean, young lady, that this exasperating young man is more than a stable boy to you. I heard how he saved you when the black horse first came. Besides his blue eyes and a handsome face, he has other good qualities. This… what is his name?"

"Johan."

"This Johan saved your life. He is strong and he must be kind for he did not retaliate when you struck him. And he is gifted, for he speaks to the horse, and it obeys him. These qualities have opened your heart in a new and wonderful way."

"But, Maria! I am a princess. He is a commoner from another country! I cannot love him."

"No, you cannot." Maria shook her head. "Your position destines you for greater things. But if you were not a princess, you might love this Johan, eh?"

Isabella sat silent for a long time, looking down at her hands... thinking. Then she lifted her head. "Yes, Maria, you are right. If I were not a princess, I could love this Johan."

CHAPTER 10: AWAKENING

*J*ohan looked at the pile of wood next to Noah's house and then picked up a round. He placed it on the chopping block and swung his axe, splitting the log chunk in half. Then he lifted a section, put it on the block and swung again. He kept at it, splitting the round into smaller pieces. When they were the right size for the stove, he split another round. He continued splitting and as he did, the pile of firewood grew around him. Sweat ran down his back, and his muscles became sore, but still he swung. He stayed there until the anger finally drained out of him. At last he stopped and wiped his face with the tail of his shirt.

"Well, little princess," he murmured, "you can thank God your precious white neck was not on my block today." He laughed and flexed his shoulders. There was no tension. "Now I can stop thinking about you and get on with my day."

But despite his resolve, the princess's lovely face kept intruding on his thoughts. It had been three weeks and his cheek had healed, leaving only a small scar, but the blow's sting still burned in his heart, an ever-present reminder.

Johan went to the well and drew two buckets of water. Then

he poured the water into the trough by the house and plunged his head in and kept it there until he ran out of breath. Huffing and blowing, he pulled out and used a towel hanging on a nail above the trough to wipe the water off his face and dry his hair. The cold water cooled his heated skin, but it did not soothe the fire inside Johan—a fire named Isabella.

Johan finished and walked toward the kitchen. He needed to leave for the stable, but he put off going for one reason—he did not want to see Isabella. Since the day she struck him with her crop, he'd done his best to avoid her, but it had been difficult. At least two or three times a week, Isabella came to the stables to ride and, though he did his best to make himself scarce at those times, he often encountered her as she paraded through with her retinue. If he met her face-to-face, he bowed and remained silent until she passed.

Isabella would walk by him without a word or engage one of her companions in conversation. Twice, Isabella requested his help with a horse, but he did not speak to her unless she spoke to him, and then he only grunted his replies.

Yet, he had to admit to himself that something attracted him to her. She was an arrogant, spoiled child, but she was beautiful. Her dark, lustrous hair, her flashing blue eyes, the delicate turn of her mouth obsessed him. Despite the way she treated him, she had captivated him since the first day he saw her. Now, she plagued him day and night.

If only I could spend the whole day with my head under that cold water...

He laughed at the thought and headed into the kitchen where Margot was preparing bread and cheese for his lunch. She finished wrapping the food in a cloth and handed the bundle to him. "That is an enormous pile of wood you split, Johan. Thank you. You cut enough for a hard Russian winter."

Johan shrugged. "I had some things on my mind and I did not pay attention to how much I cut."

"Some things? More like someone, I suspect."

Johan frowned. "What do you mean?"

Margot shrugged and pursed her lips, a twinkle in her eye. "Well... Noah tells me you had a run-in with the princess a few weeks ago. She's a handful. Did she put that welt on your cheek?"

"She's an arrogant child, Margot, who struck me when I would not do what she demanded—because what she demanded was too dangerous. And then after she forced me to comply, I had to rescue her for the second time. If I had not seized Al-Buraq's reins and calmed him, the horse would have bolted, and that girl would be somewhere in Hungary by now."

Margot laughed and patted Johan's arm. "A lovely girl like her... a handsome young man like you... Be careful, Johan. Something might happen between you two. A fine line separates love and hate. Best you stay mad at her."

"Margot! She is a princess. It is common knowledge her parents are grooming her for a marriage of state. I am a commoner. She is far out of my reach."

"Yes, that is true, but sometimes the heart does not care for political realities." Margot giggled and hurried out of the kitchen, leaving Johan to stare after her.

ISABELLA SAT at her study table in the castle library, trying to understand the complex Latin grammar her teacher, Johannes Hönter, had given her to study. "Nouns, including proper nouns and pronouns, have six cases or casus—nominative, vocative, accusative, genitive, dative and ablative." She read the confusing words out loud. "Several nouns have a seventh case, called the locative. They also have three genus; masculine, feminine and neuter; and two numerus: singular and plural."

She yawned and put the book down. Concentration was

difficult when a certain handsome, smiling face drifted into her thoughts again and again. Dark hair, intense blue eyes...

Hönter rose from his chair at the next table and came to stand by her side. "You find this boring, Princess?"

Isabella grinned up at him. "Do you want me to massage your ego or tell you the truth, Master Hönter?"

Hönter laughed. "Yes, Princess. I admit Latin is a dead language. The old Roman Empire is a dim memory, and the coliseum crumbles into dust. Yet, we need to read the language, for it is the root of the Romance languages and will serve you well in your life. In addition, knowing Latin aids a person in understanding the mass and church dogma, which will also benefit you later in your life."

Isabella put the book on her table. "I understand, Master Hönter, but Latin is so difficult. Sometimes I'd rather be a Lutheran so I could read the Bible in a living language and put this book away forever."

He chuckled. "You may as well wish for something else because you will never be a Protestant—not as long as your father and mother are alive. Now..." He sat across from her. "Let us go through the declensions—first, second, third, fourth, and fifth."

Isabella sighed and recited. "Singular—nominative; carta, dominus, puer, vinum, rex, civis, jus, redditus, res. Vocative; carta, domine, puer, vinum, rex, civis, jus, redditus, res...

HER CLASSES DRAGGED BY, but at last Isabella was free for the rest of the day. She wandered through the castle, unable to wrench her thoughts from her confrontation with Johan. She had not slept well since the day she struck him because, by nature, she was not a cruel person.

As she crossed the courtyard, she spied her father's chapel, now finished, and went into the cool retreat. Many candles burned on the hand-carved altar, and their light illuminated the beautiful sculptures, stuccos and paintings that filled the interior of the chapel and lined its walls. Above it all shone the chapel's magnificent golden dome. Isabella slipped into a pew, knelt, and tried to still her racing heart, to find solace in prayer. But though the chapel was still and peaceful and her thoughts should have risen to God, they returned to Johan.

I must do something! This torment cannot continue.

Then a scripture came to mind; one that Pieter had often read to her.

Humble yourself in the sight of the Lord and he will lift you up.

"Must I?"

The surrounding silence was almost deafening. Then again the words came into her mind.

Humble yourself in the sight of the Lord and he will lift you up.

Isabella knew what she had to do. She whispered her acquiescence to God, "Yes, Lord, if that's what you ask of me."

Resigned to the inevitable, she rose and moped toward the stables.

JOHAN WAS LAYING fresh hay in Al Buraq's stall when he heard the small sound of a rustle of skirts behind him and turned. Isabella was standing there. "Princess…" He bowed. "What can I do for you? Saddle a horse?"

A shaft of sunlight was streaming through a small round window high up on the wall. Small particles of hay dust danced in the beams like golden stardust. The light fell on her face, and Johan thought she had never looked more beautiful.

Isabella shifted from one foot to the other. "I'm here to apologize." She looked down and then up at him again. "I… I struck you, and I am ashamed, for that was wrong." She took a small step forward. "When you smiled at me, I thought you were mocking me, but now I understand you were protecting me. I have spent many sleepless nights thinking of you…" She blushed. "I mean of…" She glanced away and then looked into his eyes. "… of what I did to you. I am sorry for my rude behavior. I was the one who was insolent, not you. Can you forgive me?"

Johan set his pitchfork aside. Isabella was pale and trembling, yet she held his gaze. He wanted to take her in his arms and comfort her, tell her he accepted her apology. But he knew he wouldn't be able to release her until he had wrapped his arms around her slim shoulders, kissed her lips and stroked her silky hair.

"You are right." He folded his arms. "I did not want the horse to injure you. Al-Buraq is a handful, even for me. I never doubted your horsemanship, but he is strong and spirited. When I have worked with him for a while longer, he will be ready for you to ride."

"Ever since…" Isabella lowered her eyes. "Since the first time you saved my life, and I saw how you spoke to him, calmed him with your voice…" she looked at him again. "I have hoped you might show me more about horses. I know how to ride, but you…" She smiled. "You understand them, and they understand you."

Johan's heart pounded against his ribs. She respected him. She wanted him to teach her, to be her mentor. But that could never be. His attraction to her was too strong. He might overstep the boundary between himself and her.

"I accept your apology, Your Highness, and I forgive you." He held his voice steady. "However, as far as me teaching you, I think you forget that you are a princess, and I am but an ignorant stable boy." He touched his cheek. "You do not need me, for you have everything you need already. Your father can provide you an able horse master at the snap of his finger—one more fitting to your rank. I think it best we remain as we are. Now, if that is all, I have much work to complete before nightfall."

Johan reached for the pitchfork. Isabella turned white and then bright red as she stood staring at him. Then she wheeled and walked from the stall, her head high and her back straight. Johan never saw the tears flooding her cheeks.

CHAPTER 11: A GROWING LOVE

*B*ack straight, head high, Isabella marched to her rooms, jaw clamped and fists clenched. Once inside her bedroom, she ran and threw herself across the bed, weeping like she'd never wept before.

Her door opened, and a moment later Maria was at her side. "Why, Isabella, my darling, whatever is the matter?"

"Nothing..." Isabella cried. "Oh, everything, Maria." Head in her arms, she sobbed into the bedcovers. When she had cried the last of her tears, Isabella lifted her head. "Do you have a handkerchief?"

Maria pulled a linen cloth from her pocket and handed it to the princess. "Whatever happened to upset you so?"

Isabella did not respond.

Maria thought for a moment. "Could it be that stable boy?"

Isabella nodded and dabbed her eyes.

"Tell me what happened, Isabella, dear."

"I..." Isabella rolled over and sat up. "I went to the stables to apologize to him for my... my bad behavior... the way I acted when I struck him, and I asked him to show me how to work with horses the way he does." She paused.

"And?"

"He…" She sniffed. "He thanked me, then refused my request and reminded me that he was only an ignorant stable boy before he sent me away."

"What?"

"That's exactly what he did! He is despicable. I hate him."

Isabella slid off the bed and went to the window. She needed air, so she pulled the drapes and opened the window. A spring breeze slipped through; it felt cool against her cheeks.

Maria came and slipped her arm around Isabella's waist. "You poor dear. That must have been painful for you. But he displayed wisdom."

"Wisdom, Maria?" She pursed her lips. "Is it wisdom to treat a Polish princess in such a rude manner?"

"That is my point, Isabella." Maria placed her hands on Isabella's shoulders and turned her so they were face to face. "You are a princess, and as he reminded you, he is but a stable boy. You are miles apart in status and destinies." She smiled. "Think, Isabella! When you are a queen, Johan will still work in a stable, pitching hay. He will have a fat wife and boisterous sons he will teach to be stable boys in their time. He sounds like an intelligent young man, for he has grasped the truth, though you have not."

"What do you mean, I have not, Maria?"

"Princess, you are no longer a girl." Maria smoothed Isabella's dark hair. "You are a beautiful young woman whose passions and soft heart will draw you to a strong, handsome young man like Johan. But you must learn to be more discreet, for your feelings for him are obvious. Your parents would be furious if they discovered your secret."

Isabella covered her face with her hands. "Is it that obvious?"

"My dear…" Maria laughed. "I am not that much older than you, but I am, shall we say, more experienced in these matters. You could only be more obvious if you took the royal trumpeters to the tower and announced your infatuation to the entire kingdom accompanied by mighty blasts."

"Come, sit with me for a moment." Maria led Isabella to the couch on the other side of the room. "Isabella, you must listen. Johan has shown wisdom by keeping his distance from you. You must not allow him any further into your heart.

"I overheard your father and mother speaking of your future. They concluded the negotiations for you to marry John Zápolya, King of Hungary. Isabella! You are to be the queen of my homeland!"

Isabella frowned. "Yes, I know about John Zápolya. But he is an old man. I told my mother I am too young for him. Besides..." Isabella shook her head. "You are right, Maria. My heart belongs to another."

Maria's brow furrowed. "If you complicate this with an affair of the heart, it will enrage your father." Her eyes narrowed. "Royal princesses are born for one reason—to marry kings. The joining of Poland and Hungary will stop the greedy Hapsburgs from swallowing my country... and yours."

"But don't my feelings count for something? Don't I have a say in my future?"

"No, Isabella, you do not." Maria shook her head. "If you treasure this young man's life, you will not continue this flirtation. If your father found out someone stands in the way of his plans... Well, Sigismund could make him disappear. He would take steps to ensure you never see him again."

"Are you saying my father would have Johan killed?"

"That is one possibility if your relationship interfered with the Zápolya marriage."

"Oh, Maria, that is horrible. To think my father would have someone I love killed is... well it is just too awful."

"But it is truth. As harsh as my words may sound, if you love this young man, you will forget him and look to your future."

AFTER HE SPOKE WITH ISABELLA, Johan kept busy. He did his best to avoid the princess, but if he came in contact with her, he remained polite but distant. For her part, unless she had a specific request, she would nod and pass by without speaking. Several weeks passed this way and Johan felt like he was getting control of his feelings. But one morning, all that changed. He was grooming Al-Buraq when he heard the familiar rustle of skirts. He turned to see Isabella entering the stallion's stall. She had a determined look on her face.

It startled Johan to see her. "Your Highness, what...?"

"I need to speak to you."

"But Your Highness, we agreed—"

Isabella waved his comment away. "I didn't agree to anything. Actually, you told me how we should behave toward each other and I had nothing to say in the matter. But the way we treat each other troubles me deeply. You have been so mean." The words were barely out of her mouth when she put her face in her hands and burst into tears. Al Buraq snorted and shied away.

"Mean? But what did I do? I thought..."

The princess kept crying and her tears pierced his heart. He wanted to take Isabella into his arms and comfort her but that was impossible. He looked around to see if anyone else was with her, but she was alone. Johan did not know what to do, so he waited while the girl cried.

When she finished, she pulled out a handkerchief and dried her eyes. "I like you as a person and I admire your skill with horses. I only want to be friends. Can't we at least be that?"

Johan hesitated. "I could be your friend, but..."

"What, Johan?"

It was the first time she had used his name, which sounded

strange but wonderful coming from her lips. He looked out into the hallway and then closed the stall door.

"I must confess, Your Highness, I would like to be your friend but it seems like an impossible thing. Not only do our stations in life create a great gulf between us but I am not of your faith. I do not see how we—"

"That is of no matter." Isabella shrugged. "Many Protestants have immigrated to Poland, fleeing the problems in Germany. My father leaves them alone as long as they keep their religion to themselves."

"Your Highness, I—"

Isabella interrupted again. "You may call me Isabella. Your Highness is entirely too formal."

"Yes, Your Highness... I mean, Isabella. The problem is that I am more than a Protestant. I am an Anabaptist. You are a Catholic, and I have vowed to hate all Catholics."

He saw the startled look on her face. "Does that trouble you, Isabella?"

She put her head down and her voice was faint. "My teachers taught me about the Anabaptists. But they did not tell me why Anabaptists hate Catholics."

Johan led Isabella to a bench by the wall and sat with her, being careful not to touch her. Outside horses neighed or whistled and stomped in their stalls. The smell of sweet hay mixed with the pungent smell of liniment. Through the walls, Johan could hear other grooms working their horses. He took a deep breath and began.

"Catholics claim paying money to the priests can keep a person from hell. Anabaptists do not believe that. Nor do we believe the bread and wine of the Mass turns into the actual body and blood of Jesus. And we do not practice infant baptism."

Isabella stared at him until Johan had to look away from her shocked expression. At last, she spoke. "My teacher told me Anabaptists do not baptize infants, but what you are telling me about the Mass and indulgences is blasphemy. How will your soul get out of purgatory if the priests do not intercede for you and if your loved ones do not pay indulgences for your soul's salvation?"

Johan shook his head. "Anabaptists know the Catholic Church invented purgatory to fatten the priests' purses. Isabella gasped and jumped to her feet.

"That is a lie."

"Isabella, before you get angry, please listen for just a moment. You asked why Anabaptists hate Catholics. I am telling you."

Isabella sank down on the bench while Johan went on. "The Bible is clear. Jesus died for all people. He bore everyone's sins on the cross, and if you trust in him alone, you will go straight to heaven when you die."

Isabella shook her head. "But that is too simple. And what about the Mass? Are we not to eat the flesh and drink the blood of Jesus? The Mass has great magic."

Johan turned and looked into her eyes. "The way Anabaptists see it when Jesus broke bread and served his disciples wine he did not mean the bread and the wine were his physical body and blood. They *represent* his body and blood and the price he paid to provide salvation for all. We are to remember his sacrifice when we take the Eucharist, but we are not cannibals, eating his actual body and drinking his actual blood."

Isabella had a pained expression on her face. "But what about baptism? Are you not condemning infants to hell without baptism?"

"No, Isabella. If babies are baptized before they can understand what baptism means, when they are babies, then they go through the rest of their lives expecting to go to heaven because of an act, not a relationship with Jesus."

Johan stood and paced back and forth as he spoke. His

words came hard and fast like arrows. "Anabaptists believe a person must understand what they are doing when they accept baptism because it is such an important act. You can't accept Christ as your Savior when you are a baby, and you also shouldn't receive baptism without understanding what you are doing."

Isabella was silent for a moment. "So what you have told me is informative, but holding different beliefs is not a reason for you to hate Catholics so much, is it? What is the real reason? What have you not told me?"

Johan turned to Isabella. He felt the muscle on his jaw twitching and he took another deep breath. "My Aunt Elspeth was the most wonderful, kind woman I ever knew. She cared for everyone as Jesus commanded us to do. She was a true Christian. Yet, the Protestant Reformists in Basel arrested her and tried her and my uncle for heresy. They turned her over to the Catholic soldiers, who could have put her in prison. Instead, they burned her and my Uncle Hans at the stake.

"Because we were Anabaptists too, they forced us to flee the city. We left our farm and all our possessions behind. My mother died on the journey to Krakow. After that, I vowed never to rest until I could take vengeance on the Catholics and the Reformists who killed my aunt and uncle—and my mother, too, for she would still be alive today, if not for them."

"Johan, that's terrible." Isabella shuddered. "I know hatred exists between Catholics and Lutherans, but for religious leaders to kill innocent, good people is a sin."

"Yes, Isabella, a great sin. That is why we cannot be friends."

Isabella stood and faced Johan. "You may hate Catholics, but can you put that aside for my sake? I want to be your friend— that is what I care about. It doesn't matter what our faith is if we care for each other."

"You are right, Isabella." He took her hand and pulled her down beside him. "People should be able to choose their friends based on their behavior, not their religion. I must confess that, despite the huge gap between us, I... I..." He stopped and turned his head.

Isabella's eyes opened wide. "Why, Johan, you are blushing." She laughed, and the sound of it was like a rippling brook in a mountain meadow. "What must you confess?" She was smiling now.

"I have wanted to be your friend."

Isabella looked into his eyes and took his hand. "Yes, we will be friends." Then, without warning, she leaned over and kissed him on the cheek. Giggling, she jumped up and ran, her laughter trailing behind her.

CHAPTER 12: THE DECISION

Sigismund, King of Poland, stared at his diminutive queen, Bona Sforza. "I am still not convinced a marriage between our daughter Isabella and John Zápolya will benefit Poland, Bona." He pursed his lips. "And it will anger the Hapsburgs."

Without blinking, Bona returned his gaze. "Do not vacillate now, Sigismund. You concluded the negotiations. The Hapsburgs have only one thing in mind, husband. They want to bring the rest of Eastern Europe, including Poland, under their dominion. Zápolya has agreed to wed Isabella, and such a marriage will knit Poland and Hungary together as a bulwark against the ambitions of both the Hapsburgs and the Turks."

Sigismund walked to the window and was silent for a long time. At last he spoke. "The Hapsburg Emperor Charles and his brother Ferdinand are like hungry wolves—wanting to devour us. But to the south, Suleiman lurks, desiring to bring Christendom under the banner of his bloodthirsty prophet. The Hapsburgs now control half of Hungary. Zápolya controls the other half, but only because he has aligned himself with Suleiman."

Bona moved to stand beside Sigismund. She slipped her hand into his. "Your family once ruled Hungary, Sigismund. If this marriage to Zápolya produces an heir, a Jagiellon will inherit the throne. We have spoken of this.

"With the might of Poland behind him, Zápolya could free himself of dependence on Suleiman and quiet his country's fear of Charles. He could move his army south and become the power in the Balkans. Charles V has promised to fight against Suleiman, but he has never sent an army. I think he considers Zápolya a weaker opponent than Suleiman and so he continues this little war over Hungary. But even if Charles takes over Hungary, we must fear the Turks more, for religion drives them."

Sigismund was silent as he surveyed the verdant landscape that surrounded Wawel. The manicured castle grounds ran toward the broad Vistula River. As he watched, many ships rode its deep current bearing north toward the Baltic seaports and the Scandinavian countries. Beyond the river, golden wheat fields flowed up and over rolling hills, awaiting the harvesters' scythes. White clouds drifted across the blue sky.

He sighed and shook his head. His country was at a significant juncture in history, and poor little Isabella was a pawn in political maneuvering that was determining the shape of Europe. Sigismund turned back to Bona. "I must admit this is a delicate negotiation and you are right. Even though he makes friendly overtures, we should fear Suleiman. I prefer a Hapsburg marriage, but then Hungary would be at the mercy of the infidel Turks. I will do this, but only if we can persuade Charles not to overthrow John Zápolya if we align with Hungary."

The queen went to a table and poured them both a glass of wine. "What if we can negotiate a treaty between Charles and Zápolya that guarantees Hapsburg aid to Hungary against the Turks, instead of a Hapsburg conquest of the rest of Hungary? That would be a win for Charles because he will not have to spend his resources defeating Zápolya. It will also be a win for us since we will become known as the defenders of Christianity in Europe. Then Isabella can wed Zápolya, and we will extend Poland's influence."

Sigismund laughed as he accepted the glass of wine. "Brilliant." He lifted the glass. "If you weren't a woman, I would make you my prime minister, Bona."

Isabella stamped her foot and dropped into a chair. "I do not want to marry an old man, Father. I am too young. And when I marry, I want it to be for love."

Sigismund laughed out loud. "For love! Where did you get such a foolish notion?" He turned to his queen. "Did you hear, Bona? Our fifteen-year-old daughter wants to marry for love, instead of for the good of her country."

Bona shook her finger at Isabella. "You are a woman, a princess of the Royal House of Jagiellon. You were born for one purpose and one purpose only—to advance the power of our dynasty through marriage."

"Yes, yes, I understand what you hope to gain through your political maneuvering. But why must it be John Zápolya? Can't you find me a younger royal who... who shares the same interests I do."

Sigismund laughed again. "If you mean by interests, a handsome young prince who thinks only of bedding you, none are available—at least none who can further our goals."

Isabella hid her face in her hands. "Father, don't be crude. I am not thinking of the marriage bed, for I know nothing of such things. I mean someone young enough to appreciate riding, traveling, hunting, balls..."

"Life is more than your simple pleasures, Isabella." Hands on her waist, Bona leaned toward her daughter. "Your father and I have agreed. You will marry John Zápolya and our family will grow in power and influence. Why do you resist, daughter? You will be a queen."

"I resist mother because..."

Bona looked into her daughter's eyes. "Perhaps you resist, Isabella, because you are interested in someone else?"

"No, Mother, I..."

"You think I am not without my sources of information? The servants in this palace give me daily reports, daughter, or did you forget? And they tell me they have seen you moping around the palace, staring out the window, visiting the stable..." She raised a knowing eyebrow. "The stable! So that's it! The handsome stable boy is the one you pine after, the one who saved you. Am I not right?"

Isabella stared back at her mother, her chin lifted.

"Daughter, is it the stable boy?"

Isabella looked to her father for help, but he turned away. She whispered, "He's my friend, and that is all."

Bona came and jerked her daughter to her feet. Her face twisted with rage. "We will have him locked so deep in prison he will never see the light of day again! He should never have dared to think—"

"Mother! Please! Johan is innocent!" She tried to pull away from her mother's iron grip. "He has said nothing... nor has he ever touched me. Please do not harm him." She looked at her father. "Papa, please!"

Sigismund came to stand beside Bona. "Too much is at stake for you to dally with someone so far beneath you. If King John found out, and if he thinks you are not a virgin, he might not agree to this marriage." Sigismund took Bona's hand away from Isabella's arm. "However, I owe something to the lad, for he saved my life when he saved Isabella. And I do not wish to punish him if he is innocent as our daughter says."

Isabella grabbed her father's hand. "Oh, thank you, Papa!"

He was silent for a moment and then a thought came to him. "We have a trade mission going to England. I will send him with our ambassador to tend the horses. The trip will last for at least a year, maybe two, and perhaps the cold English climate will cool his ardor. If he is in England, there will be no distractions here when you marry John."

Isabella stared at her father. "But, Papa, we are just friends. Why send him away? What about his family, his work?"

Sigismund shook his head. "No, Isabella. He must go. He must leave the stables anyway, for I could never have him working here so you could continue your little dalliance."

Isabella sank back down on the couch.

A year, or two… We were just getting to know each other…

JOHAN WAS IN THE GROOMS' quarters when a palace servant came to tell him he had a visitor. He followed the messenger to the corridor where a young woman dressed in fine clothes was waiting. "Hello…" He'd seen her in the courtyard a time or two but did not know who she was.

She stepped close and spoke in a low voice. "I am Maria, Princess Isabella's lady-in-waiting. She wishes to meet with you in the stable. You must come now."

"Is something wrong?"

"Please come. She will tell you."

Johan hesitated. He had a bad feeling. But the girl pursed her lips and motioned with her hand, so he followed her to the black stallion's stall. Isabella was inside on the bench. She looked up when he entered, and her face was wet with tears. Johan stepped inside as Maria withdrew.

"What is it, Princess?"

"Oh, Johan, I have gotten you into serious trouble."

Johan came and sat beside her. "What do you mean, trouble?"

Isabella wiped her eyes. "My father is planning to send you away to England... for a year, maybe longer."

Johan shook his head. "Why ever would he do such a thing?"

"I am to marry the king of Hungary in a month. My parents do not want you to be an impediment to the marriage."

Johan was growing more perplexed each moment even as he felt dismay at the news of Isabella's upcoming marriage. "Isabella! What is going on? Why would I cause a problem in your marriage?"

Isabella hid her face in her hands.

Johan pulled her hands away. More tears wet her cheeks. "Isabella, you must tell me what is happening. Why would I be a problem?"

"Because... because... because I love you, Johan."

Before he could speak, the princess was in his arms, clinging to him. "I have wept, I have paced my rooms, I have sworn I would not see you again. But I cannot help myself, Johan." She looked into his eyes. "You have taken my heart, and I cannot get it back."

"Isabella, I..." And then his arms went around her, pressing her to his chest. When she looked up, he rained kisses upon her soft lips. She returned his passion, her lips on fire and her breast heaving.

At last he forced himself to pull away. "I love you too, Princess. I have loved you since the first day I saw you. But we cannot, we dare not! I am a stable boy and you are a royal princess. Such love is madness, madness!"

Isabella clung to Johan as though she would meld her body into his. "If I love you and you love me, cannot we go somewhere where I am not a princess and you are not a stable boy? A place where we could be Johan and Isabella and live our lives in peace and simplicity without the world crushing us?"

Johan held her for a long time, stroking her silky hair. He shook his head. "Isabella, we can't, we can't... we have to give this up."

She pulled herself tighter against him. "Please, Johan. You love me. I know you do. Think of something. There has to be a place we can go!"

Johan lifted her face and looked into her beautiful eyes and he felt the last resistance go. She loved him. She was his to command. "Isabella, such a place may exist. Travelers have told me stories of the Anabaptists taking over Münster, Germany, and declaring it to be a free state. They are calling the city 'The New Jerusalem.' We could go there, become invisible, and be free to live our lives together. Dare we?"

Isabella took his face in her hands. "I will go anywhere you say. I want to be with you for the rest of my life. Please, Johan, please take me away. Love me... marry me."

Johan kissed her soft lips again. They trembled under his touch. Then he broke away, took hold of her arms and held her from him. "If we are to go, we must go tonight. Disguise yourself. Will Maria help?"

"She will not be happy with my decision, but she will help me in any way she can."

"Good! Have her get simple clothing, such as a servant would wear. Trousers would be even better. If we appear to be two youths traveling together, we will not draw attention to ourselves."

"I will tell her."

"Good. We will take Al-Buraq. When my family traveled from Switzerland, we learned how to disguise our horse to appear old and worn out. The robbers ignored us. We can disguise Al-Buraq the same way. Now, go! Bring one change of clothes. We must travel light. I have money saved and I will pack food. The journey will be long, several hundred miles. We will be on the road for a month, maybe two. Hurry now. I will meet you here at midnight."

Isabella pressed into Johan's arms and they kissed once more. Then she rose and opened the stall door. She whispered to Maria. "Come! We must hurry."

She looked over her shoulder, her eyes bright. "Midnight, Johan... my love."

CHAPTER 13: THE JOINING

*a*fter Isabella left, Johan left the stables and went home. He ate supper with his family, memorizing their faces, for he knew he would never see them again. When the family went to bed and the house was quiet, he packed a knapsack, put his savings into a pouch and slipped downstairs. He tiptoed to the mantle and removed the golden crucifix from its place of honor.

I will take this to remember my Tante Elspeth.

He lit a candle and sat at Noah's desk to write a letter to his father and sister.

Dear Papa and Annalisa,

I am leaving tonight with Princess Isabella. A great love has grown between us, so I am taking her away to a place where we can be free to love each other and live a simple life as Johan and Isabella. I cannot tell you where for I do not want you to have to carry the secret and so be in danger from the king. Please thank Noah and Margot for their kindness to us. I love you both so much. If I never see you again on earth, I will see you in heaven.

Your son and brother,

Johan

He left the letter on the mantle, went to the kitchen and packed cheese, meat and bread from the larder, and then picked up his bags. He looked around the house one more time, took a deep breath, and slipped out into the night.

After the short walk to the castle, he went into the stables by a back way and hurried to Al-Buraq's stall. The horse greeted him with a nicker and pushed against his chest, searching for the apple Johan always carried.

"Yes, yes, I didn't forget," Johan whispered. "But you must be quiet, Al-Buraq."

While the horse crunched the apple, Johan saddled him. Then he waited, his heart pounding. After about half an hour, the midnight bell in the clock tower rang, but it did not bring Isabella. He rose and paced back and forth in the stall, going to the door several times to look out into the passageway. A half hour passed—still no Isabella. After an hour the bell in the clock tower rang one o'clock but still no princess. Johan turned to the stallion.

"She changed her mind, my friend. She's not coming. I should have expected it." He kicked at a bale of hay and then exhaled. "Well, Al-Buraq, with or without her, I must flee or I will spend the next two years in England." Johan put his face against Al-Buraq's muzzle and patted the horse goodbye, picked up his bag and slipped out of the stall. A few flickering torches lit the way. He took a few steps and was almost to the side door when he heard someone running down the passageway. A boy wearing a cap and trousers with a pack over his shoulder hurried up to the stall. Johan retreated into the shadows.

The boy opened the stall door and looked in. "I'm here, Johan, where are you?" He heard Al-Buraq nicker.

Johan smiled. He'd recognize that voice anywhere so he hurried back to the stall.

Isabella whirled around, her eyes wide, and her mouth open, as if she was about to scream. But then she saw him and smiled.

"Johan, it's you!" In the dim light her face shone below the boyish cap. She threw herself into his arms, "Oh, Johan, I had such a scare. I thought you would leave without me. I was ready to go when my mother came to bid me good night. She never does that. I barely had time to throw on a robe over my clothes and climb into bed.

"She talked for the longest time. She wanted to discuss marriage with me, and..." Isabella lowered her eyes. "Marriage and babies and a woman's duty to her husband. I couldn't imagine..., well, being that way with the old man they want me to marry. But I thought of you and, and... Oh, Johan, do you still want me?"

Johan looked down at the trembling girl in his arms. She was the most beautiful thing he had ever seen. Overcome by her innocent beauty and sweet smile, he leaned to kiss her. She wrapped her arms around his neck, and the fire in her kiss was white-hot. He wanted to hold her forever.

Finally, he pulled away and looked at her. "We must hurry but before we go, I need to ask you something." He paused, taken aback by the question in her eyes. "Are you sure... Are you sure this is what you want, Isabella? You have lived in luxury and comfort. From now on, you will live a peasant's life. You will milk cows and make bread and...," Johan smiled, "care for our children. Until now your life has run before you like a route on a map with no surprises. But from this day on, we will not know what tomorrow may bring. And... if they catch us, your father will hang me or throw me in prison for the rest of my life."

"Oh, Johan." She took a breath. "I have wanted to be a normal person for so long. I hate being a princess. A peasant's life sounds wonderful—if I am with you. Since the first time we kissed, my life before you became a dim memory. Now, the only reality is you and me and the adventure that awaits us."

"But, Isabella, your father will scour the country for you. We are not safe. We could call this off right now and none would be the wiser." He looked around. Behind them, Al-Buraq moved restlessly.

Isabella grasped his arms. "My father will never look for us in Germany. It's too far away." She looked up at him, her face pale in the torchlight. "Why are you saying this, Johan?" There was fear in her voice. "Don't you want to be with me?"

Johan looked down at her. "I want to be with you forever, Isabella, but if you have any fear or uncertainty in your heart—if this is just a way to escape marriage to an old man..." He paused. "Now's the time to say so."

"Yes, my parents want to force me into a marriage with a dotard whose only desire is to get a young, unspoiled girl into his bed. But that is not why I am going." Isabella tightened her hold on him. "I am certain of my love for you and my desire to be with you forever. My question for you is this—do you feel the same?"

Johan smiled. To be with this young woman was worth everything, even his life. "You are right, my love. We will put our lives in the Lord's hands. Whatever happens, we will always have these next days together. Now we must hurry before someone comes."

He strapped their bags on behind and lifted Isabella into the saddle. "Come, *leibchen*. Let us find our destiny."

FOR THE NEXT THREE NIGHTS, Johan pushed Al-Buraq hard, stopping only to camp in secluded spots during the day to avoid Sigismund's soldiers and other travelers. He kept a sharp look-out, but after dark the roads were quiet. Late on the fourth day, storm clouds gathered in the east. Far off on the horizon, lightning bolts streamed from a tumbling mass of gray clouds that were headed their way. Soon, the clouds obliterated the sun, and the fierce wind whipped the tree branches above them. Johan watched in alarm. "I don't like the looks of the storm, Isabella. We need to find better shelter because it will be *ein mordskerl.*" They gathered their things and headed deeper into the woods.

Behind them, something snapped, and he turned in time to see an oak branch crash to the ground. Al-Buraq snorted and pawed the ground. The clouds rolled across the sky above them, but only a few drops of rain fell.

A thunderous rumble followed another lightning flash and then the heavens opened and rain poured down on them. Above, the clouds heaved in a paroxysm of violence, the storm front a mass of blacks and grays lit only by the towering bolts. The trees bent before the howling wind, and the rain flew straight into their faces. In just moments, the downpour soaked them to the skin.

Johan put his jacket over her shoulders and lifted her onto the horse's back. He had to shout over the wind. "We must find a barn or a cave where we can get dry!" The lightning flashed again and, ahead of them, Johan saw a path. "There!" he cried.

The trees provided them cover, but the wind was whipping through the branches and Johan feared more limbs would come down. As he led the horse down the path, Johan glimpsed a light ahead. Step by step, lightning flashes lighting the way, he guided the nervous stallion through the forest until they entered a clearing, where the downpour hit them full-force.

Before them was a small cottage with a light in the window. Johan wiped the water from his eyes. Behind the cottage was a barn. He pulled Al-Buraq toward it, fumbled the door open and led the horse into the barn.

A lantern burned inside, and by its light, Johan could see the barn was organized and neat, with tools spaced along the walls. A cow eyed them from a stall, swishing her tail, and a goat bleated a welcome. Farther back, a large draft horse studied the newcomers, its big eyes reflecting the lamplight. The horse nickered softly.

Al-Buraq whistled a challenge, but the old horse didn't rise to the bait. The stallion stopped his pawing and stood still. Chickens clucked in their cages but soon tucked their heads back under their wings. Johan could hear the rain beating on the roof.

Johan helped Isabella dismount. She was soaked. He laughed. "You look like a drowned kitten, Isabella."

She giggled. "And you look like a drowned puppy."

He took a horse blanket from a shelf by the door and offered it to her. "You must take off those clothes and dry off."

Isabella blushed. "You must not look, Johan." She turned away.

Johan raised the blanket behind her and closed his eyes. Once, she coughed, and he opened them. Glimpsing white skin and a slim back, he turned his head away, his heart racing.

"May I have the blanket, please?"

Still facing away from her, he held the blanket behind him. Isabella took it from him. "Will you bring my other clothes, Johan?"

He was digging in the pack when the barn door opened, and an old man stepped in, a lantern in one hand and a rough shawl over his shoulders. The rain had settled to a steady downpour. "Oh..." The man stopped.... "Who are you?" he asked, "and what are you doing out on such a night?"

Isabella moved close to Johan and pulled the blanket tighter. He put his arm around her. "I am Johan, and this is Isabella. We are traveling to Münster... I mean to Germany, and we saw your light. I'm sorry I didn't ask your permission, but we were soaked and I needed to get Isabella out of the storm."

"Münster, is it? Strange doings there, I hear."

"You know of Münster?"

"Yes. Every real Christian has heard of the Münster rebellion."

Johan's heart leapt. "Are you... are you an Anabaptist?"

The old man's eyes twinkled. "Let's say many new understandings are coming to the church after years smothered by Catholicism's darkness."

Johan heard Isabella give a little gasp, and he stiffened.

The old man smiled. "Oh, I hope I didn't offend either of you."

"My parents raised me a Catholic," Isabella said. "But I... I am not offended."

"I fled Switzerland..." Johan hesitated. "Because my family believed in these new teachings. We had to flee our home."

"Switzerland! Ja, I thought so. Your accent gives you away. Why don't you both get dressed in some dry clothing and come into the house? We will talk over a cup of tea and bread and cheese. My wife and I have a bed where you can stay."

Johan looked at Isabella. She was blushing. He turned to the old man. "We cannot sleep in the same bed, sir, for we are not husband and wife... yet."

The old man looked from Isabella to Johan and back again. "So, you are running away to get married, are you?"

The two fugitives looked at each other, and Johan nodded. "It is our greatest wish. We would have married before we began our journey, but we left Krakow in somewhat of a hurry."

"Ahh..." The man studied them, as if appraising them in a new light. "Maybe you are the fugitives the messenger told us of... and then, maybe you are not." He patted Johan's arm. "No worry. I won't give away your secret. I am a pastor. If you want to keep your relationship holy before God, I can help you. My wife will be your witness, and I will marry you as you wish. Then you can stay in the house or I will make you a bed in the barn."

Johan looked at Isabella.

Her face paled, but her eyes burned with love as she looked up at him. "Please, Johan, might we?"

Johan, his heart filled with love for the beautiful girl, nodded to the old man. "It is our greatest wish. We would be most grateful for your kindness, sir."

PART IV
THIS YEAR IN JERUSALEM

AND SO, THAT NIGHT, *Isabella, the princess, wed Johan, the commoner. They were not the first to find refuge in a barn on a cold and stormy night. Johan may have thought of Mary and Joseph as he and his trembling bride made their bower in a bed of sweet-smelling hay.*

Abel's journal tells us that Johan and Isabella stayed with the old couple for several days and then left for the free city of Münster, Germany. They expected to find peace and safety—what they found was a city under the rule of madmen.

"The Price of Freedom"
From The Journals of Jenny Hershberger

CHAPTER 14: THE JOURNEY

FALL OF 1533

ohan trudged the hard-packed road, the black stallion's reins in his hand. It was more than a month since they left the pastor's house, and he was certain no one from Sigismund's guard would recognize Al-Buraq. Johan had smeared mud on the tired horse's coat, his mane was shaggy and unkempt and his proud head drooped.

Shafts of sunlight broke through overhanging clouds now and again, but a chill was in the air. In the distance, Leipzig's spires and towers marked the horizon.

Johan looked back at his young wife perched on the horse's back. She was pale and gaunt. Life on the road had not been easy for his princess. "Not much longer, my dearest." He gave her an encouraging smile. "Leipzig is before us. Travelers we met last week said a camp occupied by others going to the New Jerusalem lies on the outskirts of the city. They gave me a map."

Every day they traveled, they found the road filled with men and women going to Münster. The new Protestant rulers of the once-Catholic city were sending out messengers to proclaim that the Kingdom of God on earth was in that city and word had spread throughout Europe.

Isabella smiled a weary smile. "I am glad we have reached Leipzig. How far to Münster from here?"

Johan shrugged. "Near twenty days travel, I'm told, if we keep a steady pace. How are you feeling?"

"My stomach is tender." Isabella touched her abdomen. "And I have felt queasy the last few mornings. Maybe because we have had so little to eat."

They had stayed with the kind pastor and his wife for several days after their cottage wedding, a brief but lovely time. Since then they had been on the road to Münster and had made fair progress. But they often remained in their camp for an extra day to let Isabella rest and this slowed their journey. Once they watched from the woods as a troop of horsemen rode by on the road, the red banners with white eagles marking them as Sigismund's soldiers. And another time they disappeared into a crowd in the marketplace of a small town when Sigismund's heralds came into the village to announce a reward for Isabella's return. Now they were in Germany and had encountered no one from Poland for several days.

Just at dusk, when the shadows were growing around them, they came to the junction marked on Johan's map. The main road made a sharp turn and followed a stream toward Leipzig. Another less-traveled path went off to the right. Johan led Al-Buraq through the trees, and soon they saw a camp with many fires.

As they made their way into the clearing, a bearded, heavyset man detached himself from a group standing around a fire. He planted himself in their path and with pig-like eyes, squinted at the stallion.

"Ain't no mud can hide the lines of that horse, youngster. Where did you get him?"

"He is *my* horse," Isabella said. "I'll thank you to stand out of our way."

The man laughed. "Who d'ya think you are, Queen of Sheba?

I think you stole him, and I'm just the one to return him to his rightful master, whoever he may be."

The other ruffians guffawed and made coarse remarks. "Get the girl, too, Hans. She looks like she needs us to return her somewhere, too."

"But only after we inspect her for blemishes and such," said another. Loud whoops followed his remark.

The man called Hans looked sideways at Johan and then reached for the reins. But before he could grasp them, Johan struck him a powerful blow to the face and knocked him to the ground.

Hans lay motionless for a moment and then struggled to his feet. He touched his nose and his hand came away bloody. "You fool! I'll have your eyes for that."

Hans lunged at Johan, reaching for his throat, when Isabella screamed, "Watch out!"

Hearing the swish of steel against leather, Johan jumped back.

But Hans did not pursue him. Instead, he stood erect, eyes bulging, the point of a broadsword at his throat. A tall man held the sword.

"So, my piggish friend," the man said. "Once again you terrorize travelers before they reach our camp. Didn't I warn you against doing that yesterday?"

The blood running from Hans's nose was dark against his skin, which had turned a pale yellow. His hands shook. When he tried to speak, the man flipped the sword and struck him across the side of his head with the flat side of the blade.

Hans crashed face first into the dust and lay without moving. The man turned to Hans's companions, his sword extended. Firelight danced on the burnished blade. "You are too low to even come near a lady of such obvious breeding, but in this case, I will allow you to beg her forgiveness for your boorish behavior."

125

Pale and silent, the men glanced at each other.

"Speak!" The tall man brandished the sword.

The men touched their caps and bowed. "Begging your pardon, madam, we was forgetting ourselves," one man said. The others nodded in agreement.

"An intelligent decision, gentlemen. Now, one more thing." He pointed the sword at the still-unconscious Hans. "Take this piece of filth and leave this camp… now! If I find you here in the morning, I cannot keep my mistress…" He lifted his sword in mock salute… "I cannot keep her from taking her vengeance on you. Understand?"

The men mumbled their assent and dragged their leader's limp body into the woods.

"My apologies for the uncivil reception." The swordsman sheathed his weapon and bowed to Johan and Isabella. "My name is Frederich Weisbach. Are you hurt?"

Johan bowed in return. "I am Johan, and this is my wife, Isa.. uh, Bella. I thank you, sir, for your help, although I think I gave that lout a lesson he will not be soon forgetting."

Frederich laughed and put out his hand and Johan took it. Frederich had a powerful grip. "That you did. You have a stout arm, and you gave him more than he bargained for, I'll wager. Hans is a cretin. We have rested here for three days and I have watched him at his work. Until I arrived, he made his daily bread assaulting weary travelers. Yesterday I warned him for the last time. Obviously, he did not take me seriously. I was coming to send him packing when you struck him. A stout blow and well placed." Frederich laughed. "To have one of his victims fight back must have been a surprise."

Johan helped Isabella dismount, and she took Frederich's hand. "I thank you, too, sir. Your help is most appreciated."

Frederich bowed again. Johan thought him a strange-looking man. Tall and gangly, his Adam's apple bobbed when he spoke, but there was a friendly twinkle in his eye that put Johan at ease.

"Where are you bound, young travelers?"

Johan hesitated.

Frederich smiled again. "The New Jerusalem?"

Johan and Isabella glanced at each other.

"Do not worry, my children. I am traveling with a messenger sent from Münster to escort true believers to the Kingdom of God on earth." He patted his blade. "My mistress and I protect those bound for the city. I perceive that you may be two such seekers. Is that correct?"

Johan nodded. Frederich put his hands on their shoulders. "Do not fear. We do not let the Catholics or the Reformists tell us where we may or may not go—or whom we may baptize and when. I will take you to our leader, Michael. You can stay with us. And let us find white paint to put a blaze on your stallion's face that would make him less recognizable to the Polish king's riders, eh?"

Johan pulled back. "You know who we are?"

"Sigismund's messengers have been on the roads for weeks, Johan. They look for a young man leading a black stallion carrying a lovely young..." And here he swept another bow. "Princess?"

"Oh, no! They can't find me!" Isabella gasped. "I do not want to be a pawn in my mother's politics. I only want to be Johan's wife, nothing more."

Johan shook his head. "We hid from them many times before we crossed the border but I did not think they would come into Germany."

Frederich laughed. "If Sigismund is anything, he is persistent. But do not fear, Johan. Come with us, and we will escort you and your lady from one kingdom to another."

THAT NIGHT, after a satisfying supper of bread, cheese and German sausage, Johan and Isabella relaxed before a fire surrounded by smiling men, women, and children. The spring from which they'd drunk their fill earlier gurgled nearby. As he sang hymns and praises to God with the others, Johan looked around the group. Joy and peace radiated on their faces. He couldn't remember when he'd last sensed such contentment. Smiling, he squeezed Isabella's hand in his.

She leaned against his shoulder. "This is wonderful," she whispered. "So peaceful."

After the songs, the group quieted, and an elderly man dressed in simple clothing stood. "I am Michael Grossman," he said, "one of the twenty-five apostles sent out from Münster to tell a great message. God's wrath is coming on this wicked world, and only in Münster can we find safety."

A man stood. "But how can this be, Brother Michael?"

"I was getting to that." Michael spread his hands. "Have you heard of Melchior Hoffman from Strasbourg? He is a latter-day prophet who received marvelous revelations about apostolic Christianity and its rebirth. Several years ago, he prophesied that 1533 would inaugurate the new era."

"That's this year!" Isabella whispered.

Johan grinned. "God has timed our escape to match his return to earth."

"Hoffman prophesied that true believers would overthrow Catholicism and Lutheranism," Michael said, "and Strasbourg would be the seat of the New Jerusalem."

The man frowned. "But now we're told Münster is the site, rather than Strasbourg. Why is that?"

"Hush, brother. Please sit and have patience. I will answer your questions in time."

The man sat, and Michael continued. "Two of Hoffman's followers, Jan Matthys and Jan Bockelson, studied his prophecies. After much prayer and revelation, they discovered that he was wrong about the exact time and place where Christ would return and reign. They named Münster as the correct location and 1534 as the time." A murmur ran through the group. "In the meantime, great things have been happening in Münster. Early this summer, Bernhard Rothmann, an anti-Catholic Lutheran leader, withdrew from Lutheranism and became an Anabaptist.

"And a wealthy wool merchant named Bernhard Knipper-dolling published Rothmann's anti-Catholic tracts. His teaching convinced most of Münster to embrace Melchior Hoffman's Anabaptist theology. Then Rothmann and his allies gained control of Münster's political offices. Knipperdolling became the mayor after deposing the Lutheran magistrates. Then they drove the Catholic Bishop, Franz von Waldek, out of the city."

A cheer rose from the assembly. Many raised their hands and shouted praise to the Lord. Michael lifted his hands, and they quieted. "I have more to tell you, friends. Münster has food and clothing and warm shelter for all pilgrims. And the leaders believe in the righteous use of the sword. The apostate church will burn no more true Christians at the stake."

Johan looked at Isabella and nodded in agreement. Michael went on. "No longer will the priests steal unbaptized children from their parents and no longer will the arrogant royals lord it over the simple folks." There were more shouts and cheers. Michael quieted the group once more.

"Prophets Matthys and Bockelson have taken up residence in Münster and are preaching wonderful news. When Christ returns, he will find us living in the Garden of Eden, following his Word and living free from punishment and fear, free from the false doctrines of Satan's bishopric, the Roman Catholic Church."

Isabella pulled her hand from Johan's grasp.

He glanced at her. She was staring at Michael, her face flushed, her hands clenched. She turned to him. "Oh, Johan," she whispered. "Is the Catholic church really that bad?" She put her face in her hands and wept. Johan waited until she finished.

When she raised her head, she smiled a brave smile. "I know little about these things, Johan, only what my teachers told me. Perhaps Michael is right. I know the Catholics have hurt you." She took his hand again. "One thing I know. If Münster is all they say, a place of peace and joy, then I want to go there with you." She paused... "Can it be true, Johan?"

Johan chewed at his lip. He wanted to say yes, he wanted to believe but was the message too good, too perfect? He looked over at Frederich, who sat beside them, staring at the fire. "Frederich," he whispered, "can we believe what he says?"

Frederich lifted his head, and Johan saw uncertainty on his face. "I believe what God says, Johan. It is men I do not trust."

"Then why do you follow?"

Frederich shrugged. "A man needs to believe in something, Johan, even if he is wrong."

CHAPTER 15: MÜNSTER

"Get down, Isabella!" Johan turned on the seat and motioned to his wife who ducked under the blankets spread out in the wagon's rear. Coming toward them on the road was a group of riders with the Eagle of Poland on their banners. Johan guided Al-Buraq to the side of the highway as the soldiers galloped past the long line of travelers. Frederich strolled up and leaned on the wagon, watching as the cavalcade disappeared back toward Leipzig.

"Ah, young master, it is a good thing we found this wagon. And the paint to disguise your horse."

Johan chucked the rains and Al-Buraq stirred in the traces and moved back out onto the road. Frederich trudged along beside them. Johan looked after the riders. "You can come out now, Bella."

Isabella poked her head out. "Are they gone?"

"Yes. That is the third patrol we have seen this week. Your father must be desperate."

"Will we never get to Münster, Johan? It has been so many days."

"It takes longer when we are traveling with so many people,

but there is safety in numbers. The Polish soldiers do not look for a cart horse with a white blaze and stockings pulling a peasant wagon. Al-Buraq is a proud horse but I think I have convinced him to accept his new role, at least until we arrive." The horse picked up his ears and nickered as if to agree.

THE NEXT MORNING Isabella was sick again. Frederich brought an old woman to help her. The woman poked her head into the wagon where Isabella lay. Her white hair curled out from underneath a cap that marked her as being from Holland. She had sharp blue eyes and a ready smile. "I am Magda. My friend, Frederich, tells me you are ill. What is wrong?" When Isabella told her, the old woman climbed into the wagon and asked Isabella to unbutton her blouse. "Let me see your breasts, girl."

Isabella hesitated.

The old woman laughed. "Oh, come, come, girl. You needn't be shy with me."

Isabella did as Magda asked her. The woman glanced at her then pulled the blouse closed. "When were you last visited by the Lady in Red, dear?" She smiled.

Isabella tilted her head. "The Lady in Red?" Then she realized what Magda meant. "Oh... oh, I see. Let me think. I believe my course happened not too long after we married."

"I see." Magda lifted Isabella's chin and looked into her eyes. "So young, so young, but that's the way of life."

"What is the way of life, Magda? I don't understand."

"Girl, you are two months pregnant. You will have a baby come spring."

"A baby, but... but how?"

Magda threw back her head and laughed. "Don't you understand, girl? If you are intimate with your husband..."

Isabella hid her face in her hands. "Yes, I know how people make children, but I didn't think…"

"And why not, Bella? You are young and strong. Your Johan is a man's man." She chuckled. "Don't worry, dearest. Old Magda will be with you when your time comes. I've brought more children into this world than ships sail the Rhine."

"A baby. Oh, Johan… a baby."

LIFE TOOK on a whole new meaning for Isabella. When she told Johan she was pregnant, they were lying together in their bed inside the wagon. He stared at her for a long time and then pulled her close and she slipped into sleep in the safety of his arms. Although she was young, she did not worry, for she knew Johan would always be nearby to protect her, to give her his strength and love her. Even the morning sickness did not trouble her, for this is what she wanted above everything—to be Johan's wife and the mother of his children.

The halls of Wawel Castle were far away, in another time, another life. Now she was just Bella, wife of Johan, and soon-to-be mother of his child. The only tie to her past, the great stallion Al-Buraq, was no longer the king of the desert, but a wagon horse. She wore the plain clothes of a peasant and twisted her long hair in a simple braid. Every night, after the day's travel, she sat with the women and learned from them or watched as they did commonplace things like mending clothes. She was a quick learner and soon felt comfortable with many of the ordinary daily tasks, although some things took a while for her to perfect, like cooking.

One day as they drove, Isabella giggled, remembering the first time she cooked for Johan.

He turned in the driver's seat. "What are you laughing at, Bella?"

"The soup…" She hid her smile behind her hands.

"Ah, the soup." Johan shook his head. "Never in my life have I eaten anything like the soup."

"Was it that terrible?"

"It smelled good until you burned it," he chuckled. "That added a very distinctive aroma and a unique flavor."

"Oh, Johan." Bella laughed out loud. "I never lifted a pot or a utensil in my whole life, nor was I ever in the castle kitchen. I had not the faintest idea how to make soup."

"Well, since you've been learning from the other women, your cooking has improved."

"I'm glad you think so." Bella rose from her cushions at the back of the wagon and crawled forward to throw her arms around Johan. With her cheek against his back, she cried.

She felt him turn and then he pulled her into his arms. "What is it, little one?"

"Oh, Johan. I love you so much. You have saved me from a life that was shallow and meaningless. I want to be the best wife I can be, the best cook, the best mother…" She clung to her husband, her tears wetting his shirt.

"Come up here." Johan pulled her onto the seat beside him and put his arm around her. Al-Buraq plodded ahead, step by step by step.

Isabella watched the horse's long tail swing from side to side. Here we are, she thought, an Anabaptist stable boy and a Polish princess, now just Johan and Bella.

At last, on a bright winter morning in late December 1533, Johan stopped the wagon before the gates of Münster. Isabella sat beside him, her face thin, but her eyes bright. The pale winter sun gleamed on the massive stone battlements, and banners snapped in the breeze. The city's fortifications were thick and high, and bastions stood at strategic corners. Men with spears walked atop the walls. Frederich pointed to the moat in front of the wall. "The founders of the city diverted the River Aa to feed this ditch. It encircles the whole of Münster. They made the gate of massive timbers and great steel hinges—a defender's gate."

Johan's eyes followed the stone walls up and up until they rested on the banners atop the towers. "This is it, Bella! This is Münster. We're here!"

Isabella leaned on his shoulder. "At last!"

Frederich walked up beside their cart and put Johan's thoughts into words. "Ah, now here is a city to my liking—strong walls, stout gates, the most modern defenses. A soldier could defend this city for a long time."

"But," Bella said, "why would we need to defend it?"

Frederich shook his head. "Tell your wife what the future holds for militant Anabaptists, Johan." With that, he turned and walked away.

Bella peered into her husband's face. "What is he talking about, Johan?"

"This city is now Protestant, Bella. Bernhard Rothmann forced the Catholic Bishop von Waldek to sign an edict of toleration last February. Once he did, they drove von Waldek and many of the Catholics from the city. Since then, only Protestant clerics preach in the churches.

"While we were on the road, Frederich heard armed militant Anabaptists from Holland are on their way here. Their arrival will spark a crisis, for the Catholics and the Reformists will not give up this city without a fight. The Anabaptists here will call upon other Anabaptists to take up arms and defend the city, in case the Catholics or Reformists attack us, and I will join them, for I will not run anymore."

"But, Johan." She gripped his arm. "Is there no place where

we can live a simple life? I thought we would find peace here."
She touched her belly. "Peace for our child."

The massive gates groaned and Johan watched as they
opened and a group of soldiers marched out across the bridge.
Michael Hoffman and the leaders of their group went forward
to talk to their captain.

Johan turned to Isabella. "You and I have come to the point
in our lives where we must decide who we are. We could slink
off into the woods and find a place where no one would recognize us—live our lives pretending we believe nothing. We could
watch while the Catholics and the Reformists torture and
murder true believers and never lift a hand to stop them.

"Or we can take a stand for what we believe and make our
home here in Münster. No more running. We will fight if we
have to, but we will not fear death. And when the day comes, we
will stand before our Lord as he says, 'Well done, good and
faithful servants.' What good is our faith if we do not stand
for it?"

Bella was silent a long time, her gaze on the city wall. After
several moments she whispered, "I am wondering if your desire
to fight comes from your faith or from your hatred of the men
who killed your aunt?"

Johan frowned.

"My parents raised me Catholic," she said, "but since we
listened to Michael's teaching, I have changed—I agree with the
Anabaptist way. But I do not yet grasp onto those teachings as
something to live by as you do. I am a woman, Johan, and I am
not concerned with defending this city.

"I only want to be your wife and raise our children in peace
—I know nothing about standing for my beliefs, except that if
anyone tried to hurt you or our child, I would give my life to
stop it from happening. That is all I know..."

Johan touched Bella's cheek. "You are an amazement, Bella.
When I first met you, something drew me to you, but I also

thought you were a spoiled young girl with not a practical thought in your head. But I was wrong. You are deep, Bella; as deep as the ocean. A simple man like me could never hope to win the love of a girl... of a woman such as you, and yet you have given me your heart. I am blessed."

Johan took Isabella into his arms. After a moment, he held her away and looked into her eyes. "I love you, Bella. We will find what we are looking for here, I think."

The soldiers from the city waved them on. Johan chucked the reins and Al-Buraq stepped onto the bridge that crossed the moat.

As the wagon rolled into the New Jerusalem, Isabella looked back at Johan, love and trust shining from her eyes. "I meant what I said, Johan. If anyone ever tries to hurt you or our child, I will give my life to stop it from happening."

CHAPTER 16: WORDS OF POWER

$\mathcal{I}$nside its thick walls, Münster bustled with activity. The crowd pushed up against the cart, jostling it as they made their way through the main gate onto a broad thoroughfare, and Johan had to quiet Al-Buraq. Everywhere Johan looked, people were on the move. On every corner, merchants hawked bread and meat. Cattle, pigs, goats and chickens filled pens and cages and customers stopped to haggle prices with the vendors. Soldiers marched through the streets, their gold, red, and blue-striped banners snapping in the breeze.

Isabella sat next to Johan, her face alight as she took in the surrounding activity. Frederich and Magda walked with them, and as they drove along, a great stream of people moving like a river encircled them and drew them toward the center of the town. People were talking and laughing and all around them was motion, color and laughter. Johan stopped a man who was hurrying by their cart.

"Sir, do you know where can we find a house to live in?" He pointed to Isabella. "We are new in the city and I need a place for my wife. She's expecting our first child."

The man shook his head. "So many come to Münster."

"Can you help us?"

He pointed to a large building a short distance away. A sign advertising gold and jewelry hung above the door. "Go see the man in that shop. He owns property all over the city. Now I must go."

Frederich reached out and grabbed the man by the sleeve. "Where do you go in such a hurry, friend?"

"To hear Rothmann preach. He preaches every day in the square, against the Catholic Church, and the words are sweet to my ears." Shaking loose from Frederich's grasp he hurried on his way.

Isabella tugged on Johan's sleeve. "Can we go hear him?"

Johan jumped down from the cart. "First, I must arrange for a place to stay and then we will go." Johan walked across the street and into the shop. In about ten minutes he returned. He was smiling as he held up a key. "We are lucky. It seems they ran some Catholics out of town this morning and their house is now empty."

The stream of people heading toward the square had grown in size, and the little group joined them. Johan took the lead rope and guided Al-Buraq through the crowd, speaking to him to keep him quiet. Soon they came to the great central square of the city. A towering cathedral dominated the skyline and a large platform stood on the paved area in front of the massive doors. A large crowd of laughing, shouting people pressed up against the platform. Johan stopped the cart at the edge of the crowd.

Soon a small man dressed in simple black garb with a trimmed beard stepped up on the platform and stood without speaking. From the whispers of the surrounding people, the travelers knew it was Rothmann. He held aloft a leather-bound book and the whispering and murmuring from the crowd trailed off.

Rothmann surveyed the crowd for a long moment and then he spoke. "This is the Bible, the inerrant Word of God. As the apostle Paul wrote, these Holy Scriptures alone are enough for reproof, correction and instruction in righteousness. Almighty God has given them to help true believers live without error, equipped for every good work. Since the apostasy first began through human writing and teaching, apostates have corrupted the divine Scriptures. Now the Almighty has declared we should destroy non-biblical writings, both new and old and cling only to the Holy Scriptures."

A babble of voices arose and a woman in the back of the crowd shouted, "Amen."

Rothmann raised his hands to quiet them and then continued. "Jesus was born of the Holy Spirit, yet the sinful nature Mary received from Adam did not taint the holy flesh that formed in her womb. Thus, Jesus was born sinless and lived sinless in thought, word and deed. That is why he could take the punishment for our sins on the cross, forgive us and make us children of God."

Rothmann spoke with great power and his words fell on Johan like hammer strokes. He glanced over at Isabella. She was staring at the preacher but Johan could not tell what she was thinking.

A hum began in the crowd as people around them responded to the words.

"He's right!"

"I never heard this before."

"Amen, brother, amen!"

Rothmann raised his Bible again. "This book explains what I am trying in my humble way to make clear to you. Bear with me, brothers and sisters, while I try to open this heavenly Word to your eager hearts."

A smattering of applause followed.

Rothmann opened the book and then lifted his hand and the applause ceased. He read. "For by one Spirit are we all baptized into one body." He looked up at the crowd. "This Bible says

Christ's church is a congregation of baptized believers—adults who choose immersion in full knowledge of their decision to follow Christ. The church is *not* a congregation of infants sprinkled with a few drops from a pagan fountain, the purpose being to add them to the tax rolls, but a group of believers baptized into one church by the Holy Spirit."

At this, there was another burst of applause and then a swelling mix of "Amen" and "Hallelujah!" from the crowd.

Johan leaned over and whispered to Isabella, "He teaches the Anabaptist creed. He is not afraid."

Rothmann put the Bible down and lifted both arms. "Anabaptism is strong in Holland and we who are Dutch know baptism means to immerse or dunk in water," he shouted. "The Catholics ignore this directive from God and sprinkle babies rather than immerse adults, thus saving themselves the risk of soiling their costly robes." The crowd roared with laughter, caught up now in the force of Rothmann's preaching.

"Anabaptists choose of their own free will to follow Christ with their whole heart. They are the believing children of God. The Scriptures testify that faith comes through hearing and hearing from the Word of God. Jesus said that those who hear and receive the Word as if their soul is fertile soil would bear spiritual fruit as much as one-hundredfold. These are they who will build the true church." The crowd was with Rothmann and shouts and yells of approval filled the square. Rothmann raised his voice again, and it cut through the hubbub like a knife.

"But you cannot build Christ's church unless you preach the holy gospel. And what is this gospel?"

The crowd fell silent in expectation. Someone shouted from the back, "Tell us again!"

"Say these words after me," Rothmann demanded. "Christ died for my sins according to the Scripture."

"Christ died for my sins," Johan whispered, "according to the Scripture."

People all around them were responding. Beside him, Isabella also repeated the words.

Rothmann waited until everyone had spoken. "Christ was in the grave three days and three nights, according to the Scripture."

The crowd answered. "Christ was in the grave three days and three nights, according to the Scripture." A significant pause followed as though all heaven was holding its breath.

"Christ rose from the dead according to the Scripture, and the disciples and five-hundred others testified of the event. He is risen!"

People shouted and jumped up and down. "He is risen, He is risen, He is risen!"

Johan and Isabella shouted along with the crowd, "He is risen, He is risen!"

At last, Rothmann spoke again, and the crowd quieted. "My brothers and sisters, I have much more to say. In the days to come, I will tell you of many wondrous things of God. But now, his Spirit impresses upon my heart to ask those who receive and believe my words, are you baptized into the true church? Do you want to join today with those who are earthly citizens of heaven?"

All around Johan, people shouted, "Yes, we do! Yes, we do!"

"Then come, my people." He motioned to them. "The elders of the city are waiting in St. Lambert's Church with tanks of water. They will immerse you. Come, come I say, and join the heavenly throng around our gracious God's throne."

One by one, and then in small groups, onlookers left the crowd and walked the steps into the church.

Isabella leaned over and tugged Johan's sleeve. "Johan, I want baptism, for they only sprinkled me as an infant. Please."

Magda nodded. "I, too, wish baptism."

He nodded and helped her down from the cart. He tied Al-Buraq to a nearby hitching post and, grasping the elbows of the two women, he let the flow of the crowd propel them toward the steps leading up to the cathedral's open doors. At the bottom of the steps, Johan glanced around, looking for Frederich.

At first, he didn't see him, but then, as the crowd parted, Johan saw him standing by the cart. Leaning on his sword, Frederich watched as the frenzy of the moment carried the bulk of the crowd toward the doors of the cathedral.

"Frederich," Johan called, "come, come let them baptize you!"

Frederich smiled and shook his head. He pointed to the cart and mouthed the words, "I will stay and watch the horse."

And then the people closed around Johan and the women, and the eager throng swept them up the steps and through the doors into the dark coolness of the ancient cathedral.

LATER THAT EVENING, Johan and Frederich sat by the fireplace in a small house the shopkeeper had rented to them on Bridge Street, near where the River Aa flowed under the wall. Bella and Magda had gone to bed, and the two men sat in silence. Johan sipped beer from the stein he'd picked up at the market and Frederich smoked his pipe. Finally, Frederich grinned.

"So the former were Catholics, eh." He looked around the room. "They left in such a hurry they could not take their furniture or their firewood, or even their food. It seems we arrived just in time."

Johan looked around the room. It had taken a while to find the place after the baptism, but just at dusk they had pulled up in front. The house was old and small, crammed in between two larger, more ornate houses, but in the back there was a shed for the horse and a yard where they put the cart. Inside it was dark but comfortable and the fireplace worked. "I don't mind inheriting their things. Serves them right. They were Catholics weren't they?"

Aunt Elspeth's crucifix stood on the mantle. The fire's glow reflected from the window and gleamed off its golden surface. Johan took another sip of beer and then looked over at Frederich. "Why did you not go to the baptism, Frederich? Did you not find Rothmann's words compelling?"

Frederich took a long pull on his pipe. "Yes, his words were compelling; too compelling."

"What do you mean?"

Frederich drew long at the pipe again and then let the smoke out slowly. The white cloud hid his face. "Powerful men hold power over others, whether they're great speakers, great soldiers or gifted scholars. Often they use that power to benefit only themselves. As a soldier, I have seen this many times, but Frankenhausen was the worst." He paused, staring into the fire. "It is a sad tale."

"Tell me the story, Frederich."

Frederich sighed. "Ten years ago, a German named Thomas Müntzer preached that God wanted to set up a new world order, one where the aristocracy did not enslave the lower classes. This was during a time of social upheaval and widespread religious doubt, and his preaching rang true with many impoverished farmers and peasants. The nobles squelched scattered uprisings in southwestern Germany and Alsace in the past, but no major revolt occurred until Müntzer organized the peasants. His powerful preaching drew many to him."

Johan peered at Frederich across the hearth. "Were you one of those peasants?"

Frederich shook his head. "No, I was a Landsknecht, a mercenary with a group from North Germany. Young and foolish, I thought the life of a soldier was romantic and glorious. Our masters paid us well and gave us the best weapons. No one could overcome us.

"I served in the household of George of Saxony. Spies reported that Müntzer was leading an army to the city of Frankenhausen to challenge the nobles. When he arrived, thousands of peasants joined him. They occupied the town hall and stormed the Count of Schwarzburg's castle.

"We marched to the castle to meet them. On the night before the battle, several of us slipped into their camp disguised as peasants. Müntzer was preaching and goading the peasants to fight, great swelling words that hypnotized even me. But when I looked around, I realized that despite this man's promises, the peasants didn't have a chance. They had only pitchforks, farming tools and clubs, while we had swords, mounted cavalry and cannon. Their leader was sending them to their deaths." Frederich closed his eyes.

Johan sipped his beer and waited. He dreaded what Frederich would say next, but the man was baring his soul and he knew he shouldn't interrupt.

"In the morning, the Count of Schwarzburg demanded that the peasants leave his castle and turn over Müntzer. They refused, so we attacked—the blood and killing crazed our men. Seven thousand peasants died that day, yet throughout the battle, Müntzer stood on the parapet screaming at them, promising them victory. What they got instead was death. We had men among us who were like animals. They butchered the men, raped the women and impaled little children on pikes. One man in particular comes to mind, a man named Jügen Fromme. He earned the name 'Butcher of Frankenhausen.' What he did made me sick. I will never forget him." Frederich paused and swallowed. "But it was not Fromme's doing that lead to the massacre. Müntzer sent them into a battle he knew was hopeless. Good men died, compelled only by words, and men revolted against authority, led by a rascal who used them only for self-gain."

"What happened to Müntzer?"

"We captured him, tortured him, and then executed him. His powerful words came to nothing. Those gullible men gave their lives following his false teachings."

Frederich stood and walked to the window. "After that, I left the mercenaries. I heard Michael Hoffman preach and decided my sword would be of better use defending him than killing helpless peasants." He shook his head. "I am not a spiritual man, Johan—fighting is all I know. But one thing I have learned— never listen to the words of men who are using words to get you to do something for them if it will cost you but not them. Hoffmann convinced everyone to accept baptism today. What will he ask of you next? If you want to follow someone, follow Christ alone. That is why I did not go to the baptism today. I did not hear the voice of the Spirit, only the voice of a man."

CHAPTER 17: THE PROPHET

*J*ohan laid down his hammer and stretched his back. January in Münster was cold, but the forge he labored over was red hot and kept him warm. He had found work with the city's best-known blacksmith, where the things his father had taught him in the farrier shop worked in his favor.

His days were long, for the city needed to build or repair much ironwork, and he was never without work. He worked hard. Isabella's belly grew larger every day. Soon, he'd have a child to support, as well as his wife. And there was also Magda, who stayed with them to care for Isabella.

The year 1534 had rung in with uncertainty. Münster had not become the city of peace like Michael Hoffman and others had proclaimed. Instead, near-daily conflicts flared between the Anabaptists, the Protestant Reformists, the Aristocracy and the remaining Catholics. But Johan lived with that, knowing he would pay the price for freedom.

The Catholic Prince Bishop von Waldek had struck a truce by signing an edict of religious tolerance within the city limits. When he did, Rothmann and the Anabaptist elders permitted him to return to Münster, but constant conflict plagued the city. Gangs of Anabaptist youth roamed the streets, looking for Catholics and Lutherans to harass.

Rumors abounded. Some said a massive army financed by Holy Roman Emperor Charles V was marching from Koblénz to liberate the city from all Protestant sects and return the Catholics to power. Another speculation suggested a ten-thousand-man Anabaptist army had assembled in Holland was even now marching to defend the city against any attacks by armed Catholic or Reformist forces. Johan never shared the rumors with Isabella, for they frightened her, but somehow they always reached her ears. Almost every evening, he had to calm her, often taking her hands and praying with her, or holding her in his arms and comforting her.

As Johan was returning from work one day, he heard a great commotion as he was passing the cathedral square. Bernhard Rothmann's voice rose above the din. "Quiet, quiet, all of you. Jan Bockelson, God's messenger and the right hand of Jan Matthys, the prophet, has come from Holland to speak to you."

The tumult quieted and a clear, strong voice rang out. Drawn by the power in the words, Johan turned his steps into the square. A tall, handsome, blonde man was standing on a butcher's cart in front of St. Lambert's Church. He held out his arms.

"I am Jan Bockelson from Leiden. I bring you the word of the Lord."

A hush spread over the plaza.

"We are in a terrible age," he said. "Sin and wickedness abound everywhere. The streets of the cities of Europe run red with the blood of true believers. The devil's agents do their evil work everywhere. Do you want to know who those agents are?"

Someone shouted, "Tell us!"

Bockelson signaled for the crowd to move closer. "Satan's greatest emissary in this world sits on a bloodstained throne in

Rome. He calls himself Papa Clement, but his real name is Apollyon, for he has come from the abyss to turn this world to his master's way by teaching you the Catholic Church's false doctrine."

"No!" cried a man. "The pope is true. He is Christ on earth. He—"

Before he could finish, Johan saw three men dressed in black clothing surround the man and strike him with clubs. In seconds, they drove the man to the ground. Johan edged close to the cart, his stomach churning. The man lay on the pavement, blood running from his nose and mouth. It was clear to Johan the Catholic was dead.

Bockelson pointed to the prone body. "The agents of Apollyon are among us," he cried. "Besides the adherents of the Pope's demonic church, many follow the apostate, Martin Luther. His teachings are a deception designed to keep you in what he calls the Protestant church, but it is also Satan's church. We know Martin Luther is of the devil because he burns true believers at the stake for rejecting infant baptism. Luther, his fellow apostate, Zwingli, and the Catholics hunt us like dogs when it is we, the Anabaptists, who hold the true faith."

He paused, leaning toward the onlookers. "But the greatest terror is right here among us—the so-called Prince Bishop, Franz von Waldek. Even now, he plots to drive all true believers from this city."

At the clatter of hooves on cobblestones, Johan turned. A group of mounted men rode from Market Street into the square. They forced their horses through the crowd until they reached the cart where Bockelson was standing.

One man, dressed in the uniform of a Catholic commander, pointed his finger at Bockelson and shouted, "I am Berthold von Wessel. I serve the Prince Bishop. Disperse this crowd and..." He edged his horse closer to Bockelson. "Leave this city at once under punishment of death! You are disturbing the peace."

Bockelson laughed. "And I thought you were here because you wanted the word of the Lord! This city is not at peace, but the prophet will bring peace. Jan Matthys of Haarlem is the prophet. I am the prophet's servant."

"Does the prophet know Prince von Waldek has forbidden preaching in the streets?"

Bockelson drew himself to his full height. "It is God who commands us to preach, and his law supersedes the blustering of the beast von Waldek. This city belongs to God, not the bishop and, despite his arrogance, he has no authority here."

Von Wessel looked around. The people had closed in on his horsemen and Johan could see fear come on his face.

"God may own the city, but..." his voice shook... "But my men patrol it. If you continue to resist, I will have your head." Von Wessel nodded to his men, and they urged their horses through the crowd and rode away.

Laughing, Bockelson pointed at the retreating soldiers' backs. "See how the minions of the devil fear the Most High God! He has locked their swords in their scabbards and filled their hearts with terror."

He turned to his listeners. "This is our city, the city of the living God. No more will the Catholics and the Reformists slay the true believers. The only blood that shall run in the streets of Münster will be theirs!"

A great shout went up from the crowd.

"You must choose," Bockelson shouted. "Will you be a citizen of the world, a world that has come under God's judgment and will soon experience his terrible wrath, or will you choose the Kingdom of God? No middle ground is available—you cannot halt between two opinions. Serve the Lord or serve the devil. Which will it be?"

"We will serve the Lord!" the onlookers yelled. "We will serve the Lord!"

Bockelson looked down and beckoned to someone. Out of

the crowd stepped a tall man wearing a long black coat and a black hat. Taking Bockelson's hand, he climbed onto the cart and turned to the audience. A dark curling beard adorned his face and, even from a distance, Johan could see he had piercing blue eyes.

Lifting the man's hand high, Bockelson exclaimed, "Here is the prophet, Jan Matthys. He will tell you the word of the Lord for these times." With that short introduction, Bockelson leaped off the cart.

The onlookers clapped, but Matthys's stern face brought them to silence. "In a vision, God's holy angels carried me down from heaven. I saw this city, Münster, ringed with fire. Outside were the troops of Satan and inside, standing on the walls, filling the streets, were the saints of God, the true believers. I stood on the wall and looked out on the armies that surrounded this place, and fear gripped me.

"But then a mighty angel came as I stood alone on the wall, and he said, 'Do not fear, for I will open your eyes.' And he opened them..." Matthys's voice rose. "And I saw the armies of the Lord camped round about this city. The troops blazed with light. Each one stood twelve-feet tall, and the demon horde cowered before them."

Along with the others, Johan pressed closer, hanging on the man's every word. "Then the angel said, 'Look into the city and tell me what you see there.' I looked and the saints of the city stood clothed in shining garments. They shone like the sun, and in the hand of every saint..." Matthys paused... "In the hand of every saint was—a sword!"

The throng screamed. People shouted, clapped their hands, and jumped up and down.

Arms high, Matthys proclaimed, "And the gates of the city swung open and the army of the saints rode out. The ground ran red with the blood of the enemies of God, and the Lord himself came down and trod the winepress of his wrath. He dipped his garments in the blood of those who served the devil. And the King of kings dwelt in the New Jerusalem, the city that men once called Münster!"

Men and women alike screamed and cried out like tortured animals. Many fell to the ground, writhing and twisting. Women rushed to touch the prophet and his messenger, shouting, "Hallelujah! Praise God! May his kingdom come! Come, Lord Jesus!"

Filled with emotion, Johan called out, "Amen, brother, amen, brother," again and again. The prophet's words stirred him as preaching had never stirred him in his life.

Matthys waved his hands back and forth over the people. "Hold, brothers and sisters, silence!"

When the spectators had regained their composure, he said, "The weight of suffering of the saints has piled up before God. We will never again stand mute while the flames lick around us, or the torturer applies the knife. The priests will no longer rip our babies from our arms and force them to accept the devil's baptism. We are the army of God. He fights for us, he goes before us, and he is our rear guard. Do you want to be in this army, or do you want to be outside the gates of this city, cast into outer darkness?"

A man yelled, "What must we do, Prophet?"

Though he did not shout, Matthys's voice carried to the back of the square. "Brother Rothmann baptized many of you, but most of you have not received the true baptism. Come now. Receive the true baptism."

There was a stir and then a group of Catholic nuns made their way out of the press and knelt before the prophet.

Matthys lowered to one knee. "What do you desire, my sisters?"

"We wish to be free," one nun said. "We wish to take the true baptism."

Matthys jumped off the wagon and signaled the people to

move back so that all could see. "Then take off your habits and uncover your heads."

The nuns hesitated and looked at each other.

"Take off your habits!"

The nuns obeyed. They stood before the people with shorn heads lowered.

Matthys embraced each one then turned to the crowd and pointed at the women. "See how the Catholics violated these dear sisters. The glory of a woman is her long hair, but the beast von Waldek forced them to look like men. It is a travesty."

He spoke to the nuns. "God calls you out of the cold convent prison, where you wear out your knees kneeling before the icons and symbols of a demonic religion. Come now and rejoin humanity. Become a true believer. Accept baptism and join our movement."

He turned and motioned to waiting men who lifted huge urns of water and carried them onto the church steps. The nuns fell to their knees. As the prophet called out, "We baptize you in the name of the Father, the Son and the Holy Spirit," the men held the urns aloft and poured the water over each woman. Matthys laid his hand on each head. "Rise in freedom and newness of life."

The nuns leaped to their feet, their soaked black robes clinging to their bodies, laughing and praising God. The onlookers laughed and cried and clapped. Soon, dancing men and women filled the cathedral square. Many knelt beneath the urns to receive baptism. Johan remained by the cart watching in wonder.

Maybe we have found heaven on earth...

CHAPTER 18: THE SIEGE

*I*t was the first week of February. Johan and Isabella were sitting in the kitchen when Frederich came in, shaking the snow off his boots. Johan noted the sour look on Frederich's face as he pulled a chair up to the kitchen fire.

"What is it, Frederich?"

"Matthys has taken over the city council and granted full religious freedom to the Anabaptists."

"But that is good, Frederich! At last we have a place where we can be free to live our lives as we choose."

"Good for the Anabaptists, bad for the Catholics and Reformists, Johan," Frederich growled.

"What do you mean?"

"Matthys demanded the deaths of all Lutherans and Catholics in the city. The council was reluctant to sanction mass murder, so they settled for the expulsion of all non-Anabaptists. The expulsions will begin next week. Anabaptist patrols are scouring Münster warning those who refused adult baptism to leave the city. It is a sad day for religious freedom."

Johan looked away. "But they are Catholics… Reformists. We should drive them out. They have no place here."

Frederich shook his head. "They are more than Catholics and Reformists, Johan. They are people."

~

BY MID-FEBRUARY, the new rulers of Münster forced over two thousand residents to leave the city. Johan and Isabella watched from the window every day as friends and neighbors trudged through the snow. The refugees' breath frosted in the bitter air and many had blankets around their shoulders. Sobbing children stumbled along beside adults—people with their worldly possessions piled on carts and carried on their backs. Men and women who had lived their whole lives in Münster were being driven from their homes by neighbors who had once been their friends.

"This isn't right, Johan." Isabella turned from the window. "These people are not only being forced from their homes, it is also the middle of winter. I'm sorry, but I cannot see Christ in this."

"The Catholics and the Lutherans are murderers, Bella." Johan nodded his head. "If you had known the terror we faced at their hands and the grief the death of our loved ones caused, maybe you would not be so eager to have them for neighbors. To live in a city we can call our own and not fear persecution will be a great thing."

At the sound of crying, Isabella looked again. She pointed out a group of small figures trudging through the falling snow. "These poor children are freezing out there. They did not murder innocent believers. Was it not the leaders who commanded the masses to perpetrate the massacres?"

"Yes, Bella, but each man answers to his own conscience. If a priest or a pastor ordered me to kill someone innocent of any crime except following his or her conscience, I would not do it.

Yet people just like these laughed and celebrated while my Aunt's body fed the flames."

"Will there not come a day when men can live in peace when each religion has tolerance and compassion toward others?"

Johan shrugged and rose to stir the fire with a wrought-iron poker and add more wood. "I don't see that day ever coming, dearest, short of the return of Christ to this earth. Men should live that way, but sad to say, we are born evil and not good."

The door opened, and Frederich hurried in, a bitter blast of cold following close behind. He stepped to the hearth and poured himself a cup of the tea steaming there in a cast-iron pot and slumped in a chair. The look on his face did not portend good news.

Johan looked up from the fire. "What is it, Frederich?"

"Terrible happenings, Johan." Frederich's Adam's apple bobbed up and down in his agitation. "Von Waldek has done what he promised and hired the Landsknecht, the mercenaries I told you about. I was standing guard on the wall and saw them marching into camp outside the city. I recognized their banners. Many of them are probably my old battle mates, men I fought with at Frankenhausen. They are dangerous men, ferocious fighters. Even now, they are digging siege lines around the city. I fear after these last refugees flee, no one else will leave... or enter Münster."

"Do you mean von Waldek will keep everyone out of the city?" Isabella asked. "How will we get food? Supplies?"

"Yes, he will do just that. And as for supplies, there will be none coming in. Soon Matthys will have us on short rations. I am familiar with sieges."

As Johan contemplated what this new development meant for them, he heard shouts in the lane and looked out the window. Men dressed in black and carrying stout cudgels were marching toward their house. "All citizens are to go to the cathedral square at once," one of them called. "The prophet, Jan

Matthys, has a word from the Lord. Everyone must go now, no exceptions."

They banged the doors on both sides of the street with the cudgels and shouted, "Go to the square. The prophet requires your attendance to hear the word of the Lord."

Across the street, their neighbor leaned out his door. "What's the racket? What's happening?"

Three messengers halted. "Are you deaf, man? Every citizen is to go to the square now, no exceptions."

The neighbor grunted. "It's late in the day. I need sleep. Someone can tell me what he says." He turned to go inside.

Johan watched as one of the prophet's men grabbed the neighbor's arm and threw him to the ground. The other two kicked him, pulled him to his feet and shoved him toward the square. "No exceptions," they shouted. "No exceptions. Every citizen must attend." When a club thudded against their door, Isabella cried out.

Johan put his arm around her and held her close.

"Come out, come out!" a deep voice commanded. "Every citizen to the square."

"Now it begins." Frederich shook his head. "The city of peace is turning into the city of Matthys and Bockelson. Quick! Rouse Magda and don your coats. We don't want those ruffians breaking in here." Frederich opened the door. "Stop your pounding; we are coming out."

By the time they reached the square, darkness had fallen and torches ringed the plaza. As always, the residents gathered before St. Lambert's Church. A confused mutter ran through the crowd. Many were angry because Matthys's men dragged them from their dinner tables or fires and forced them out into the bitter cold.

Isabella, Johan, Magda and Frederich stood at the edge of the multitude. Then the crowd parted and Jan Matthys, dressed in black and accompanied by Bockelson, Rothmann, and Bernhard

Knipperdolling, the new mayor of the city, made his way to the platform set up in front of the cathedral. Matthys mounted it with measured steps and stood for a long time, gazing at the now silent crowd. At last he spoke.

"The beast von Waldek has issued an order." He held up a piece of paper. "He had this nailed to the city gates. In it he threatens to arrest and imprison everyone who accepts the true baptism."

Matthys let out a derisive chortle, and the crowd laughed with him. Soon, the square was ringing with raucous guffaws mingled with shouts and threats against von Waldek. Johan felt his spirits lift at the calm demeanor of the prophet. Frederich shook his head while Isabella and Magda stood silent.

Matthys raised his hands for silence. "He tried to send his men into the city with more of these cursed proclamations. They did not get far. Now, we will tell Apollyon's agent what the one true God says." He signaled to men standing at the side of the platform, bearing the bundles of von Waldek's proclamation. They threw them to the ground in front of Matthys who jumped down, grabbed a torch from a guard and set it to the pile of paper.

The crowd moved back as flames flared to life. Johan and his group could see the fire burning from where they stood. Matthys stepped back up on the platform Hand his words cut like knives. "The fire of God's wrath is coming for the God-haters and the sinners who have not received the true baptism. I have seen a great vision. The Lord Jesus himself will return to this earth on Easter of this year. He expects to find a purified city, one fit for his rule."

His voice rose. "If you have not received the baptism, you are to leave this city at once. If you repent and receive baptism tonight, God will forgive your sins. You no longer can hesitate. This is the hour of cleansing." The fire from the burning procla-mations cast a ghastly light on Matthys's face and Johan could smell the acrid smoke. He saw that Isabella was trembling in the cold and he put his arm around her.

Gangs of men dressed in black pushed through the crowd, questioning each person. "Are you a true believer? Have you received the baptism?"

They separated those who refused to answer or refused to reject Catholicism or Lutheranism from the crowd and shoved them all toward Münster's main gate.

One man broke free and ran to where Matthys stood. "I'm a citizen of this city. I was born in Münster. My whole life is here. If you throw me out, my family will be destitute."

"You might have repented, but now it is too late." Matthys peered down his nose at him, his lips curled in a sneer. "You could have rejected your sin and joined us, but you refused. The Lord demands to have a pure city for his throne." He turned to the guards. "Drive him out. Drive them all out!"

Matthys's ruffians drove the unrepentant ones toward the gate, bludgeoning them with cudgels or poking them with spears. "Out, you godless whelps of Satan! Leave our city." Screams and cries filled the square as they forced hundreds out of the city. One thug, a young man, approached them. "Have you received the true baptism?"

Johan, Isabella and Magda nodded their assent, but Frederich stood silent. The guard reached for his arm but Frederich's sword was at his throat before he even touched him.

"Do you question the faith of one of God's soldiers?" Frederich demanded. "You beardless pup, you do not understand who you are accosting."

The young man hesitated, and Frederich thrust the sword deeper. The man jerked back, his neck bleeding. "No... I'm sorry, sir. I do not question your faith." Johan watched as the man turned and hurried away.

"But, Frederich," Johan whispered. "They have not baptized

you. If you want to stay in the Kingdom of God, they must baptize you."

Frederich put his hand on Johan's shoulder. "They can baptize me, my young friend, but not because I believe this city to be the Kingdom of God on earth."

"Why then?" asked Isabella.

Frederich sheathed his sword and patted the scabbard. "Because I fear a time will come when you will need my mistress to protect you."

AFTER THE FINAL expulsion of Catholics and Reformists, Frederich's fears came true. Von Waldek ringed Münster with soldiers who blocked any supplies from coming into the city. Expecting such a move by von Waldek, Matthys and Bockelson had stockpiled weapons and food. Tubs of soup soon appeared on street corners. All the men of the city were armed and given daily instruction in military preparedness.

Matthys preached fiery sermons that warned of the coming wrath, now only weeks away. The Lord was coming, and they would turn their weapons against a godless world as Christ led them forth from a purified, sanctified city to scour the earth and bring in his one-thousand-year reign.

Johan felt concern and doubt as the city changed before his eyes. He went to Frederich. "What will we do, my friend? Isabella will deliver our baby soon."

Frederich shrugged. "Matthys is not the only one who saw this coming. I have also been preparing. Come with me."

He led Johan down to the small cellar. There were boxes of foodstuff and bags of grain and flour on the shelves. Johan turned to his friend in surprise. "Where did this come from? Why didn't you tell me?"

Frederich put his hands on Johan's shoulders. "Had I told you, Isabella would have found out and she would have given it to the refugee children. I am sorry about their fate, but my concern is for you and Isabella and Magda. Seek the safety of this house when you can and look forward to the birth of your child. And don't worry, God is watching over you… and he has set me as his sentinel."

CHAPTER 19: THE TERROR

*G*reat anticipation grew in Johan's heart as Easter, Jan Matthys's prophesied day of the Lord's return approached. The days were warming, more people were in the streets, and the excitement was almost tangible as Johan walked through the city. Münster was alive!

Matthys, Bockelson and Rothmann preached the Anabaptist creed in the square day and night, and unruly young men crowded the streets, vandalizing remaining Catholic convents or churches and looking for any who had refused the baptismal tanks. By mid-March, there were only Anabaptists in the city.

The constant demand for ironwork to strengthen Münster's defenses meant Johan's work at the blacksmith's shop continued uninterrupted, but other things were changing in the city. As supplies dwindled and trade ceased, the city council assigned the now jobless merchants and tradesmen to other tasks. As he made his way to work each morning, Johan often passed squads of men receiving military training in the square or going to clear the brush and debris from the area just outside the city walls and cart it away.

In the little house on Bridge Street, Isabella's day

approached. Magda ordered her confined to bed and cared for her like a mother. Johan did his best to keep the tumult and changes in the city from Isabella and Frederich somehow kept their small store of provisions replenished, so, inside their four walls, the little family enjoyed a sense of peace. But there was no peace in Münster.

Rothmann had preached that everything Christian brothers and sisters own belonged to everyone in common, so in mid-march, Matthys made a stunning move. To abolish debt, he had the city's archives, documents, contracts, accounts and ledgers burned in the square and all private debt abolished. The poorer people of the city, now free of their debts, rejoiced and danced around the huge bonfire while the once-rich landowners sulked in their houses.

ISABELLA, though confined to bed, did not rest. Her back hurt, her legs hurt. She could not find a comfortable position to sleep.

Magda smiled at her discomfort. "It's God's revenge on women for getting Adam exiled from the garden."

This statement, though told in jest, did nothing to cheer Isabella. She often found her emotions getting the best of her and she would weep for no reason. She knew Johan was trying his best to keep her humored, but the fact did not help her vacillating mood swings

The morning she demanded sweets, he smiled and said, "We have no sweets, Bella. And even if there are sweets in Münster, they would cost a king's ransom and I would scarce have the wherewithal to buy them."

Isabella narrowed her eyes. "When I lived at Wawel Castle, I could have sweets any time I wanted." Isabella pouted. She was acting like a spoiled child and she knew it, but she didn't care.

Johan straightened. "Well, Princess, in case you hadn't

noticed, we are no longer at Wawel." His eyes flashed. "We are in the Kingdom of God in Germany, where no sweets are available and will not be available until Easter when Jesus returns to establish his Kingdom. If you can curb your desires for two weeks, perhaps he can find you some."

Isabella's heart skipped a beat. Johan had never spoken to her in such a way. She burst into tears. "I'm sorry, Johan, I didn't mean that. I don't, don't... want... I don't want to be at Wawel... I want to be here with you."

Johan eyed her for a long moment, and then, without a word, rose and walked out of the house.

Sobbing, Isabella rolled to her side and buried her face in her pillow.

Magda came and patted her back.

"He's left me," Isabella cried. "I acted like he was my servant, not my husband... after everything he's done for me."

"Now, now, my darling girl. He'll be fine." Magda smoothed Isabella's hair. "Things have changed since the prophets came to Münster, but not for the better. Johan sees this and, though he won't say it, I believe he regrets bringing you here."

"Could not we leave then? I would be happy in a tiny cottage in the forest, like the one the pastor who married us lives in."

"Matthys has declared that no one can leave." Magda sighed. "And von Waldek has ringed the city with his soldiers, so no one could leave even if Matthys allowed it."

"But what does that mean, Magda?"

"It means that soon the city will run out of food and supplies."

Fear stabbed Isabella's heart like a knife. "But... my baby? How will we feed and clothe our baby, Magda?"

Isabella wept as Magda took her in her arms. "Don't fret, my darling. The Bible says we should not worry but instead make our needs known to God, and he will guard our hearts with peace through his Son, Jesus. Let's ask him to help us find a way out of this mess, eh?"

They prayed for the baby, for Johan, for the city, and for God to do his will in their lives. When they finished, Isabella turned to Magda. "You are like a mother, Magda, and I will never forget the kindness you have shown us."

"Just let me stay with you, my dear girl, for you have become like my daughter."

～

HOURS LATER, after what seemed an eternity to Isabella, Johan returned. He came into the bedroom, kissed her forehead, and knelt beside her bed.

She whispered, "I'm sorry for what I said, Johan."

He placed his finger on her lips, reached into his pocket, and pulled out a small paper-wrapped package.

Isabella pushed upright, leaning against the headboard. "Johan, what is this?"

A smile tugged at the corner of his mouth as he handed it to her.

She opened it and gasped. Inside, two candy-coated objects glistened in the candlelight. Wide-eyed, Isabella stared at Johan. "Comfits! Cherry comfits! Oh, where did you find them, Johan?"

"I went to the confectioner's shop, the one over by Market Square. At first, he told me the prophet had confiscated his sweets and his sugar. But when I told him my pregnant wife craved one small sweet, he winked, said, 'Wait right there,' and slipped into a back room.

"A moment later, he returned with these. He told me his son and daughter had left with the Catholics and had taken his grandchildren with them. He had no little ones to enjoy his sweets. These were the last he had. So here they are, for you."

Johan looked away for a moment and then back into Isabella's eyes. A tear glistened. "I apologize for speaking to you in such a harsh manner. I will never do it again."

Isabella smiled at her husband. Love shone from his eyes, his wonderful blue eyes. And then she knew God had given her an incredible gift in this man—a man who treated her with kindness and generosity. He was not of noble birth, but he was splendid in all his ways. This simple gift revealed to Isabella, the depth of his love for her and she knew she would not fear, no matter what came. He would keep her and their baby safe. She rolled the sweets back in the paper.

"Aren't you going to eat them, my dearest?"

"No, Johan. I will keep them forever. Whenever I am feeling cross or unhappy, I will look at them and remind myself that God has blessed me with a wonderful husband. Thank you, thank you, Johan." She threw her arms around him and she was no longer afraid.

EASTER APPROACHED, and like the trees that broke the long sleep of winter and clothed themselves with blossoms, Münster came alive—alive with hope and anticipation. Everywhere that Johan went in the city he heard it on the lips of the people—Jesus would return on April fourth and drive the hated von Waldek and his mercenaries away from the city. The larders would be full again and their stomachs filled. Then the Lord would lead the Anabaptists on a victorious campaign to bring his Kingdom to a cursed, sin-filled world. The night before Easter, Mayor Knipperdolling hosted a celebratory banquet for the city's leaders. Among others, Matthys, Bockelson and Bernhard Rothmann were present. Because he now served as Matthys's chief bodyguard, Frederich Weisbach was also in attendance.

When he returned home shortly after midnight, Frederich had much to report to Johan, who had waited up to talk with him. They sat at the table, sharing meat and cheese and a skin of wine Fred had "requisitioned" from the mayor's loaded table.

"I tell you, Johan..." He shook his head. "The prophet and his friends are living like kings over at Knipperdolling's mansion. They have an abundance of meat, cheese and bread... and more, while the rest of Münster starves.

"And...," he picked up a sausage slice, "even though the prophet has outlawed drunkenness in the city, they consumed enough wine tonight to float the Dutch fleet."

He grunted. "Not only do they allow themselves the luxury of endless food and drink, they engage loose women to entertain the council members, including that tart, the prophet's wife.

"She couldn't keep her eyes—or her hands—off that handsome scoundrel, Bockelson. And he appeared to relish her attention." Frederich paused. "Divora, yes, that's her name. I'll wager she's more at home in a brothel than at the mayor's table."

"I don't understand." Johan rubbed his forehead. "God's prophet living like, like..."

"Yes, living like conquering Romans." Frederich bit into the sausage and washed it down with his wine. "Johan, the Kingdom of God in Münster is not what the common man sees. Bockelson is a traitorous dog that has his eyes on seizing the prophet's power. From what I saw tonight, he has talked Matthys into a hare-brained scheme that cannot succeed."

Johan frowned. "What is that?" Frederich's words made little sense. What did anyone's schemes matter if Jesus was coming to reign within hours?

"While they were all gathered after the feast, Knipperdolling asked, 'How shall we celebrate Easter?'"

Frederich's revelation surprised Johan. "But Matthys has predicted Jesus's coming tomorrow."

Frederich shook his head. "He is not coming, Johan, and they all know it. Bockelson, who was more than half-stewed, lifted his cup and declared, 'We should attack von Waldek's troops.' After a moment of stunned silence, Rothmann chimes in. 'We might break the lines. We have two thousand fighting men. If we charge von Waldek's camp, it might be possible to overwhelm them.'

"Without even a moment of hesitation, Bockelson says, 'No, that's too many.'"

Johan frowned. "Too many? Why, with the men and arms we have here, we could rout that band of drunkards in a heartbeat. Von Waldek may have more men than we do, but they do not have a cause and would bolt at the first charge. We should have done it long ago."

Frederich nodded. "They might run and they might not, Johan. Those are Landsknecht out there, but defeating von Waldek is not Bockelson's immediate plan, and the prophet doesn't see it."

"What would he have the prophet do, Frederich? With Jesus as our Commander—"

Frederich chuckled and took another swig. "Bockelson looked straight at the prophet and said, 'Remember Gideon.'

"Then Matthys's eyes wandered, as they do when he gets one of his religious fits. 'Gideon, yes, Gideon...' He said it over and over. Gideon is one of his favorite Bible characters. The prophet is always referencing him. Well, Bockelson took advantage of that knowledge. 'The Lord does not give victory to strong men,' he said. 'He gives it to faithful men. Gideon routed the Midianites with three hundred soldiers. Think of the glory God would receive if you conquered von Waldek with fewer. And think of David, who had only a sling and a stone.'"

Johan stared at Frederich, his mouth open. "What was Bockelson suggesting, Frederich?"

"By then, I could tell Rothmann was getting nervous. 'We must use our resources wisely,' he said. But right then that slut Divora told him to shut up and listen to Bockelson.

"Matthys lifted his arms and raised his face to the ceiling, his eyes rolling in his head like he's about to prophesy. He told us to be quiet and then said, 'If we attack with two-thousand men, it will be too many,' like it was his idea.

"Right then I saw Bockelson give Divora a sly grin, and there was betrayal in their eyes. Matthys jumped to his feet and ranted and raved about how the Lord will give him a mighty arm and the power to crush the enemies of the Kingdom. On and on he rambled. He finished by saying, 'If the Lord does not come in the flesh tomorrow, he will come in the Holy Spirit's power. He will send me out under the anointing of God to battle the giants the devil has set against us.'"

Johan gasped. "All this time, he's been saying Jesus is coming in the flesh. I don't understand. Has he been lying? Isn't he a man of God? What will happen tomorrow?"

"Matthys plans to march out to face von Waldek with thirty men—and only thirty men—at his command. That is what the prophet swore to do if Jesus doesn't return in the flesh..." Frederich shook his head. "And I know he will not."

TRUE TO FREDERICH'S PREDICTION, Jesus did not return on Easter to liberate Münster. Instead, Johan and Frederich watched from the wall as Jan Matthys, the prophet from Holland, rode out of the city gates dressed in armor, a sword at his side. Thirty men accompanied him.

Johan saw von Waldek's soldiers slowly rise as they watched the rag-tag band approach. Even from that distance, he could see the amazement on their faces as they stared at the pathetic figure. One soldier stepped forward with his hand raised but when Matthys rode forward and struck him down, von Waldek's mercenaries surrounded them and made quick work of the blustering fool and his men. As Johan watched, his faith crumbled into tiny bits. He turned to Frederich. "It was all a lie, Frederich... it was all a lie."

Frederich stared at Johan with great sadness in his eyes and then took his arm and led him away.

That night, the citizens of Münster did not see von Waldek's camp burning, or the ground stained red with the blood of the mercenaries. They did not celebrate their prophet returning into Münster under the banner of victory. Instead, the morning light revealed his grinning head impaled on a stake outside the city gates.

CHAPTER 20: THE COMING OF
THE KING

ohan spent the next morning sitting in silence, rising only to go with Frederich to view the frightful display of Matthys's severed head on a stake before the gate and the dumping of his body outside the walls by von Waldek's soldiers. Matthys had met his death, even as Frederich had foretold, and great despair came on Johan, like a black vulture settling on the dead carcass of some mangled creature. When they returned to their house, they found some of their companions from Leipzig waiting. Michael Hoffman, Pieter, and a few others sat in silence in the darkened room with Magda and Isabella.

Johan had seen little of Michael since their arrival and the man's appearance shocked him. On the journey from Leipzig, their leader had preached with power and was sure that God was at work in Münster. Then he was full of the Spirit of God, but today, he was a different man. His face was gray, he seemed shrunken in stature, and his voice was only a whisper.

"What shall we do now, Michael?" Pieter asked.

"I do not know, Pieter." Michael shook his head. "The prophet was so sure of himself, so sure Jesus would return yesterday, that I gave myself over to his coming. I am ashamed to say I made no plans except to follow our Lord in the great cleansing.

"Frederich was right." Johan dropped into a chair. "We placed our faith and trust in men—first Michael, and then Matthys. We should have placed our trust in Jesus and only him. Now, we have no leader, and von Waldek surrounds the city, locking us inside. The prophet's words blinded me. He spoke with such power. If I could, I would take my wife and leave this place..." He slumped down in his chair.

Isabella came and knelt beside her husband. "We dreamt of a city with no fear of persecution, a place where we could live in peace with our friends and await the great day of the Lord. Even yet it could happen."

"No, Isabella." Frederich stirred in his seat. "What we wished for will not happen in this city. I fear the traitor Bockelson, for he is the one who convinced Matthys to ride out in his foolish attack, and he alone will benefit by Matthys's death. Mark my words—first, he will falsely reinterpret what happened to Matthys, and then he will take power."

"That cannot be true, Frederich," Pieter said. "Bockelson has the Lord's Spirit heavy upon him. There must be another reason this happened."

Frederich laughed, but his laugh was bitter. "Why is it that when someone fools a man, he will bet his money the second time instead of admitting his stupidity? I was at the meeting where Bockelson manipulated Matthys to his death. I saw the sly looks that passed between that rogue and Matthys's trollop of a wife. We must be on our guard. I warn you. If you continue to follow Bockelson, he will lead you to great sorrow." He folded his arms. "I will say no more."

IT DID NOT TAKE LONG for Frederich's words to come true. The day after Matthys died, Jan Bockelson issued a sorrowful statement and declared he would seek the Lord. He stripped himself naked and lay for three days as if in a trance in the cathedral square. On the third day, he arose, clothed himself with white garments and called everyone to the square. Johan went with Frederich. Standing before the crowd with outstretched arms, he held his head high and his words rang with power and assurance.

"If you cannot see what happened here, then you do not have discernment in your heart. What Jan Matthys prophesied came true. Jesus returned on Easter, but not in the flesh. He sent the Holy Spirit, and the Comforter has taken possession of this city."

The crowd murmured, for they were a people desperate for answers. "It doesn't feel like the Lord has come," someone shouted from the back. Bockelson lifted his arms higher to silence the nay-sayers. Johan looked at Frederich who shook his head. Bockelson spoke again.

"I know you want answers, and I will give them to you. The death of a prophet *always* foretells the coming of the Lord. God sows seeds of righteousness in ground watered by a prophet's blood. The prophet did not die in vain, for he was Elijah come to earth again. Like John, he was the forerunner for Jesus's return.

"The Word of God says this. 'Behold, I will send you Elijah the prophet before the coming of the great and dreadful day of the Lord.' And like Elijah, God took our prophet up to heaven, where he now stands at the right hand of God with others martyred by the kings of the earth—Steven, Paul, John the Baptist and Peter."

"He's a false prophet," Frederich whispered to Johan. "He distorts the Word of God to his own ends. Jesus is the only one who stands at the Father's right hand."

Bockelson's voice rang throughout the square. "Now the prophet stands with a great company. And he urges us from heaven to continue the great fight. Empowered by the Spirit of God, we shall resist and overthrow the beast von Waldek. While I lay in a trance, the Lord visited me. He told me to take up the sword of the prophet and lead the battle. And he told me..." He paused.

Now the crowd was with him. Shouts rang out. "Hallelujah!" "Amen!" "What did he tell you?"

"The Lord told me to marry Divora, the prophet's wife so you might have an unbroken line of leadership in this great undertaking."

Someone yelled, "Praise God! Bockelson is our new leader," and the crowd took up the chant.

Johan could not believe what was happening. "Frederich, he is lying."

"Yes, Johan, he is. But these foolish sheep will follow him to hell. Mark my words, worse is yet to come."

Bockelson stepped to the edge of the platform and pointed at the gate. "Out there," he shouted, "the beast von Waldek is laughing at your prophet and holding him in derision."

Johan wondered if he yelled because he wanted von Waldek to hear him.

"Why do the heathen rage and the people imagine a vain thing?" Bockelson paced the platform. "The kings of the earth set themselves up, and the rulers take counsel together against the Lord and against his anointed, saying, 'Let us break their bands asunder, and cast away their cords from us.'

"Yet, the Lord sits on his throne, and our prophet stands beside him, and together they laugh. They hold von Waldek and his lackeys in derision. Even now, they plan their great assault, an assault that will drive our enemies straight to hell!"

The crowd erupted in cheers and shouts.

Frederich spat on the cobblestones. "They will forget

Matthys was a false prophet, that nothing he said came true. They will follow Bockelson until every one of them is dead. It is no wonder God calls us sheep." He turned and walked away, leaving Johan to watch the madness that now engulfed the Anabaptists.

~

JOHAN'S ANGER grew as the events of the following days unfolded. Four days after his speech, Bockelson revealed his true colors. He abolished the town council and appointed twelve elders whose names he had "received" from God. However, they were Bockelson's friends and supporters—Rothmann, Knipperdolling and others—men with battle scars and a desperate loyalty to the new prophet.

Then he reorganized the city's economic life. Bernhard Knipperdolling, no longer the mayor, became the Swordbearer; responsible for executing those who violated a new set of Draconian laws in which death was the penalty for crimes from adultery to complaining. Other supporters appropriated the service occupations in the city. Foodmasters ran the public kitchen. Fishmasters, Meatmasters, Shoemakers, Masters of Ironwork and a host of others took over private businesses.

Then came the crowning insult. Johan and Frederich were present at another meeting in the cathedral when Bockelson proclaimed the reinstitution of old testament polygamy. When he announced the new order of things, there was a stunned silence and then all hell broke loose. One man jumped to his feet. "I won't do that to my wife." Another yelled. "Political innovations are one thing, but polygamy is too much." Other men shouted their objections.

Bockelson listened in silence until they finished. And then he pointed at the rebels. "God does not need you to finish his work," he cried. "He can raise up saints from the stones. If you disobey this revelation, he will smite you. Your bodies will rot outside the walls where we will throw them, and your souls will rot in hell. I am the prophet now and if I am the only one left in Münster, then my wives and I will inherit this city and raise up a new line, Kingdom citizens who listen to their prophet and do the work the Lord commands us."

He gave a signal with his hand and a group of armed men marched into the room, surrounding the men inside. After a short resistance, the leaders bowed to Bockelson's wishes. Five days later, Bernhard Rothmann called another meeting in front of the cathedral and proclaimed that every man should take more wives. "There are eight-thousand women, but only two-thousand men left in the city. In the name of the Lord, the prophet commands you to take these women as wives and multiply."

Johan returned home and told Isabella the news. "Will you take another… another wife, Johan?" Her lip trembled.

Johan took her in his arms and laughed. "That strutting fool will take as many wives as he wishes, but I will never follow. Besides," he chucked his wife under the chin, "I have my hands full with just one."

JOHAN WAS RIGHT. Bockelson led the way by first marrying Divora, the wife of the dead prophet. Then he requisitioned a spacious mansion on the cathedral square for himself, and within days of marrying Divora, took fourteen more wives, every one of them young and beautiful.

JOHAN WAS in his shop one morning in September when Frederich came in the door in a rush. "You better come and hear this, Johan. What I feared is happening."

The two men hurried to the square. On the platform was someone they did not recognize. He was shouting at the people to be quiet.

Frederich whispered. "They say his name is Johan Dusenscher, and he is from Warendorf—a great prophet. But I believe him to be a friend of Bockelson, brought here to cement Bockelson's rule."

The prophet Dusenscher finally got the crowd quieted. "I have come with the word of the Lord," he announced. "I have had a great vision. In that vision the Lord showed me the last David, the king foretold by the prophets and by John the Apostle." He paused and then shouted out. "That king is Jan Bockelson!" Pandemonium broke out as the two men watched.

"Now the deceiver reveals himself, Johan." Frederich gripped Johan's arm. "Now comes the end. We must get out of this city."

BUT THERE WAS no way out for Johan and Isabella and their friends. Bockelson had set his loyal men everywhere and no one could even approach the gates on punishment of death. Three days later, in a driving rain, the coronation took place. While the new elite gathered inside the cathedral, Münster's citizens waited outside to greet their new king.

Many other changes swept the city following the coronation. Bockelson conscripted men to build defenses and removed the wealthy from their mansions, seizing their wealth and their goods. Ordinary folks who saw hard times coming hid food in attics and beneath floorboards. Frederich's preparations served them well, for with wise use the little family had enough to eat. They had to be careful for Bockelson confiscated all the nonperishable food his soldiers could unearth for his own storehouse.

And then one day the soldiers came and took the great black stallion, Al-Buraq, to be the king's personal charger. Word of Johan's skill with horses had come to the new king's ears and, since there was no more iron in the city, Bockelson appointed Johan as Stablemaster of his new domain.

CHAPTER 21: A SON IS GIVEN

"*J*ohan!"

Johan groaned and rolled over.

"Ahhhh!" The cry was louder this time and accompanied by a shove.

Johan sat up. Dawn was breaking through the window. "What, Bella? What is it?"

"It's time, Johan. My water has broken. The baby is coming. Get Magda."

"Are you sure, Bella?"

Isabella drew her knees up, squeezed her eyes shut and hissed, "Get Magda, now!"

Johan bolted from the bed, pulled on his trousers and ran for the door. He raced down the hall and pounded on the door of Magda's tiny room. "Magda, Magda!"

The door cracked open, and the old woman, already dressed, stepped into the hallway. "Her time has come, eh? I knew today would be the day."

"What can I do, Magda?"

"After you get me hot water and towels, you can do what fathers since Adam have been doing. Go get yourself a draught of ale—you'll need it. Then go to the basement and wake up Frederich, so he can make fun of you while you pace about the great room—and then wait. Leave this to God... and me." She smiled. "And please pray."

"But she's so young, and she's such a little thing, Magda!"

"Your Bella may be small, but her hips are ample, perfect for bringing children into this world. She is a healthy girl, and her spirit is strong. You need not fear. I will make sure everything goes well."

The time of delivery was short, though Isabella cried out many times. Frederich laughed at Johan's discomfort and assured him that pain and yelling was a part of childbirth. "I am the oldest of twelve children, Johan. I've seen this many times. She'll scream for a while and then, boom—a baby."

After one horrific scream, a blessed sound issued from their bedroom; a baby's cry. Johan took a swig of ale and rushed to the bedroom door. Moments later, it opened and Magda stood there smiling. She handed him a bundle wrapped in cloth. "You have a healthy boy, Johan. Every finger and toe is in its place. He has a head full of black hair and a big set of lungs." She laughed. "Your wife is fine. She is resting and waiting for you."

Baby in his arms, Johan pushed past Magda. Isabella was lying on the bed, dressed in a fresh white nightgown with a soft bolster supporting her. Her dark hair fanned across the pillow. Her face was pale, but her eyes shone and a tired smile touched her mouth.

Johan placed the baby in her arms. Isabella looked up at him, her eyes shining. He'd never seen his wife look more beautiful. The color was returning to her pale face.

Kneeling beside the bed, he asked, "How are you feeling, my precious wife?"

"Happy but tired, husband."

"You look beautiful, Bella. And you've given me a handsome son."

Isabella opened the cloth and smiled at their baby. He was a big boy, with startling blue eyes and a shock of dark black hair. His features were strong but still misshapen from the birth. "What shall we name him, Johan?"

"I've been thinking about that, Bella. He is the firstborn and we shall call him Abel." Johan took the tiny hand in his and looked down on his son.

"May the Lord bless thee and keep thee: the Lord make his face to shine upon thee, and be gracious unto thee: the Lord lift his countenance upon thee and give thee peace, Abel."

The baby screwed up his face, which reddened, and then he let out a loud howl.

Johan looked at Isabella. "So much for peace, eh my son?" They both burst out laughing.

Magda peeked into the room. "How is our little one doing?"

"He's crying," Isabella said. "What is wrong, Magda?"

She chuckled. "He's only hungry, Bella." She stepped into the room and motioned for Johan to leave. "Go on with you while I teach Bella how to feed your baby."

Johan kissed his wife on the forehead, kissed his tiny son and rose from the bedside. "Thank you, Bella, for this fine son."

FOR A MONTH, the little family stayed secluded. The baby was healthy and soon, with Magda's patient help, Bella learned her role as a mother. It took Johan a while to get used to getting up to bring the baby for the night feedings, but the joy he felt because of his son countered any aggravation.

Even during severe rationing, Frederich continued to come up with food for them, so Johan did not have to worry in that respect. Johan suspected that Frederich was 're-appropriating' it from the king but he did not ask questions. Johan now worked in the stable where his skill with horses gave him grace with the city leaders. He was not in the inner circle, but they appreciated his skills and did not require him to attend the constant "gatherings" and "training" that plagued the other men. Bockelson also overlooked Johan's refusal to take more wives.

Johan visited Al-Buraq every day and took good care of him. Bockelson could only ride the horse if Johan was at hand to manage him. Soon, the king gave up trying to take the horse out on his own. Johan was glad that Al-Buraq was in the king's stable. The stable was well-guarded, and it was not likely the hungry people of the city would break in and eat him.

The leaders in Münster cut the food ration in half. Frederich understood what was happening in the city. He was a shrewd bargainer and traded some of their goods for weapons. When Johan asked the reason for the weapons, Frederich said, "The situation in the city is bad. We might need to fight our way out of here. Before the end of all this, the food situation will get very much worse. I've been in sieges before. Mark my words, my young friend, terrible days are coming."

FREDERICH HAD his ear to the ground, and he picked up information that only the inner circle was privy to. In early August he reported to Johan that the news of Bockelson's decree of legalized polygamy had reached von Waldek. The Bishop immediately sent out riders who passed the news to aristocrats and clerical leaders all over Germany. Word came from outside sources that the outraged Archbishop of Cologne and the Duke of Cleves had promised to replenish von Waldek's disgruntled army with fresh troops and supplies.

Within a week, those standing guard on the walls saw fresh men marching into von Waldek's camp. In the third week of August, two enormous guns provided by Phillip of Hesse rolled in. Phillip also provided a contingent of gunners and plenty of cannon balls and powder. Von Waldek wasted no time in starting an attack.

For days on end, the big guns pounded the city gate, leaving it in shambles. The men of Münster massed at the gate and prevented any attacks there. But the gunners also blasted a wide notch in the wall near the St. Mauritz gate and this became the weak point in the city's defenses. But just when von Waldek was ready to attack, a heavy downpour of rain filled the moat around the city to overflowing. Undeterred, von Waldek ordered his men to construct straw pallets on which to float across. On August 31, 1534, the long-planned assault of Münster began.

"JOHAN! WAKE UP!" The need for urgency in Frederich's voice, coupled with the hammering on their bedroom door, roused Johan from sleep. He'd been dreaming of the meadows at the foot of Deer Mountain. In his dream, he was lying in the grass, the sheep were grazing nearby, and Isabella and Abel were asleep on a blanket under the giant ash tree that crowned the knoll.

White clouds drifted by the peaks that surrounded the mountain. Below him, green pastures, dotted by the houses and cottages of his neighbors, eased down the mountain toward Basel. A lone eagle circled high above and Johan had felt peace; the peace he'd had before...

"Johan! Get up, now!"

Isabella sat up as Johan stumbled from the bed to open the door. Frederich's face was pale and grim. "The word has come. Von Waldek is attacking the city. We must go to the defenses."

Johan hesitated, but Frederich grabbed his arm. "I know what you are thinking, lad. How did the Kingdom dream come to the point where we are defending an insane Dutch liar? *Es ist eine Hölle einer Verwirrung!* But I tell you, von Waldek's men are here for one purpose—to kill every man and rape as many women as they can find."

Quickly Johan threw on pants and a shirt then pulled on his boots. Frederich handed him a leather jerkin.

"Wear this. It will protect you from sword thrusts."

Isabella sucked in a sharp breath.

"Not one Anabaptist will be alive inside this city if von Waldek's men get in, Isabella." He handed Johan a sword. "Take this, strap it on and follow me. Stay right with me and do everything I say if you want to live."

"Johan!"

He turned.

Isabella was sitting up in the bed, clutching the covers to her breast. "Don't go, Johan."

"You heard Frederich, Isabella. Von Waldek is attacking the city. They need all able-bodied men. I must go and fight."

"But what about us, Johan?" she asked, eyes wide. "What about Abel and me and Magda?"

"If I do not go, Isabella, von Waldek's soldiers will break in, and they will kill us all, including the baby."

Frederich smiled at Isabella. "Do not worry, Isabella. Is he not with Frederich Weisbach, the greatest swordsman in Münster? Johan will return to you, I promise."

At the sound of shouts outside the house, Frederich grabbed Johan's arm, and the two men ran down the hallway. Johan opened the door. Men in black shirts were running up and down the street.

"Alarm, alarm!" they shouted. "To the walls! Von Waldek is coming! Report to your positions at once."

Men streamed out of the houses and into the streets, all of them armed for battle. It surprised Johan to see many women among them. The women carried axes and clubs, their arms were bare and their hair tied back. When Johan and Frederich reached the square, commanders were shouting orders. One man, Gerlach van Wullen, who was a leader of the guards, grabbed Frederich. "You! Weisbach! Bring your friend and come with me. We go to the notch. That is where our defenses are weakest."

In the company of dozens of men armed with muskets and swords, Johan and Frederich followed van Wullen toward the gate. When they arrived, he ordered them to climb to the top of the thick walls. "Weisbach, you're in charge here. I will be on the other side of the notch!"

Johan gasped when he saw what they were up against. Across four hundred yards of denuded landscape, hundreds of Landsknecht soldiers armed with muskets, crossbows, knives, pikes and swords marched in formation toward the city, their gaudy orange uniforms plain to see in the bright sunlight. Many of them carried scaling ladders. They were singing a German fighting song.

The soldiers looked fierce and determined and tramped to the sound of huge kettledrums. The booming beat sent a shiver down Johan's spine. From time to time, a monstrous explosion shook the wall as a huge cannonball crashed against it.

"They will float across the moat and then put the ladders against the wall," Frederich shouted to his men. "Keep your heads down until they climb the ladders. They will stop firing the cannon when their men reach the moat. When they come across and are scaling the ladders, do your best to knock them back down." He grabbed up a pole lying on the ground and handed it to Johan. "Use this."

As Frederich had predicted, when von Waldek's men reached the moat, the drums stopped beating and the cannons stopped firing. Below them, fifteen hundred men threw straw pallets into the water, loaded on their equipment and swam the pallets across.

Van Wullen shouted, "Fire!" and a ragged musket volley

rained down on the swimmers. Stinking brown smoke filled the air and the noxious fumes made Johan cough. That first volley killed many Catholic soldiers, but many more reached the other side of the moat with their weapons and ladders intact. In minutes, they'd placed their ladders against the walls, focusing on the massive notch that the cannon had blasted in the wall.

With a great shout, the Catholic troops scaled the walls. And through the smoke, Johan saw the heads of the enemy coming over the wall. He used the pole and shoved one ladder over. The men fell screaming to the ground below. Soon, however, the ladders were too many to knock down and the Catholic troops clambered up into the notch and clambered over the debris toward the defenders.

Frederich turned to the men behind him. "Draw your swords, men. Remember, you are not fighting for the king, you are fighting to keep these animals away from your wives and children. Johan! Stay beside me." He lifted his hand and signaled the men forward. "Now! Attack!"

CHAPTER 22: THE BATTLE

*I*sabella sat in the bedroom holding Abel and listening to the roar of the cannon followed by the sounds of musketry and men and women screaming from the wall above their house. Magda sat with her. They could smell the acrid smoke from the muskets, even through the drawn shades. The baby was crying, frightened by the loud noises and the shouts of the combatants.

Johan, Johan! Oh God, please keep my Johan safe.

THE SUN WAS SETTING when she heard the door of the house open and the sound of voices from the front room.

"Johan!" Isabella rushed into the hallway. Frederich stood in the doorway with his shoulder under Johan's arm, supporting him. Johan's face was pale. He had a blood-stained bandage tied around his head and blood matted his hair.

Isabella stared at her husband. Her heart leapt into her throat and she raised her trembling hands to her face. Frederich glanced at her. "Ah, my dear, have no fear. I have brought your man home to you. His wound is not serious. One of their men got past my sword and fetched the lad a terrific clout to the head with his cudgel before I could stop him." Frederich, though splattered with blood, smiled a battle-weary smile. "That mercenary will go no more a'cudgeling."

"But the blood…"

"The red badge of courage, Bella. Johan fought like a man. Aside from the little mistake of turning his back to that one soldier, he did well. With a little scrubbing and a few hours of sleep, he'll be as good as new." Frederich grunted. "Although the ringing in his head may persist for a few days."

"I'll be all right, Bella." Johan grimaced. "I only need to lie down for a while, and then I'll be as good as new."

"Take him to our bed, Frederich." Isabella flew to the kitchen where she grabbed towels and wet them in the water bucket they kept on the counter. Rushing into their bedroom, she knelt beside Johan. "Close your eyes while I remove this nasty bandage and wash the blood from your face and head."

"Do you need anything more from me?" Frederich looked ready to topple into bed himself.

"Nothing I can think of at the moment." She smiled a small smile. "Thank you for bringing him home."

Frederich tipped his hat and left the room. Magda came in, holding the baby. Seeing the shocked look on her face, Isabella smiled. "Frederich says he will be fine, Magda. I've just got to get him cleaned up." Taking great care, she unwound the stained rag from her husband's head, wincing at the sight of the ugly gash above his ear. The skin had split, but with a little probing, she assured herself the wound was superficial, as Frederich had said. She dabbed at it with a damp towel and wiped the blood from his hair and face.

"Oh, Johan, Johan, my dearest," she whispered. "If I had lost you…" She stroked his stubbled jaw.

Johan opened his eyes and placed his hand over hers. Tears ran down his temples into his hair.

"Johan, what is it, husband?"

"I'm sorry, Bella. I didn't mean to cry." He swiped at his eyes with the backs of his blood-splattered knuckles. "I did the unthinkable—I killed men today, many men. It was...." He squeezed his eyes shut.

"Oh, my dear." Isabella put her head on Johan's chest.

He wrapped his arms around her. "When the Catholics came over the wall, all I could think of was protecting you and the baby. Ever since I left Switzerland, I thought killing Catholics and reformists would be easy after what they did to my family. But when I saw men dying and heard their terrible screams... Oh, Bella..." Johan curled on his side, buried his face in the pillow and sobbed. Isabella, who'd never heard her husband utter such heart-wrenching cries, held him until his tears subsided. At last his breathing evened out, and he fell asleep.

Just before dawn, Johan's groans awakened Isabella. He tossed back and forth, crying, "Frederich, help me! Help me!" She could feel him trembling. "No," he muttered, "get back, I don't want to kill you... Oh, no, don't!" Johan screamed. "No, no..."

Isabella shook his shoulder. "Johan, wake up. You're having a terrible dream."

"What?" Johan clung to her arm. "Bella. Oh, Bella."

"What is it, my dearest? The battle?"

Dim light filtered between the heavy curtains. The baby, disturbed by the sounds in the room, stirred in his crib and then quieted. Isabella could see that Johan was looking at her. She'd never seen his face so sad. He drew her close. "I have been wrong," he murmured in her ear. "In my hatred of those who persecuted us, I thought it would be easy to take revenge on them, but it was not. To kill another human being is beyond horrible... Oh, Isabella, I keep seeing their faces—the surprise, the sadness as I killed them. I can't get them out of my mind."

She pulled him close. "Perhaps if you told me about the battle..."

"But I've always kept hard things from you, Bella."

She lifted her face and looked into his eyes. "I am your wife. I am no longer a weak little girl. When I married you, I accepted that I would share everything with you, the good and the bad. So tell me so I can help you carry this burden."

Johan sighed and then propped himself up in the bed and pulled her close. His voice was a whisper. "We were up above the St. Mauritz gate, where von Waldek's cannons had torn a huge hole in the wall. They crossed the moat on rafts, brought their ladders to the gap and climbed up the wall. We were pushing the ladders off with poles, that was all we had, but on the other side of the notch they had logs they threw over the wall. The logs crushed the Catholics and knocked them off the ladders. They fell screaming to the ground, their arms and legs twisted and shattered.

"Our women on the wall poured burning pitch and lye onto the soldiers. When it hit them, they shrieked like fiends from hell. But that didn't stop their musketeers, who maintained a steady fire from beyond the moat. I kept my head low, but others did not. Men fell all around me. One with half his face shot away fell right beside me."

Isabella touched his face. "Oh, my poor Johan."

"They knew the notch they had blasted in the wall with their cannons was our weak point, and they concentrated their fire there. Their muskets kept those of us with firearms down and drove the women away. They had many more men than we did and so, in time, a host of them climbed the ladders and surged through the gap into the city. We attacked from all sides, fighting hand to hand.

"And then this terrible rage came over me. Screaming like a madman, I swung my sword this way and that way. Up, down, all around, following Frederich as he cut a swath through the hordes."

Johan took a ragged breath. "Isabella, I don't know how many men I killed or wounded, but I stabbed and slashed and stabbed and slashed until I could not lift my arms. I followed Frederich, and we killed so many of the enemy that they fell back from our onslaught. One young boy refused to retreat..." Johan stopped.

"Go on, husband. I can bear it."

"He... he was so young, maybe fourteen or fifteen. He rushed at me with a pike. I deflected his thrust with my sword and grabbed his arm. When I looked at his face, I knew I didn't want to kill him. He wasn't even old enough to shave. I thought of his mother, or perhaps a sweetheart waiting for him as you were waiting for me. I screamed at him to stop; that I didn't want to kill him, but he dropped his pike and came after me with a short sword. He wouldn't quit, Bella. He wouldn't quit."

Johan was shaking. He moaned. "I saw so much hatred in his eyes. I remembered you and the baby waiting here alone, and I had to fight back. If I did not kill him, he would kill me. I... I stabbed him..." He swallowed. "I stabbed him so hard my sword ran through his body. He screamed and screamed and tried to get away from me, but my sword held him fast. Then his life was ebbing away, and he lost his strength. I watched his eyes go blank as he fell to the ground."

Johan was panting now. "I was trying to wrench my sword out of his body when something struck me from behind and knocked me senseless. When I awoke, Frederich was carrying me away from the battle. He told me we had driven von Waldek off and won the battle. Oh, Isabella, Isabella, my hands are forever stained with blood..." Clinging to her, he cried, "We must leave this place, Isabella. Christ does not rule here. This is not the Kingdom of God. It is hell on earth."

∼

But Johan could not flee the troubled city with his family. It was impossible. After the victory, Bockelson became even more controlling. He issued an order that no one was to leave Münster under punishment of death. He set trusted guards at every gate and ordered the defenses strengthened and the wall at the St. Mauritz gate rebuilt. Most of the men in the city worked to build great earthen mounds outside the walls to prevent the easy approach of troops and inside everyone worked together to repair all that von Waldek's bombardment had damaged.

Frederich came home one day and the look on his face was sour. "Citizens can no longer bargain for food at the central market, Johan. Bockelson has set up a central food distribution point where we will all receive our rations. And he has commanded all citizens to grow gardens and raise pigs. However, I still have connections with those who have gone underground so the hard times should not catch us short when they come."

For Johan, the most galling development was the great entertainments Bockelson staged, where he was the center of attention and acclaim. On the nights the king presented these spectacles, he called the people to the cathedral square with trumpet blasts.

One night when the trumpets sounded, Isabella came to Johan in the kitchen. "Can I go with you tonight, Johan?" she asked. "I am so tired of staying in the house. I haven't been out since Abel was born."

"It's not a good idea, Bella. The king has a wandering eye and you are beautiful."

Frederich poked his head in the door. "Johan is right; it is not safe for beautiful women to be on the streets."

Isabella stuck out her lower lip. "But, Johan, you and Frederich will be with me."

Magda came in holding Abel. "Oh, take her with you, Johan," Magda said. "The poor girl is going crazy cooped up here. She needs to get out, to experience life again. Don't worry; I'll take care of my darling Abel. Let her go with you."

"Please, Johan, please!" She grabbed Johan's arm.

Johan sighed and nodded. Frederich shook his head. "Women," was all he said.

Locking the door behind them, the trio joined the crowds hurrying to the square. Men in black urged the crowd forward, crying, "Come see the king! Come see the king."

WHEN THEY ARRIVED at the square, Isabella sucked in her breath. The whole area was lit with torches and lanterns and dozens of white banners with a golden emblem floated above the platform. Trumpets gave sporadic blasts summoning the people and soon they packed the square. Frederich leaned close to Isabella.

"When the king appears," he murmured, "don't let the splendor put you in awe, my dear. Bockelson is a master manipulator and a charlatan." He swept his arm out, pointing to the throngs of worshipers. "He has stolen their freedom, and their wealth and what does he offer them? A spectacle. Yet the sheep flock to him with eyes ablaze, like children at a carnival."

Isabella felt her heart pound and, for a moment, she felt like she was back at Wawel watching one of the great royal pageants. Then trumpets blared and a group of beautiful women wearing pure white robes entered the square. In the lead came a voluptuous dark-haired woman bearing Bockelson's personal dark-blue banner. Someone had emblazoned the new symbol of the city, an orb of the world pierced by two swords on it. The words, "One King of Righteousness Over All," flowed across the bottom. With another flourish of trumpets, Bockelson appeared, also dressed in white with a golden crown on his head.

"He is such an arrogant man," Frederich whispered. "For one thousand years, Catholic Europe has recognized that the pope and the emperor held the two swords of power, spiritual and secular. Now he has taken both for himself. And the reference to the king on his banner does not refer to Christ."

"Who are the women?" she asked.

Frederich snorted. "Those are his wives, selected and sometimes taken by force from among the most beautiful women of the city. Leading them all is the creature, Divora, former wife of the prophet Matthys. She was the instigator of the fiasco that led to the prophet's death—all so she could crawl into Bockelson's bed."

As the spectacle rolled on and on, two men in the square were watching Isabella. One had pig-like eyes and heavy jowls and the other, a thin man, wore the mayor's sash on his chest. Meanwhile, Bockelson was strutting back and forth on the stage receiving praise and bowing. The pompous antics of the king distracted Isabella and Johan so that neither noticed the two men whose attention was on Bella—but the sharp eyes of Frederich Weisbach missed nothing.

CHAPTER 23: BETRAYED

*P*rince Bishop Franz von Waldek smashed his fist on the table. "What do you mean the troops are deserting?"

The commander of his troops, Wilkin Steding, stood at attention before him, looking out of place in the luxurious tent. Though it was a cold December night, sweat trickled down his forehead.

"They are deserting in greater numbers every day, Your Highness. The men are angry that the attack did not go well, and since their defeat, they have nothing to do."

Von Waldek slammed his fist down again. "You were the one who planned that attack. I should have replaced you the moment that rabble of farmers armed with pitchforks drove you out of Münster."

"It was not a rabble." Steding lifted his chin. "They had professional swordsmen amongst them and they fought like berserkers."

Von Waldek blew out a long breath. "What is our troop number?"

"We are down to eight hundred men, sir, who all want their wages before Christmas."

"Oh, yes, paid before Christmas." Von Waldek snorted. "Why? So they can slip away to the nearest town and celebrate in some tavern or a brothel?"

"Well, Your Highness, it is the way of soldiers."

"Not the way of my soldiers!"

One of von Waldek's aides entered the tent. Von Waldek looked up in irritation. "What?"

"Your Highness, the guards captured a man who says he's from the city. He begged them not to kill him until he had spoken to you. He says he has a message for your ears only; a message that could turn the tide of battle."

Von Waldek picked up a goblet of wine and took a sip. "He's saying that to save his skin because he knows we kill everyone who attempts to leave the city." Von Waldek shrugged. "Oh, well, it's been a dull evening. Let's see what this lout has to say. Afterward, we'll put him to the sword."

The aide left. In a moment he lifted the tent flap and entered, a short man with piggish eyes and heavy jowls behind him. He was holding his cap in his hands and bowing as he came. He blinked his eyes in the dim light of the tent. A small fire burned on a grate and the smoke meandered upward and out of the hole in the tent's top.

Von Waldek waved the aide out. He stood up and approached the prisoner. "Well, what is it? Spit it out!"

The fat little man looked sideways at the commander. "Perhaps if you and I could speak alone, Your Highness…"

Von Waldek laughed out loud. "Oh, by all means. Are you one of Bockelson's demented angels on a suicide mission? You get me alone and murder me. Are those your instructions? Do you think I am mad? My commander shall remain." He turned to his general. "If he makes one false move, drag him out and turn him over to the men for a little winter sport."

The man bowed again and again, sweat running down his jowls and dripping on the dirt. "No, Your Highness. I am not here to kill you but rather to give you information."

"Stop!" The prince bishop raised his hand.

The man straightened and looked around, his piggish eyes squinting in the smoke.

"Who are you?" von Waldek demanded. "And how did you get out of the city?"

The man shuffled his feet. "My name is Heinrich Gresbeck." His voice was low. "I was a carpenter in Münster. When that strutting popinjay Bockelson took away my trade, I tried to escape, but it was not until tonight that I slipped out with four other men. They sneaked through your lines, but I let your men capture me. I have something to tell you that will be of great interest."

Von Waldek frowned. "How did you get out?"

Gresbeck held up a wooden key. "With this."

Stedman leaned forward, looking at the key. "Where did you get that?"

"I made it, Your Highness. When Bockelson closed my shop, he put me to work at the Holy Cross Gate, strengthening the wall. Near the gate is a small door. We used it to get outside to work on the outer defenses because they lock all the doors and gates of the city from the inside to keep the people in. The elders of the city gave me the key, but I had to give it back when we returned. One night while we were working, I made a wax impression, and I carved this from it. It works like the original."

"You mean you could open that door to my troops?"

Gresbeck bowed again. "Yes, Your Highness."

Von Waldek approached and took hold of the man's jacket. "Why shouldn't I take it right now and let myself in?" he hissed.

Gresbeck swallowed hard and trembled. "Because I have more to offer you, Your Highness. I saw someone in the city who may interest you; a woman."

"A woman?"

"The princess of Poland, Your Highness."

Von Waldek's eyes opened wide. He glanced over at Stedman, then turned back to the man cowering before him. "You mean Isabella, Sigismund's missing daughter?"

"Yes, Your Highness. I saw her with my own eyes at one of Bockelson's entertainments. There is a man named Johan Hirschberg who came to the city with a magnificent black stallion. Bockelson appropriated it for his stables, but I've seen the horse. Last year, Sigismund's riders traveled all the roads near and wide with a reward poster. They were looking for the king's daughter who had run away with a man named Johan Hirschberg. Someone reported this Hirschberg to be riding a black stallion stolen from Sigismund's stables. I know the horse I saw is that horse since Johan Hirschberg was riding him."

Eyes wide, Gresbeck waved his arms. His jowls quivered. "The night I saw this woman she was with Hirschberg. A shawl covered her up, but she pulled it away from her face for a moment. I was in Poland a few years ago and I saw Isabella riding in a carriage with her mother. She was beautiful, and she had dark hair. The woman I saw in Münster was that same Princess Isabella, I am certain!"

"Good Lord! Sigismund's daughter in the city!" Von Waldek glanced at Steding and then pointed a long finger at Gresbeck. "You will wait outside until I summon you." He opened the leather pouch lying on the table and withdrew a golden coin. "Take this as a down payment on your information. If it is true, you will receive further payment and I will allow you to leave Münster with your life. If you are false...," He narrowed his eyes, "you will suffer the tortures of the damned."

~

When Gresbeck had slipped under the flap, von Waldek paced from one end of the spacious tent to the other. "Do you understand what this means, Steding? We can tell Sigismund we know the whereabouts of his daughter. He is a very wealthy man. Knowing his daughter is in the city, he will do anything to get her back. That means money, more troops and more guns." He pounded his fist in his hand.

"Krakow is a twenty-day journey from here." He stopped, palm lifted. "Send four messengers on your fastest horses to Sigismund's court. No, better than that, I want you to go with them, Steding. Tell Sigismund we know where his daughter is and we can deliver her... for a price.

"I will go to the district council and let Germany's lords know we can get into the city undetected. But I will not inform them of Sigismund's daughter. I will only tell them we need money and more men. When the time is right, we will send our troops into the city.

"But we must be sure the Polish princess remains unharmed. That is where Gresbeck comes in. When we attack, I want him to capture her and sneak her out of the city. We will destroy Bockelson's army, and you and I will escort the princess to Krakow. Think of the glory and the money. But I won't go before I see that ignorant Dutch actor skewered on a stake before the city gates."

Four months later, in April 1535, Franz von Waldek sat in the dining room of the country house a few miles from Münster he now used as a headquarters. Sitting across the table from him was a man named Wirich van Dhaun.

"I am not happy that the German nobles have saddled me with you as the new director of my siege, General van Dhaun."

Van Dhaun smiled at the prince bishop, but it wasn't a pleasant smile. "You are eager to take Münster back, Your Highness. However, the lords of Germany made me director of this siege as a condition for lending more money for this battle."

"Yes, but your plan to starve them out instead of taking the city now is galling. We have enough men for a direct attack," von Waldek insisted. He stood, emphasizing his words with his hands. "We can send an advance team through the door to open the gates and let our men in to annihilate Bockelson's army."

Van Dhaun set his drink on the side table. "I will not waste our troops' lives again by attacking a band of fanatics. They defeated you once, and being religious zealots, they will fight to the death to preserve their little kingdom." He shrugged and smirked. "My way is the better way."

Von Waldek eyed him for a long moment and took a sip of wine. "So, as you said before, you will starve them out?"

"That is my plan. We will starve them out."

"My men stopped supplies from reaching the city but did not break their will. Why will your siege succeed?"

"You failed because you had a disinterested group of unpaid soldiers who preferred to sit around their campfires drinking ale and singing bawdy songs. Your blockade was as porous as a sponge and supplies continued to get into the city. I, however, will guarantee that not a mouse gets through my lines. Even now, the men I brought with me are digging a network of trenches, which they will man day and night. Gresbeck tells us there is little food left in Münster. The ring of steel I am forging will starve the citizens of Münster into submission. In one month, two at the most, Bockelson will come crawling out of those gates, meek as a lamb."

At the sound of a commotion outside the window, von Waldek turned—a troop of horsemen was trotting into the courtyard.

"Now who could this be? Are you expecting cavalry, van Dhaun?"

Van Dhaun shook his head, a puzzled expression on his face.

Someone pounded on the door, shouting, "He's here, Your Highness, he's here!"

Von Waldek rose and threw the door open. "Who's here, you fool?"

"Sig... Sig... Sig..."

"Spit it out, you idiot!"

The young man sucked in a breath, blew it out and stood tall. "Sigismund, Your Highness, King Sigismund of Poland!"

"Sigismund!" Van Dhaun jumped to his feet. "What in the world is he doing here? Krakow is six hundred away miles from here. Surely he is not interested in the affairs of a minor church official..."

Von Waldek waved him to silence. "Do you think he might be interested if his runaway daughter is in the city?" He turned to the servant. "Bring him in, fool!"

The servant hurried out.

"Isabella—in Munster?" Van Dhaun raised an eyebrow. "Now I know why you wish to gain entrance so soon. You hope to receive the large reward Sigismund has offered, no doubt." The general chuckled. "Well, Your Highness, since I am in charge of the siege, it would seem I am your partner in this venture."

Von Waldek glared at the general. "This is not your business."

Heavy footsteps sounded in the hall and an instant later, Sigismund I, King of Poland, burst through the door.

"Where is my daughter? What has become of her?"

Von Waldek stepped back before the force that was Sigismund. "Your Majesty." Von Waldek bowed deeply and then raised up. "Welcome to my headquarters. Let me offer you some refreshment—"

Sigismund strode across the room. Before von Waldek could

dodge him, the king clamped his brawny fist around von Waldek's throat.

"You know who I am?" the king growled.

"Yes, yes, Your Majesty. You are Sigismund—"

"Do you understand what I can do to those who thwart me?"

Von Waldek choked out his answer. "Your fame... precedes you, Your Majesty..." Von Waldek struggled to breathe.

General van Dhaun had edged toward the door.

"You will tell me where my daughter is, now!" The king's fierce face was inches from von Waldek's and the prince bishop could see a vein working in the king's temple.

"Please... Your Majesty. I can't breathe."

Sigismund shoved him into a chair. "Talk."

Von Waldek rubbed his throat. "We, uh...," he glanced at van Dhaun. "We believe your daughter is in Münster."

"Believe?" Sigismund roared and reached for von Waldek's throat again. "You *believe*?"

Von Waldek held up both palms to ward the king off. "A spy from within the city has informed us of a beautiful woman there who lives with a man named Johan Hirschberg. They came to the city with a splendid black stallion."

"Hirschberg!" Sigismund stepped back. "Yes, yes! That's the man. He has my daughter *and* the horse?"

"Yes, Your Majesty."

"What are you doing to rescue her?"

Von Waldek nodded to van Dhaun. "This is the director of the siege, General Wirich van Dhaun. He believes the best way to conquer the city into submission is to starve its citizens. We have constructed siege works to cut off supplies. If all goes well, the city should surrender within a month. Meanwhile, our spy will guarantee that someone captures your daughter and sneaks her out of the city."

Sigismund looked from man to man. "Yes, that is a good

plan, for I want no harm to come to Isabella. If you attack the city, she might get hurt. I will give you thirty days."

Von Waldek breathed a quiet sigh of relief. "Yes, Your Majesty, we guarantee no harm will come to her." Behind Sigismund, he could see van Dhaun's face. It was hard to miss the doubt there.

CHAPTER 24: DEADLY DAYS

APRIL / JUNE 1535

ing Jan Bockelson stood atop Münster's thick wall, watching von Waldek's soldiers at work below. Not five hundred yards from the wall, hundreds of men were digging long trenches. Soon, the siege lines would encircle the city.

Behind the trenches, amidst hundreds of tents, men bustled back and forth. Carts loaded with cannon balls and war supplies crowded the network of roads leading to the siege lines. In the distance, timber-laden wagons pulled by teams of horses approached the camp out of the surrounding forest. Along the line, men were building sentry blockhouses.

Bockelson smiled a grim smile and turned to his new chief bodyguard, Jügen Fromme. "Life will become very hard for the people, Jügen, but it is important that the king's household and his elders are well-fed. I trust you made preparations."

Fromme, a thickset man with an ugly scar running down the side of his face, nodded. "Yes, Your Majesty. I have only been here two days but I know your people have been gathering supplies for months. Knipperdolling tells me you will have less than before, but you will have enough."

"Enough to last until May?"

"Why May, Your Majesty?"

Bockelson swept his hand over the enemy's activities. "The Lord has shown me salvation will come to this city on Easter when he will end the siege, and von Waldek will come crawling on his knees to beg my forgiveness.

"Then our army will go forth to bring down Satan's kingdoms. By the end of June, we will conquer Rome, and I will take my place as the rightful ruler of the new Christian empire." Bockelson could see his words entranced Fromme, and he smiled. "I will reveal my revelation to the people tonight."

He suppressed a snicker. *These fools are so easy to sway. My years as an actor stand me in good stead.*

"Forgive me for asking, Your Majesty," Fromme said, "but why must we endure this siege and suffering? Why can't the Lord come now?"

Bockelson whipped around. "Oh, ye of little faith! Had you been Peter, you would have drowned the moment you stepped out of the boat." He shook his finger in the trembling man's face.

"Understand this, Fromme! This city is full of malcontents and complainers, murmurers like those who plagued Moses. The Lord will send a baptism of fire to purge Münster. Those who stand strong will receive a great reward." Eyes narrowed, he lowered his voice. "You came with good recommendations, Jügen, but I am taking a chance since I do not know you. I would not have made you my chief bodyguard unless I believed you had certain... shall we say... qualities. Loyalty, faithfulness and a willingness to do anything I command. I trust you will be one saint who stands up to the test, Jügen..."

"Forgive me, Your Majesty!" The bodyguard bowed, his face a mask. "You can trust me. I will be true. I will be a faithful one. Call on me, and I will do whatever you ask."

Bockelson looked again at von Waldek's soldiers to prevent

Fromme from seeing the smile that tugged at his lips. "I know, Jügen, I know."

～

HOLDING ABEL IN ONE ARM, Isabella pushed the heavy drape to the side. Her neighbor was skinning what looked like a squirrel. She frowned. That wasn't much meat to put in their supper pot.

Frederich came in the door and hung his hat on a nail. "Good morning, Isabella. What do you see there?" His advice to store food for hard times had served the small family well. They rationed their supplies, yet it was enough to keep Isabella strong and healthy so she could feed the baby.

"Good morning to you, Frederich. I'm watching our poor neighbor skin a squirrel. That family has six children, but the squirrel is so scrawny, it will not even flavor their soup." She turned back to the window. "The king declared we should share our food. Maybe we could do that. I feel sorry for those who do not have enough when we have plenty."

Frederich frowned. "Do not feel sorry for the fools who swallowed that liar's poison. While people in the city go without food, the king's table groans with meat, cheese, bread and wine. A righteous king would share with his people."

"The king has wine, Frederich? He made drunkenness punishable by death."

"Yes, and demanded everyone surrender their barrels, which then ended up in his private larder. Your concern is with Abel and his well-being, not the neighbors. If we are to escape this city, we must be strong and alert. We will not share what little we have stored."

"But will we escape, Frederich?"

"Johan and I have searched the walls and so far we have not found a way out. But we will. I am worried about you, Princess, because I saw that pig, Gresbeck, eyeing you when we went to the square that night. I do not trust him. Knipperdolling saw you that night too, and I'm sure he told the king about you."

Isabella smiled at her friend. "Is that why you have neglected your duties and stayed close to the house?"

"Yes, that is why. But they don't bother me about it...," he patted his sword, "because they know my mistress has a temper. Anyway, Bockelson has Jügen Fromme to guard him and he trusts him more than me. They will call on me if they need me."

"You are a faithful friend, Frederich. What would we do without you?"

"Thank you, Princess. I will not stay in this madhouse any longer than I have to, and I will bring you all out with me. That is my promise."

BEFORE SUNRISE EASTER MORNING, Johan left Frederich to watch over Isabella, Magda and the baby, and went to the cathedral square to await the second coming of the Lord Jesus Christ. Bockelson had proclaimed for weeks that this was the day. He'd even had a platform with a chopping block erected in front of the church and promised the people his bodyguards would behead him if his prophecy did not come true.

Excitement was high. Women sang and men marched around the square waiting for the Lord to lead them out through the gates to conquer von Waldek. Yet, their leader, the king, was nowhere in sight. At noon, when the sun was blazing above them, one of his elders announced that Bockelson was communing with the Lord and receiving instructions.

Around one o'clock a huge roar shook the square. Johan recognized the sound as a cannon salvo and ducked under a parapet, but many people lifted their arms and turned round and round, staring into the heavens and shouting, "He's come, he's come! Jesus take us to glory!"

There was another salvo and, to everyone's surprise, metal canisters rained from the sky and burst open on the pavement, filling the square with leaflets that fluttered about like huge moths. The canisters struck a few people, and they staggered about with hands pressed to their bloody heads.

Johan picked up a leaflet. It offered mercy to any who would open the gates and von Waldek's signature was on it. Mid-day came, and many people passed out from lack of water and the stifling press of the crowd. Johan stood at the edge of the crowd, watching the menagerie of people crying out to God, or wandering around, waiting for either the Lord or Bockelson to appear. Then it was early evening and still no trumpet blast from heaven, still no hosts of angels hailing the Lord Jesus's return to earth.

When midnight passed, the disgruntled crowds gathered outside Bockelson's mansion. "Where is the Lord?" they shouted. "Why has he not come?"

At one o'clock Bockelson walked out onto a balcony. Instead of marching him to the execution platform, guards tore it down.

Someone yelled, "Where is the Lord, Bockelson? Or is this another of your lies?"

Johan smiled a grim smile.

It's another one of his lies, you fool.

Another man called out, "The enemy is still at our gates. Where is our deliverer?"

Bockelson raised his fists and screamed at the people below him. "You impure, godless creatures! Why would Jesus come for people whose only concern is the things of the flesh! Flesh! Flesh! That's all you know.

"The Lord came today, but it was a spiritual event. He cleansed the true believers from their sin and purified them for the battle ahead. The rest of you will die under von Waldek's swords. Go home. Confess your sins and prepare your hearts, for the real battle is coming soon."

The crowd erupted into yells and taunts. "Liar! False Prophet. Murderer."

Bockelson drew himself to his full height. "Go home or I will call down the fire of the Lord on you, you evil creatures of Baal."

The woman in front of Johan turned to her husband. "What if he can do that?" she whispered. Johan watched as others, who must have feared the same, gave a few more shouts and catcalls and then melted away into the night. Within minutes the square was empty.

Johan made his way home. Frederich was waiting at the door. "Tomorrow, Johan, the people of this city will realize that, once again, Bockelson has taken them for fools. Then the situation will get ugly, for the only control Bockelson has now is through his armed loyalists, who won't hesitate to cut down dissenters. We must find a way out of this hellhole before it is too late."

IN A CASTLE BORROWED from German aristocrats, Sigismund of Poland sat on an imposing throne and stared down at von Waldek, who stood before him, van Dhaun at his side. "Well, Prince Bishop? I thought Bockelson would come crawling out in a few weeks. It is now June, and still they hold out. I have waited a month. My wife fills in for me well, but important matters of state await me. I will leave in three days. What is your plan to save my daughter now? I can tell you that if you do not act, I will return with my army and when we finish with Münster, there will be no city for you to return to."

Von Waldek cleared his throat. The jowls on his florid face trembled as he faced Sigismund. "Your Majesty, we..." He nodded at his general... "We have a plan."

"Go on."

"My spy says the siege has reduced Münster's citizens to

eating cats, dogs and rats. Many are near starvation. Their resistance is low, and they have lost confidence in their king. We have a way to get our men into the city and open the gates. But before we do so, our spy will seize the princess and bring her to you."

"Why has not your spy already taken her from Hirschberg?" the king asked, a grim look on his face.

"The best swordsman in the city guards her day and night. Gresbeck cannot get close to her."

Sigismund took von Waldek by the arm. "Explain this plan of yours."

Von Waldek was shaking in Sigismund's grasp. "Gresbeck has made a model of the city which includes her home. My soldiers know where to find her during the battle and will bring her out. We will attack in two days."

"I agree to your plan if that is the only way." Sigismund scowled. "But if harm comes to my daughter or if she has already starved to death, I will make you wish you had never been born. I am only sorry that I did not bring my army the first time I came. Your incompetence wears on me. You may go."

Sigismund watched as von Waldek backed out of the room, bowing.

AT THE SOUND of a loud crash that shook the house, Johan jumped out of bed. Before he reached the door, it slammed open and black-garbed soldiers surrounded the bed, swords drawn. A squat, ugly man with a scarred face held a sword to Johan's throat.

Isabella screamed, and the frightened baby cried.

The soldiers parted. Mayor Knipperdolling strode into the room and pointed at Isabella. "Yes, that is the woman I saw in the square." He smiled. "I told the king of your beauty. He wishes to grant you the honor of making you his wife."

Isabella pulled the covers to her shoulders. "I am already married," she whispered.

Knipperdolling waved a piece of paper in the air. "A writ of divorcement, signed by the king."

"No!" Johan moved toward Isabella, but the guards pressed the sword against his neck. "That writ is useless. I will not divorce my wife."

"In this city, the word of King Jan Bockelson is the law." Knipperdolling nodded to the soldiers. "Take her to the king. And you, Fromme, take the man to the jail."

"Please," Johan pleaded, "give us a moment to dress."

Knipperdolling nodded, but the men did not leave the room. Johan and Isabella put on some clothes. Magda had appeared at the door.

Johan mouthed the words, "Get Frederich and Abel."

She nodded.

Knipperdolling shoved her into the hall. "Away with you, old hag."

The soldiers forced Johan and Isabella from the room. Jügen Fromme separated them at the front door. He handed Johan over to two of the guards who bound his arms behind him. "Take him to the palace and put him in the deepest dungeon. I will deal with him later."

Isabella struggled, trying to wrench away from Knipperdolling's men. "Johan, Johan!"

Johan turned as the guards led him away. "I will find you, Bella. I will come for you!"

CHAPTER 25: THE DOOR

JUNE 1535

*F*rederich Weisbach hurried down the street to the house by the wall. He had a terrible feeling. It was early in the morning and he had been away from the house far too long.

Something is wrong!

Just at dusk, he was returning home from gathering more supplies when a group of Bockelson's soldiers stopped him.

"Come with us, Weisbach. You are to report to the king's house," the leader sneered. "The king has need of you tonight."

The look on the leader's face told Frederich that the king would brook no insolence in the matter. When they arrived, they sent him to the dining hall where Bockelson was entertaining his wives. As the hours passed, Frederich tried to find excuses to go, but each time the king found a different pretext to detain him. Frederich grew nervous.

Something is up and I am not there to protect Isabella.

It was close to midnight when the king retired to his bedchamber and Frederich was free to go. Now as he approached the house, he saw Magda waiting by the door. When she saw Frederich, she beckoned to him with her hand.

"What is it, Magda? What has happened?"

Magda looked around and then drew Frederich into the house. She closed the door behind them and then burst into tears. "They have taken Johan and Isabella!"

Frederich grabbed her arm. "Who has taken them?"

"Knipperdolling and a man named Fromme."

Frederich's mouth opened. "Fromme! Was he ugly, with a scar here?" Frederich touched his face. Magda nodded as Frederich shook his head. "So the Butcher of Frankenhausen has found a new home."

Magda looked at Frederich. "You know this man?"

"Later! Just tell me what happened."

Magda wiped her eyes with a handkerchief. "The king issued a decree divorcing Isabella from Johan and he plans to add her to his harem."

Frederich grimaced. "So that is why he kept me at the palace. He knew I would kill anyone who tried to take the princess. Where is Johan?"

"Fromme's men took him away to the jail." She broke down and sobbed. "Oh Frederich, my girl, my girl…"

"Pull yourself together woman! Get the baby ready and pack clothes and food for all five of us. We will leave as soon as I find Johan and Isabella."

"But, how…?"

Frederich swept his sword out and bowed. "I don't know how, Magda, but God will guide my mistress and me. Pray for us."

ISABELLA STOOD BEFORE BOCKELSON, arms folded and head held high.

A salacious grin spread across his face, accenting the lust in his eyes. "Knipperdolling was right," he purred... "You are exquisite. I wish to honor you, my lovely, by making you my wife."

"I cannot marry you!" Isabella lifted her chin, "because I am already married, to the man I love. Not even a real king could change that, and you are not a king."

He recoiled as though she'd slapped him. "Not a king? How dare you!"

Isabella drew herself up. "You are an imposter who gained ascendancy over this city through betrayal, murder, and lies. Your promises are empty, and your prophecies are false."

Bockelson's eyes flashed and his face flushed as scarlet as his robe. "I am the king," he screamed. "You will do what I command."

"I will never marry you," Isabella insisted. "If you try to force me, I will kill you. If I cannot kill you, I will kill myself. But you will never have me. Never!" Isabella looked around the room for a way of escape, but there was none. She took a breath. "I am Isabella, the princess of Poland. My father is Sigismund, the king. If you harm me, you will never leave this city alive."

Bockelson glared at her, fists clenched, shaking from head to toe. Sucking in a ragged, noisy breath, he stepped closer. "Maybe you are a princess, and maybe you are not. But Sigismund is far away. Even if you are his daughter, I am king *here* and I am God's anointed. To defy me means death."

Isabella felt a cold chill pass down her spine. The look on Bockelson's face was a mix of sheer lust and total rage. He took hold of her with a powerful grip.

"You are hurting me!"

Bockelson leered at her. "I will do more than that if you do not obey." He leaned close and his breath was thick with the smell of wine. "Are you sure you do not want to marry me?" he whispered.

Isabella lifted her chin and looked him straight in the eye. "Never!"

Rage distorted Bockelson's face, and he flung Isabella to the ground. She cried out in pain. He turned to Fromme.

"Put her on a cart and take her to the square. Have the guards summon the people and tell Knipperdolling to bring his executioner's sword. When the head of this princess rolls on the cobblestones, the people will know what it means to defy their king."

~

HUDDLED ON THE COLD, rocky floor of his prison cell, Johan hugged his knees for warmth. Torchlight outside the door's barred window flickered against the dungeon's dank, slimy walls. From beneath a pile of stinking straw, a rat squeaked, its beady eyes reflecting red. A cold draft of air sent a chill down Johan's back.

"Ah," he whispered to the rat, "a survivor. You must be one of the few rodents left alive in this city. God help me be as fortunate as you."

Just then he heard voices and then there was a dull thud followed by a groan and a heavy thump. He held his breath, listening.

Footsteps approached, and the torch's blaze silhouetted a man's head.

Johan jumped to his feet and stepped back, ready to face whoever was coming.

Keys jangled, metal rasped against metal, and the door creaked open.

"Frederich!" Johan lowered his hands. "But how—?"

"Later. Come with me. We must find Isabella."

The stench of the dungeon filled Johan's nostrils, almost making him gag. As they crept into the outer chamber and toward the stairs, they passed an unconscious guard lying in a heap against the wall. Johan could hear moans from other cells.

At the top of the stairs, a second man lay prostrate in a pool of blood, sword still in his hand.

Frederich paused. "Alas, I regret having to kill this man," he murmured. "He was a friend, but he would not relinquish the keys, and drew his sword. He should not have."

They hadn't walked far when Frederich pulled Johan into a side corridor. "We will leave by the guard's entrance."

They crept out into the street, slipping from doorway to doorway. Then they heard trumpets blaring from the square. Frederich motioned, and they slipped into the shadows. A troop of men came marching down the street. "The king commands all citizens to gather in the square," their leader was shouting. "Today is the day of judgment for those who defy him." Behind the troop came a cart pulled by several men. Two soldiers and a woman were in it. The woman lifted her head.

Johan whispered, "Isabella!" and started toward the cart, his heart pounding.

Frederich grabbed his arm. "Wait!"

Stepping alongside a soldier who followed behind the cart, Frederich whispered, "What has she done?"

"She defied the king—refused to marry him." The man's eyes glistened in the torchlight. "Now, he will cut off her head." He lifted his sword high. "No one, man or woman, defies King Bockelson."

HEINRICH GRESBECK STOOD beside the body of the single guard in the tunnel leading from the small door in the wall. A knife protruded from the guard's back. He opened the door with the wooden key. Wilkin Steding and a picked force of four hundred soldiers crowded through the door into the tunnel. They were dripping wet from swimming the moat. Steding grabbed Gresbeck by the arm. "Where is the princess, Gresbeck?"

"When I got to their house, I was too late. There was an old woman there. After some persuasion, she told me that Bockelson had taken the princess to be his wife."

Steding shrugged. "She may be von Waldek's concern but she is not mine. My only concern is to take this city." Steding gathered his men around. In the distance they heard trumpets. Steding turned to look. "Something is happening in the square. That is good. It will give us the chance to move into the city undetected." He turned back to his men. "When we get to the square, we will seize the main armory and the battlewagons." He pointed to one of his commanders. "You will take your men to the Holy Cross Gate to let von Waldek and van Dhaun into the city. Now let's go!"

As Steding and his men slipped into the square, there was a commotion on the opposite side. They took cover in the shadows. A large group of people entered the square, following a cart that held two men and a woman. When they arrived at the platform in front of the cathedral, the men pushed the woman off the cart and she fell onto her hands and knees on the cobblestones. The crowd parted and a man wearing all white with a crown upon his head came out of the church. He held a scepter in his hand.

"It's the king," Gresbeck whispered to Steding, "Bockelson."

Steding put his hand on Gresbeck's shoulder. "Run to the gate, Gresbeck, and make sure our men have taken it. Tell the prince bishop where we are."

Gresbeck nodded and ran for the Holy Cross Gate.

FREDERICH AND JOHAN followed the cart into the square. Now they watched as Bockelson paraded to the platform. Knipperdolling was waiting, wearing his executioner's robes. Jügen Fromme was with him, his sword at the ready.

Frederich took Johan by the arm and pulled him forward. "We must get closer," he whispered.

All eyes were on Isabella and the king. The crowd quieted as she knelt on the stones and Bockelson sauntered to her side. She lifted herself and looked up at him, utter contempt written on her face.

"This woman has refused to become my wife, refused her king," he whined. "What should I do with this one?"

"Let her go," a man yelled. "You already have fourteen wives stolen from among us."

Two soldiers broke from the ranks and made their way through the crowd toward the place from where the shout had come. A large group of loyal women who stood beside the podium shouted, "Kill her—kill the traitor to our king!"

Frederich and Johan edged forward until they were in the third row in front of the platform.

Bockelson raised his scepter. "The people have spoken! I should not defy their will. But I will show you all that I am not only just, but merciful." He took Isabella's hand and raised her up. "Will you not reconsider? Will you not marry me?"

Isabella looked at the lustful face before her. "I would choose hell before I would choose you."

Johan's heart leapt at the sight of his beautiful wife defying the king as absolute rage contorted Bockelson's face. "Then hell you shall have!" he screamed. He struck her and she fell to the ground. He turned to Knipperdolling. "Remove her head," he screamed again.

Knipperdolling raised his sword. Johan started forward, rage against the beast that struck his wife burning in his heart. He cried out as he tried to force his way through the crowd. "Isabella! Isabella!"

At that moment, Steding turned to his men. "Now is the time to attack," he yelled. "Cut straight through to the king and take him, dead or alive. Now!"

The mercenaries burst into the square screaming like banshees, hacking their way through the crowd which broke and ran before their merciless attack. Women were screaming, the men were yelling. Knipperdolling looked up, saw them coming, threw down his sword and scrambled away. Bockelson dropped his scepter and ran toward the cathedral, leaving Jügen Fromme alone with Isabella. He watched as the terrified Bockelson bolted through the cathedral doors, and then he turned to Isabella. He put his hand on the hilt of his sword and drew it.

Before Johan could get to the platform Frederich, grabbed his arm. "Run to the stable and fetch the horse. We will need him."

"But, Isabella—"

"I will bring her, I promise. Meet us at the house. Go now!"

Johan bolted toward the stables as Frederich leaped onto the platform and shoved Fromme away from Isabella.

Jügen Fromme stumbled and then came to his feet. His mouth dropped. "Weisbach!"

Frederich swept a bow. "So! You remember me, Fromme. I am honored."

Fromme's face paled. "What are you doing here?"

"I have come for the princess."

Fromme's mouth dropped open and his face twitched. "The king told me that a great swordsman guarded her, but I did not know it was you!"

"No time for reminiscing, Jügen."

Fromme's face went pale, and he tried to pull out his weapon, but Frederich's sword swept up.

Fromme stepped back, staring down at the bright red stain spreading on his shirtfront.

Frederich bowed again. "Retribution for the wives and children of the peasants you murdered at Frankenhausen."

Fromme tried to say something, but no sound came from his

mouth. His eyes glazed, and he fell face forward onto the cobblestones.

Frederich turned to Isabella. "On your feet, Princess." He pulled her up. Two guards ran toward them but Frederich stepped in front of Isabella. The grim look on his face and the swish of his sword cutting the air unnerved them and they turned and disappeared into the screaming crowd. Frederich grabbed Isabella's hand and together they ran toward Bridge Street.

Frederich went ahead with his sword and the crowd parted like the red sea before him. From the center of the crowd more screaming arose. Frederich looked and saw a gang of Anabaptists running into the square, drawn by the sounds of battle. They rushed at Steding's men, driving them back toward the Holy Cross gate. He looked once more and then they were out of the square and running.

Frederich and Isabella rushed breathlessly through the streets. In a few moments they arrived at the house. Magda stood by a few bundles she had packed holding Abel, who was crying. Isabella grabbed Abel and clutched him to her breast and he quieted at once. At that moment, Johan rode up on Al-Buraq. He leaped down and took Isabella in his arms. "Bella, Bella."

"No trouble, I see," said Frederich.

"The stable was empty; everyone was in the square."

Al-Buraq sniffed the baby and then snorted impatiently.

Frederich grabbed a bundle and strapped it behind the saddle. "The horse is right. We must go now. We must get out of the city." They tied the other bundles on and then Johan lifted Isabella and the baby onto the horse's back. He turned to Frederich and nodded. "Ready, Frederich. But how do we get out?"

"We must find the place where the mercenaries got through. Follow me!" The old woman hesitated. "Come, Magda, I will carry you." He whisked her into his arms and they started off.

"The cross, Johan!" Isabella cried. "Did you get Elspeth's cross?"

Johan dashed inside, where the golden cross stood like a sentry on the mantle, reflecting the flickering light from the candles burning in the room. Johan picked it up. He remembered the night his family had fled Basel—the light gleaming on the cross when he took it from its hiding place.

"Johan! Come now!" Frederich shouted.

Johan darted out to the street, grabbed the reins and followed Frederich through the streets. Women's screams and men's shouts filled the darkness. As they were making their way around the square, some men came running out of a side street and blocked the way. They wore the black of Bockelson's guards. The leader saw Frederich. "It's Weisbach. Halt!"

Frederich put Magda down and pulled out his sword. Just then more men wearing the uniforms of the Landsknecht soldiers burst out of the same side street. The guards turned to this new danger and Johan pulled the horse past them. Behind them, the sounds of sword clashes and more running feet echoed off the walls. They came to the street leading to the Holy Cross Gate. Frederich brought them to a halt. "Von Waldek's soldiers must have come from somewhere near here since they came from this direction We must find the way they got in."

The musketry and cannon blasts had started fires in the city and now the sky was lit with a spectral glow. Screams and shouts echoed through the city. Frederich turned this way and that, looking for the way von Waldek's men had entered the city. Just then they saw a fat man go running past.

"It's Gresbeck," Frederich shouted, "and he looks like he knows where he's going. After him." They followed Gresbeck until he reached an opening in the wall. A short distance away, Frederich could see the Landsknecht soldiers massed around the Holy Cross Gate fighting with Bockelson's guards. The fat man glanced back at them. He stared at Isabella for a moment and then turned and ran into the opening.

"I've been here before, Johan. It's a tunnel under the wall. There's a stout door at the end, but it's always locked. They must have gotten it open. That's our way out."

AT THE HOLY CROSS GATE, Steding's one hundred men overpowered the guards and opened the gate. As the heavy wooden doors swung open, there was a braying of trumpets and Franz von Waldek rode into Münster mounted on a white horse. A bishop's miter was on his head and black armor clothed his squat body. Soldiers poured in behind him on foot. Gresbeck was running alongside von Waldek, shouting. He grabbed von Waldek's leg. "Over there, Your Highness! The Polish princess!"

Frederich lowered Magda to the ground and helped Isabella off the horse. At the entrance, he turned to Johan. "Get them out of here. I will bar the way."

"No, Frederich!" Johan grabbed his companion's arm.

Frederich smiled a sad smile. "Christ told us what the greater love is. Go now and know I have at last served God in my own way. Go!"

Just before he went into the tunnel at the bottom of the Münster wall, Johan looked back.

Sword drawn, Frederich was taunting the mercenaries. "Come closer, you men. Come and taste cold steel."

The soldiers rushed at Frederich and he disappeared in a melee of bodies and flashing swords, shouting, "Run, Johan, run!"

Johan whispered, "Farewell, friend."

ISABELLA HELD the baby and stared at the oncoming soldiers.

Von Waldek was urging them on. "Get her, get her! Kill the others!"

Fear overcame her, and she stopped, at the mouth of the tunnel, confused...

And then Johan was with her. His powerful arms wrapped around her, infusing her with his strength.

"Come, my love," he murmured. "This way."

Together they ran. Abel's tiny arms clung to her. Al-Buraq went before them, Magda leading him. Isabella stumbled in the gloom, but Johan's arms lifted her and guided her. And then she saw it... a small, open door at the end of the tunnel.

"Through here, my dearest," he whispered.

Johan's strong hands guided her through the gate. Behind them, a hoarse voice shouted, "Find them, find them now! Kill him and bring her to me, alive."

Then they were through the door and out into the darkness. Together they hurried along toward the river. His hands guided her, kept her on her feet and strengthened her but she could not see the path. His voice urged her on.

"This way, Isabella. Lift your feet, run like the wind. I am with you; I am always with you..."

PART V
THE WAY OF PEACE

AFTER MÜNSTER, THE CATHOLICS *and the Reformists hunted the*
Anabaptists like animals. During this time of terror, a new Anabaptist
leader arose. Menno Simons was a Catholic priest who lived in Frisia,
North Germany in the 1500s. When his brother, Pieter, died in
another Anabaptist uprising, Menno experienced a spiritual and
mental crisis.

As he studied Christ's words of love and non-violence, Menno
found that new way. He became the shepherd of a flock that was
founded in Frisia but grew to include many congregations in Germany
and Holland. Those congregations became the Mennonite Church, and
from the Mennonites, the Amish Church was born. Fifteen generations
ago my ancestor, Johan Hirschberg, sat at the feet of Menno Simons
with his wife, Isabella, and their son, Abel, and learned the way of
peace...

"The Way of Peace"
From The Journals of Jenny Hershberger

CHAPTER 26: BLOEMKAMP ABBEY

*J*ohan turned as Frederich's last words echoed in his ears. Isabella was standing at the tunnel mouth with Magda. The baby was crying, and the horse was stamping. Johan could see the terror on Isabella's face. He ran to them.

"Lead the horse through the tunnel, Magda," he shouted. "I will bring Isabella and Abel."

He took Isabella in his arms. "Come, my love," he murmured. "This way."

Together they ran through the tunnel and down the path as von Waldek's soldiers destroyed the Kingdom of God on earth. Behind them they could hear the shouts of the soldiers and the screams of terrified women. A thick pall of smoke rose over the walls, lit by the flames from burning buildings and when he looked back, Johan could see a horde of men with torches rushing through the now opened gate.

When they came to the river, he put the two women and Abel up on the horse and urged Al-Buraq into the water. Al-Buraq swam across with the women on his back and Johan clinging to his tail. On the far bank he led the horse along the river, watching for soldiers. When he came to the guard post where the siege lines reached the shore it was empty and unguarded. Johan led them past and in a short while they were in the woods that surrounded the city.

When they came to the road beyond the woods, Isabella leaned down from the horse. "Where are the soldiers, Johan?"

Johan looked around. "They must have followed von Waldek into the city to join in the sport."

Isabella grimaced. "Sport?"

Magda put her hand on Isabella's shoulder. "You are so innocent, my little one. Any men who survived are being executed, and the women are being raped."

Isabella's face paled. "That is terrible." She was silent for a long while and then looked at Johan. "Where shall we go, now?"

"I don't know, Isabella." Johan shook his head. "We cannot go back to Poland."

"We shall go to my home in Friesland," Magda said. "It is not far, maybe ten days' journey. My brother lives in Pingjum on my father's farm. He will shelter us until you can find work, Johan. Then you can decide what the next step will be."

FOR THE NEXT several days Johan led his small band toward Friesland. He avoided the main roads and slipped into the woods to camp at night. When their supplies ran low, Johan went into a small town with some of their remaining coins in his pocket. While he was purchasing a few things he heard the shop owner talking to another man.

"So the Catholics took the city back?"

"Yes, they broke in and slaughtered everyone. They burned most of the city."

"What happened to their king?" the shop owner asked.

The customer shook his head. "I think they captured him,

but I don't know. A sad ending to a foolish rebellion." The two men were still talking as Johan paid for his goods and left the shop. He stopped at the outskirts of town and a great sadness filled his heart. He thought of his friend, Frederich, who had laid down his life for them.

If only those foolish men had been faithful to Christ, like Frederich was, we might have seen a great thing. I will never trust men again.

AT DUSK on the tenth day, they passed through a small town. They hadn't gone far beyond it when they came upon the charred remains of a large and once-magnificent building. The timbers gave off a burnt smell, and terrible holes, like great staring eyes, marred the walls that were still standing.

"I don't understand," said Magda. "This is the Abbey of Bloemkamp. It was the loveliest abbey in all of Friesland. What could have happened here?"

As they stood staring at the great devastation, a farmer came along on a horse-drawn cart loaded with hay.

Magda hailed him. "Hello, friend. What happened to the Abbey?"

The farmer reined his horse to a stop. "Have you not heard of the terrible battle here?"

Before Magda could speak, Johan said, "We have been in Germany for some time and have not heard of such a thing."

"It was the Anabaptists."

The three travelers glanced at each other. Isabella spoke. "Anabaptists?"

"They came with three hundred men and women and seized the Abbey in March. A man named van Geeslen commanded them. Pieter Simons, brother of the priest, Menno Simons, was second in command. They hoped to conquer the entire province and turn it to their beliefs."

Magda pulled on Johan's sleeve. "I know Menno Simons... and Pieter. They are from my village, Pingjum."

Johan pointed to the destroyed building. "But what happened to the Abbey?"

The farmer shook his head. "The nobles ordered Georg Schenck van Toutenburg, the imperial stadholder, to recapture the place. He thought it would be easy, but they could not drive the Anabaptists out." He pointed to a small knoll a few hundred yards away.

"From that hill, van Toutenburg bombarded the monastery with heavy artillery. After he knocked down the walls, he stormed it. He had to lead his soldiers into the fire four times. They captured several positions, but the church remained in Anabaptist possession."

The farmer shook his head and looked up at the charred remains. "Right here is where van Toutenburg broke their defense. They killed many Anabaptists in hand-to-hand combat. Of the ones who did not lose their lives in the struggle, they beheaded thirty-seven on the spot and took over one hundred men and women to Leeuwarden, where they executed fifty more."

"What about Pieter Simons?" Magda asked.

The farmer stepped down from his cart and beckoned the travelers close. "I found Pieter after the battle, wounded and near death." The farmer looked around, but no one else was on the road. "He died at my home, a repentant man. We all knew about the revolution in Münster and hoped that it would end our persecution... I mean, the persecution of simple believers. But then word came it was not going well there..." The farmer paused.

Johan stepped closer. He looked hard at the farmer's face. "You said 'our persecution.' Are you an Anabaptist?"

The farmer paled. "It was a slip of the tongue. I have a family..."

"Do not worry, friend, for we are also Anabaptists."

Magda touched the farmer's shoulder. "What about Pieter?"

"Before the battle, Pieter heard the reports from Münster. After van Toutenburg killed all his friends, it became obvious to Pieter that God was not smiling on a violent overthrow of Europe by the Anabaptists."

Johan nodded. "We were some who escaped from Münster. It was a terrible day. Von Waldek had broken in as we fled. Do you have any news from there? I heard two men speak of it while I was in a shop, but they did not know much."

The farmer nodded. "There was a rider who came through yesterday. Von Waldek recaptured the city. He killed over six hundred Anabaptists before the city surrendered. They took Jan Bockelson, the mayor, Bernhard Knipperdolling, and another Anabaptist elder named Bernd Kretchtinck prisoners. Bernhard Rothmann, the preacher who instigated the rebellion, died fighting. Von Waldek has turned the city back to Catholicism the city and forbidden any Anabaptists or Protestants to remain."

"We left our friend Frederich Weisbach behind, fighting so we could escape." Isabella wiped a tear from her cheek. "He warned us that Jan Bockelson was a liar and a false prophet, but we all wanted to believe. To our sorrow, we believed Bockelson... for a while."

The baby fussed. Johan helped Isabella down from the horse and led her to a shady spot. The farmer and Magda followed.

Magda shook her head. "The women of the city were the ones who encouraged Bockelson. He was a handsome devil and most of them dreamed of bedding him, I think." She spoke to the farmer, "Please tell us your name, sir."

"I am Julius de Boer." He smiled.

"And how did you know Pieter?"

"He preached at our church, saying things that were new and exciting. Many tried to shout him down, but many defended him." He rubbed his chin. "Strange how the truth can make a person angry, yet it will set them free. My wife and I had him to our home many times before the battle. He taught us about baptism and how we should wait until we are old enough to know what receiving Christ means. He also said—"

Johan interrupted the farmer. "You said Pieter repented."

"On the last night of his earthly life, I was sitting with him while he read from his Bible, that part where Jesus says, *And unto him that smiteth thee on the one cheek offer also the other, and him that taketh away thy cloak forbid not to take thy coat.* He looked over at me with tears in his eyes and said, 'Julius, I have been wrong. Christ does not tell us to conquer the world for him. He will do that when he returns. What he tells us to do is to win the hearts of our enemies with love. If my enemy smites me on the cheek, I am to turn the other cheek. And listen to this...,'

"He turned the pages of his Bible until he found the scripture he wanted. He read from Matthew, chapter five and verse forty-four, where it says, *But I say unto you, love your enemies, bless them that curse you, do good to them that hate you, and pray for them which persecute you.*

"Then Pieter gave a great sigh. 'You must tell my brother. Convince him that Catholicism is wrong, that Luther is wrong, and the Anabaptists' violence is wrong. The lost people of this world will never see Jesus unless they see him in us—in our words, in our deeds, in our behavior. Tell him, Julius, please...'"

Julius lowered his head. "And then my friend and teacher, Pieter Simons, died. I would carry his message to Menno if I could, but I am known in Pingjum as an Anabaptist and Pieter's friend. If I visited Menno the authorities might arrest me. I have my crops to get in so I cannot risk it. Perhaps you can go for me. You are a stranger and you could visit Menno without raising suspicion. You can tell him what Pieter learned. Perhaps it will help him. He is a great Bible teacher. And if he is anything like Pieter, he is a kind man. He needs to hear his brother's last words. In the meantime, please stay with my wife and me for a few days and rest. She makes the best *stamppot* this side of Leiden."

"*Stamppot!*" Magda clapped her hands. "I have had none for years."

"Your kindness is most welcome," Johan said. "We need rest. It has been a long, hard journey. And I will think about what you have asked, about visiting Menno."

Isabella slipped her hand into Johan's. "I know little about these things. My parents sheltered me from the world. But I know the violence and hatred I saw in Münster cannot be how Christ would have us live."

Julius nodded. "I have heard Menno preach and if someone could persuade him to come out of the darkness of Catholicism, he would be a great leader of men."

Johan looked at the farmer's innocent face. The familiar sadness came over him.

It was men like you, who trusted and believed, that followed Bockelson to their death. I do not think I am ready to surrender my life to another king.

CHAPTER 27: FINDING THE WAY

The refugees stayed with Julius and his wife, Sonja, for a week. For Isabella, Magda and Abel, the sojourn was a time of rest and refreshing. Julius's wife fed them well, the beds were comfortable, and the women enjoyed helping in the kitchen. But for Johan, the flat plains of Frisia only made him restless. One morning, he was sitting alone on a small knoll behind Julius's house. Towering white clouds filled the sky and several small birds that Johan did not recognize flittered among the branches on a nearby tree, but Johan took no joy in it. His thoughts were heavy when Julius came to him.

"*Goedemorgen,* Johan."

Johan nodded.

Julius sat beside him. "Perhaps the plainness of our country unsettles you, my friend. But these lands lead to the sea, and Frisia is a country of the sea. Have you ever seen the ocean?"

Johan shook his head. "The mountains of Switzerland are my home. When we left, we journeyed east on the Rhine River." He sighed. "How I miss the Hirschberg."

"The Hirschberg?"

"Hirschberg is a Swiss word and means 'Deer Mountain.'

Our family name came from that mountain, an enormous granite monolith that seems to spring out of the soul of the earth. God set it like a jewel in the heart of the Alps. Splashed among its gray cliffs and escarpments like strokes from an artist's brush are green valleys you follow up into the mountains, higher and higher until you can almost touch heaven.

"Our home was halfway up the mountain, near a small village. My father's farm comprised two hundred acres of fertile black soil. We raised goats and hay and other crops. My mother, who was an excellent cook, had a large garden." He smiled. "Our table was never empty."

Julius nodded as though he could see the setting. "I see why you miss your mountains, Johan."

Johan looked over at the farmer. "I had peace on that mountain. My father would send me climbing with the goats, and I would stay in the high meadow all day. Up among the clouds, I found great peace. Yes, Julius, I miss the mountains. I felt close to God there."

"Perhaps I am too bold," the older man said, "but maybe the peace that comes from outside is not the peace we truly seek. Each of us must allow God's peace to settle in our hearts." He put his hand on Johan's shoulder. "I need to go to the village of Zurich to deliver a load of hay. It is only a few hours. Come with me. I will show you the ocean, and you can decide which is more magnificent—the endless sea or your wonderful mountains."

SEATED beside Julius on the hay wagon, Johan smelled the salt air and heard the seagulls' sharp cries long before he saw the ocean. As they crested a small hill, Julius stopped the horse and Johan climbed from the wagon. He walked out on the beach until he came to the edge of the water.

The sun was sinking in the west, a great golden ball that sent a sparkling highway across the water to his feet. Strange white birds circled above him, their cries haunting and lonely. The waves came in, swirling onto the shore and retreating, only to rush in again. Long strands of a strange brown plant lay in piles, giving off a peculiar musty odor like nothing Johan had ever smelled.

Julius came and stood beside him. "Pieter once told me the people of the world are like this ocean, tossing and turning in their unrest because they do not know the kindness and love of our great Savior. You have seen much in your young life, but even in these few days, I have seen the unquiet in your heart. Yet, you say you have received God's love and salvation. Perhaps it is not peace you are looking for, but a purpose, *Ja?*"

Johan lifted his gaze to the clouds. A pale rose blush lit their edges. Above them, as the sun disappeared, tiny pinpoints of light appeared in the ever-deepening indigo of approaching night.

He sighed. "When we go to Magda's village I will visit this Menno Simons. Perhaps he can help me. You say he is a great teacher of the Word. I need someone who can open the words of Christ. I need to settle things in my heart. After what I saw in Münster, I now realize violence is not the way Christ would have us live, but I still carry this anger in my heart.

"I told you about my Tante Elspeth." He turned to Julius. "Before she died, she told me not to be bitter against her persecutors. With her great wisdom, she understood, but I did not. I have been carrying this hatred for too many years and so I have no peace. And yes... I also have no purpose. I thought being a husband and a father would be enough, but a man needs more than that, I think."

~

THE NEXT MORNING, Johan harnessed Al-Buraq to a small cart Julius loaned them. "I do not use it often," he said, "and it is not far to Pingjum. You can return it when you settle in."

The two men embraced, and Johan marveled at how God could bring perfect strangers together in love. They left, waving a sad goodbye to Julius and Sonja, who stood beside the small gate that led into their yard. Isabella and the baby were on the seat with Magda and Johan walked beside the cart, leading Al-Buraq.

After a few hours travel, Magda stood up in the cart and cried, "There it is. My village!" On the distant horizon, a church steeple glistened in the morning sun. She had been holding Abel, and she lifted him. "See, Abel, it is Pingjum, Pingjum."

Magda sat again. "How good to come home for I have been away for so many years." She pulled Abel close and wept.

Isabella put her arm around their faithful friend. "You should not be crying, Magda, you should be laughing."

"Yes, Bella, you are right!" She grinned a toothy grin and giggled like a young girl. Isabella giggled and then the two women burst into laughter.

Johan looked up at the two women and smiled. Soon he was laughing too. He shook his head.

Were you a stranger passing on the road, you might marvel at the sight of four travel-worn people, one leading a great stallion, with two women and a child pulled behind in a cart, all laughing as they went along the way.

WHEN THEY ARRIVED in the village, Magda directed them to pull up in front of a shop in the main square of the village. She looked around. "It is many years since I left, but nothing has changed." An old man wearing spectacles came to the door and squinted up at them. "Can I help you?"

"Maarten?" Magda leaned toward him. "Do you know me?"

"Magda?" The old man stepped closer. "Magda, is that you?"

She laughed, and the sound of it was like a stream rippling over polished stones to Johan's ears. "It's me, you old fool. I see your eyesight is going the way of your good looks."

"Magda, Magda!" The old man did a little dance in the street. He turned to the shop doorway and shouted. "Annika, come. Look who has returned from the dead!"

A white-haired woman appeared in the doorway. She stared for a moment and then her face lit up. "Magda, my sister!"

Johan lifted Magda down, and he and Isabella watched as the three old people embraced with the embrace of loved ones long parted. Annika kissed Magda many times. "I thought we'd never see you again." When at last they released each other, their wrinkled faces were wet with tears. Maarten looked at Johan. "God has answered my prayers. Thank you for bringing her home."

Annika wiped her eyes and blew her nose on an embroidered handkerchief. She motioned at those on the wagon. "And who are these? Your children?"

Magda waggled her finger under Annika's nose. "I never married, as you might well remember. But these dear souls are like my children. And the little one…" She took Abel in her arms as Johan helped Isabella step down from the cart. "The little one is like my grandchild. We have traveled a long journey together, all the way from Münster, and even before."

Maarten and Annika looked at each other and then at the travelers. "Münster?" Maarten asked. "All Europe knows of the rebellion there and the terrible bloodshed. They say many Anabaptists perished."

"Few escaped." Johan shook his head. "Many died because they believed in a man rather than the word of God."

"Is that not the way in all religions?" Maarten shook his head. "For centuries, it has been the same. First came the

Catholics with all their rules and lavish lifestyles. Then Luther told us the pope was wrong. Conrad Grebel and Felix Manz came next, telling us our baptisms were of no consequence. As Pontius Pilate once asked, 'What is truth?'

"But, enough of my wayward thoughts." He waved aside his comments and turned to the doorway. "Enter our humble home. If our sister loves you, we love you."

"We were just sitting down to our mid-day meal," Annika said. "We have fresh milk for the little one, bread warming in the oven, cheese from our goats, sausage from one of our pigs, and a bottle of delicious wine to refresh your spirits. Come in, come in."

Annika led the way through the shop and into the living quarters. After washing the dust from their hands and faces, they sat at Annika and Maarten's table. At first, Abel hid in his mother's arms, peeking shyly out at the old couple, but soon the excellent food and kind words put him in a merry mood. He ate well and then in no time, he was asleep in Isabella's arms.

Annika beckoned Isabella and led her to a small bedroom with a bed and a cradle. She smoothed the blanket in the cradle. "My son, Wilhelm, slept here when he was a child. Alas, he is in heaven with his father." Annika dabbed her eyes with a hanky from her pocket. "Put the little one here. You and your husband may have the bed."

Abel slept while the other five talked long into the night. After a while Isabella became sleepy. Annika led her to the bedroom. "Sleep well, child, for the Lord watches over this house." Shortly after, Magda and Annika also slipped away to bed.

Johan and Maarten sat by the fire long into the night, sipping Frisian beer and smoking Maarten's long Meerschaum pipes. The fire crackled and popped, and soon the conversation turned to Münster.

"Was it as bad as they say, Johan?"

"Worse. We got out before the city surrendered, so I don't know all the details of what happened after, but von Waldek was a butcher. Before we left, hundreds of starving Münster women begged Bockelson to let them leave the city with their children. Bockelson sent them out, but not without calling down the wrath of God upon them. And von Waldek was the hand of that wrath, for he killed every woman and child who stumbled out of the city and planted their heads on stakes in the ground in front of the gates."

Maarten repacked his pipe. "Back in the early days, messengers from Münster came to our church. We had a great debate. Many of us knew Anabaptists whom the authorities had murdered, and we supported their cause. But many had been to Leiden and heard Matthys and Bockelson preach, and they counted their teachings as ravings of madmen. Then, one night the priest Menno Simons came."

Johan sat forward in his chair. "Menno Simons? Is he still in the village? We have come from Bloemkamp with a message from his brother."

"From Pieter? We heard he died. How do you have a message from him?"

"Julius, the farmer who brought Pieter out of the battle and cared for him until his death, told us the message. It is one of repentance I think God would have me share with Pieter's brother. Is he here?"

"No, the church transferred him to Witmarsum. They felt he was asking too many questions, so they put him in a parish where they could keep a closer watch on him."

"Where is this Witmarsum, Maarten?"

"A short way down the road. I will tell you how to find his house and send you with a letter of introduction. He is a good teacher, but the other priests dislike the strange ideas he has come up with." Maarten leaned close and lowered his voice. "Menno is on to something. You have an honest heart, and he may trust you, when he trusts few others. Your wife and child can stay with us while you visit him."

TWO DAYS LATER JOHAN HIRSCHBERG, Swiss Anabaptist, stable boy to kings and husband of Princess Isabella of Poland stood at the door of an unimposing house in Witmarsum, Friesland, on a warm summer day. A man dressed in the robe of a simple Catholic priest answered Johan's knock. A long, well-kept beard adorned his face, and his eyes captivated Johan. In them he saw kindness, warmth and the real love of Christ.

The man smiled at him. "Yes?"

"I am Johan Hirschberg." Johan held out the letter from Maarten. "I come with a message for Menno Simons."

For a long moment, the man studied the brief missive and then smiled at Johan.

"I am Menno Simons."

CHAPTER 28: MENNO

*M*enno Simons nodded. "What is your message for me?"

"I..." Johan hesitated. "I have a message from your brother, Pieter."

Menno drew back, his eyes narrowed. "My brother is dead, murdered at the Abbey of Bloemkamp."

"Yes, yes." Johan lifted his hand. "But he lived several days after the battle in the home of Julius de Boer, who tended his wounds. Pieter asked Julius to deliver a message to you, but he could not come for he is a suspected Anabaptist. So he asked me to come in his stead."

Menno stood aside. "Please come in, Johan." Menno waved him into the simple room. Book-filled shelves lined the walls and a small fire burned in the grate. A steaming teapot, a loaf of bread, a hunk of cheese, and a pitcher of milk stood on a bare wooden table beside a large open book.

"I was just sitting down to eat," Menno said. "Would you care to share my table?"

Johan nodded. "Please, I would be grateful." He had left early before the household awakened and had not stopped for breakfast. Menno brought two cups and sat across from him. He cut the bread and cheese.

Johan looked at the open book. "Is that a Bible?"

"Yes, this is one of the Dutch Bibles printed at Antwerp. I try to read in it every day. I am ashamed to say this, but when I became a priest in 1515, I had never read the Bible, for I felt it would influence me away from the teachings of the church. That shows you how foolish men can be."

As the two men enjoyed their simple repast and made small talk Johan learned that Menno had been born in Witmarsum but had moved to Pingjum as a child. While Menno poured more tea and sliced another chunk of cheese, Johan shared a little about his childhood in Switzerland. Menno listened, smiling at Johan's description of the Alps.

"I have heard of the beauty of your Alps, but I have not yet seen them. Perhaps someday..." He set his tea down. "If you don't mind me asking, how did you get to Friesland from Switzerland?"

Johan hesitated. He had told no one his secret although Frederich and Magda both knew who he and Isabella were. He looked into Menno's eyes.

Lord, can I trust this man?

Although not audible, the response was immediate. *Yes.*

He smiled. "The story is long."

"I have all day. More tea?"

"Yes, please." Johan slid his cup closer. "My family became Anabaptists not long before the persecutions in Basel began. The Reformists arrested my aunt and uncle and turned them over to the Catholics, who burned them at the stake for repudiating infant baptism."

Menno frowned. "Oh, dear God," he whispered.

"My family fled Basel, but my mother died in Görlitz. My father, sister, and I buried her there and continued to Krakow, where my father and I found work in the stables of Sigismund, the King of Poland. It was there I met my wife."

"Oh, are you married?" Menno seemed surprised. "Where is your wife?"

"She stayed in Pingjum with our child and our friend Magda and her brother and sister, Maarten and Annika."

"Would that be Maarten de Jonge?"

"Yes, the same."

Menno smiled. "Pieter and I knew the de Jonges well when we were children. And how did you come to know Magda?"

"We met her when we were traveling to Münster to escape trouble in Poland."

"Trouble?"

Because he felt God had told him he could trust this kind man, Johan told him his story. "My wife is Isabella, Princess of Poland, and daughter of King Sigismund and Queen Bona. I met Isabella when I worked for her father as a stable boy and we fell in love. We kept our love secret for a long time, but then her parents tried to force her into a political marriage, so we left Krakow. An old Anabaptist pastor married us in the woods somewhere in Germany. We left there and traveled to Leipzig where we met Magda. From there we traveled to Münster."

Menno's brow creased. "We have heard of the missing princess, even here. Did you go to Münster because you believed the reports of a New Jerusalem and an Anabaptist empire?"

Johan shrugged. "We thought we could just be Johan and Bella and live a simple life, waiting for the return of Jesus to establish his Kingdom on Earth."

"But I see it did not turn out like that."

"No, it did not." Johan grimaced and felt a chill run down his back. "Matthys and Bockelson led the people astray with lies and false teaching, yet the Anabaptists succumbed to their promises and their demands. By the time von Waldek marched in, those who hadn't prepared for the siege were eating rats and leather and dying in the streets. But they followed Bockelson, believing Jesus was coming any day. That belief ended when von Waldek broke into the city and killed them all."

Menno offered Johan more tea. "My first introduction to the Anabaptists occurred a few years ago when the Catholics beheaded a man named Sicke Snijder at Leeuwarden for being rebaptized. The concept of rebaptism sounded strange because I was a Catholic priest. But for the first time, I searched the scriptures and could find no mention of infant baptism."

Menno took another piece of bread, broke it, and handed some to Johan. "I discussed the issue with my pastor, searched the church fathers' writings, and even read the works of Martin Luther and Heinrich Bullinger. That was when the Catholic Church sent me here…" He smiled, "To keep a closer eye on me, I think. There is a large monastery here and I must make weekly reports to the Abbot." He shrugged. "It is my penance for questioning the dogma, I suppose." Then Menno looked at Johan. "So, Johan, you are an Anabaptist then?"

"To be honest, I do not know what I am." Johan shook his head. "My aunt taught against infant baptism, and her teachings brought her death. She also taught that men and women should love one another. The Catholics and Reformists drove us from our home and my mother did not survive the journey. I hated them for what they did to us. When I came to Münster with Bella, the experiences of my past filled me with hate and I wanted to strike back at those who caused me so much unhappiness. Yet, when I killed my first Catholic soldier…"

Johan folded his arms on the table and put his face down. "He was only a boy, and yet the hatred on his face… I could not comprehend that men could have such hatred for one another," he sobbed.

Johan heard Menno sigh and get up from the table. He came around and put his hand on Johan's shoulder. "So many questions, eh? The Anabaptists here preached and practiced what they called *Believer's Baptism*. Then disciples from Münster came and stirred up the village. Many left to go to the 'New Jerusalem,' as they called it. I felt they were fanatical and misled, but I admired their zeal. Their views of the Bible, the purpose of the church and discipleship intrigued me, but still the militant stand they took..." he paused. "The hatred they held for the Catholics did not meet Christ's standard for love."

Johan felt Menno pat his shoulder. "You are a good man, Johan Hirschberg, and you have opened your heart. So now I know I can trust you, I would hear the message for me from Pieter. What is it?"

Johan sat up, wiping his face with the back of his hand. "On the last night of Pieter's life, Julius was sitting with Pieter, who was reading to him from the Bible. Pieter read the verse where Jesus says, *And unto him that smiteth thee on the one cheek offer also the other, and him that taketh away thy cloak forbid not to take thy coat.*"

Menno leaned forward, amazement on his face. He shook his head. "But the last time I saw Pieter he wanted to kill every Catholic and Reformist. I don't understand."

"Pieter told Julius that he had been wrong to fight the Catholics and the Lutherans, that Christ does not tell us to conquer the world *for* him. Instead, he tells us to win the hearts of our enemies with love. And then Pieter read to Julius from Matthew chapter five and verse forty-four. *But I say unto you, love your enemies...*"

Menno whispered, "... bless them that curse you, do good to them that hate you, and pray for them which persecute you."

Johan looked at Menno. There were tears in the priest's eyes as Johan went on. "Pieter told Julius, 'you must tell my brother. You must convince him that Catholicism is wrong, that Luther is wrong, and the violent Anabaptists are wrong. The lost people of this world will never see Jesus unless they see him in us—in our words, in our deeds, in our behavior. Go to him and tell him, Julius, please.' Those were his final words. At the end, your brother was thinking of you, Menno."

Menno's face twisted. He stood and went to the window and harsh sobs racked his body. "Pieter, Pieter..."

Johan watched as Menno poured out his grief. In a while, Menno turned. "I thank you, Johan Hirschberg, for delivering this message from my beloved brother. It has shaken me to the core. I pray to God that he would forgive my unclean walk and unprofitable life. I have not followed Christ as I should have."

Menno returned to the table and sat across from Johan. "If you would care to stay, I would welcome your company tonight. Perhaps we can explore the Word of God. You seem like a man who has many questions as have I."

Johan nodded. "I would be honored, and yes, I have many questions. Let us finish this good bread and then perhaps you would open the Bread of Life."

That night, a fire warming their bodies and a candle lighting the text, the two men poured over the scriptures. They talked of the true church, something Menno saw as a bride, pure and unstained, waiting in the dark night of the world for her bridegroom to come and take her to the Father's house. Johan listened as Menno strode about the room, speaking of the life of Jesus, how he showed grace and mercy. And Johan told more of the terror of Münster and the violence that only led to the death of gullible people who followed men instead of Christ.

At one point, Menno slammed his fist into his palm. "I fear the Münster rebellion has only created a cauldron of hate and fear that the established church will visit on the Anabaptists for years to come. If it were not for that, I might follow the Anabaptist way, but I still have questions. How can I reconcile it with the Catholic teachings? A great gulf lies between Melchior Hoffman's teachings and the Pope's infallible words. Does the Eucharist become Christ's flesh? Was Mary also born of a virgin and her grandmother before that and so on back to Adam?" Menno threw up his hands in despair. "I don't know, Johan. The practices ingrained in my flesh want to overpower the truth I find here." He held up the book.

Johan nodded. "Perhaps if we believed God is who he says he is in his Word, and that he does what he says he will do, and that he has given us everything we need in the Bible…"

Menno's face lit up. "Yes, yes, the apostle Peter said the same thing." He turned the pages. "Here, in second Peter one and three it says *According as his divine power hath given unto us all things that pertain unto life and godliness, through the knowledge of him that hath called us to glory and virtue.* And how do we find that knowledge of him?"

Johan put his hand on the Bible. "I believe all knowledge of Christ is in this book."

~

As Johan prepared to leave the next morning, Menno said, "Last night, I realized I need someone like you to challenge me, to ask questions, to assist me with my studies—to be my friend. Would you consider bringing your family here to live with me in the rectory?"

Johan's mouth dropped open. "Me? But I am just a stable boy…"

"No, Johan, you are much more than that. You are a man with deep thoughts and a tender heart. I'd like you to be my assistant, to do the mundane tasks around the church like cleaning, maintenance and so forth, while I study and conduct parish visits. But I would also like you to be my sounding board, someone I can come to when I lose my way. I have much to discover, but I cannot embark on this journey by myself. I will give you and your family a place to stay, your board, and a small allowance the Church allows me to use for help."

Johan looked long and hard at the gentle face of the Catholic priest.

So this is where you've been leading me, God, this is the purpose for which I was born.

He smiled and took Menno's hand. "Yes, we will come."

CHAPTER 29: THE CALL

1535

$\mathcal{I}$n August 1535, Isabella, and her family moved to Witmarsum, Friesland. Magda put up such a fuss while they packed that when they arrived, Isabella asked Menno if the old woman could join them, and he agreed to send for her. Isabella was glad when Magda came for she took over the running of the household. Much to her satisfaction, Isabella had a peaceful place where she could learn the real joy of being a wife and mother and soon the girl who had once been the spoiled and pampered daughter of a king was one of the best bread makers in Friesland. She learned the finer arts of cooking and sewing and managing a household, and at last, the Hirschbergs became just Bella and Johan.

In the days that followed, Isabella watched Abel grow strong and healthy. Johan took up the duties of Menno's right-hand man—taking care of the non-clerical work needed in the small church and parish. Isabella watched Johan slowly change as the bitterness and anger dropped away. She was proud of her husband for he often went with Menno to the houses of the poor of the village and while Menno brought comfort and spiritual solace, Johan would busy himself repairing a leaking roof or re-mortaring a cracked chimney.

The most amazing part of their new life for Isabella was to watch as her husband fulfilled Menno's need for a sounding board. Johan was a man of the world, in tune with the everyday life of the common man, while Menno spent his life in spiritual pursuits. Thus, each man served the other, for when Johan foundered in the mundane, Menno lifted him up to sublime heights and when Menno lost touch with the reality of daily living, Johan pulled his feet back to the ground. It was during their time together that Menno forged many of the ideas that in time became the basis of the developing and redefined Anabaptist faith.

It was a season of peace for Isabella. Life became centered on raising her son and blessing her husband. Her former life as a princess was like a strange dream and soon even the terrors of Münster fell behind her. Johan was her protector and guide, they lived in peace and they sat at the feet of a gentle teacher who led them into the amazing world of God's Word.

She started a journal and filled it with entries that showed her she too was growing in her walk with the Lord. One morning she was writing and when she looked at the words, she felt that the terrors and hardship of Münster were far behind her.

Life is perfect. In the quiet peace of a pre-dawn Friesland morning, I rise from my bed and walk through the fields surrounding Witmarsum—the smell of the ripening hay and the sound of the full-eared corn rustling in the cool breeze that came from the sea comfort me. The cry of the gulls carried inland on the sea breeze are haunting but only lead me to a deeper contemplation of the world and its ways.

ISABELLA OFTEN THOUGHT of the vast gulf between the aristocratic class and the people of the land. She was with Menno one morning and a question came unbidden to her lips.

"Menno, why has God set a few men to rule over others?"

He smiled and put his arm around Bella's shoulders. "Ah, my dear, you ask the same questions I hold in my heart."

"I only ask because I think of the wealth and privilege I enjoyed as a child while the poor often had nothing. It is something I often ponder."

Menno nodded. "As I examine the Word, I see that God did not want kings for Israel. Saul became king only because the people demanded it. I think it is the same way with the Catholic Church. Nowhere do I see a pope mentioned in the Bible, and yet the church tells us we must follow a ruler who is not Christ, but a mere man. Men will always have their king. I think either that should change, or I should change. But that would mean leaving the church." Menno sighed.

Isabella loved the man with all her heart and she went to him and kissed him on the cheek. "I wish that life would go on forever in this way—simple, peaceful and flowing from my past into a future that is yet unseen. I pray that we can be this way forever, for at last, I am the person I hoped I would be."

Menno shook his head. "I, too, wish that, my dear. But I fear that all good things must end or change—events are moving around us. I think they will bring great pressure to bear on the paradise we have found."

ONE NIGHT ISABELLA had a dark dream. She was in Münster on the night they escaped and she went through the door at the end of the tunnel but on the other side was only deep darkness. She looked around, but Johan was not there. It was dark, so dark, and Abel was no longer with her. Hands reached out for her out of the darkness, but they were not the familiar hands of her beloved—they were grasping and treacherous hands and she knew if she let them take her she would never escape.

She awoke with a cry, "Johan! Johan!"

Johan awakened at the sound of her cry and put his strong arms around her. "Bella, Bella, my love, what is it?"

"A dream, Johan, a terrible dream. We were in Münster. I was running, and you were with Abel and me and then you were both gone, and I was alone—alone in the darkness. And there were others there, but they did not love me. They only wanted to use me. I cried out for you, but I could not find you— I could not find you anywhere, and Abel... My sweet Abel... Oh, Johan, what does it mean?"

"It is nothing, dearest—bad memories from the days of Münster. Go back to sleep, for it will pass."

"But, Johan, it frightened me..."

From that morning on, unease lurked in the back of Isabella's mind. She tried to put it away, but it stayed with her, so she went to Menno. When she walked into the room where he was writing, he put down his pen.

"Good morning, Bella. What brings you?"

"I had a dream, Menno. I have dreamt of Münster before but this time I was alone with no one to help me. There were men who wanted to take me, to use me in their plans. Oh, Menno, what does it mean? I have a sense of foreboding that will not leave me."

Menno sighed. "Yes, Bella, I, too, am disturbed by these times. The horrors of Münster and Bloemkamp often trouble my spirit. The blood of those misguided people falls so hot upon my heart that I cannot find rest in my soul. Though they were in error, these zealous children gave their lives for their beliefs. They humble me and challenge me to speak out against the fallacies of the Catholic Church. But I continue in my comfortable life because I am lazy. I want to escape the cross of Christ and enjoy the physical comforts of this world."

Isabella looked at Menno. His words troubled her heart. "I sense something ahead, Menno—trouble coming our way. Johan has told me that the authorities are persecuting Anabaptists with greater vigor. I fear our days of peace in this lovely place are ending although I would have them go on forever."

"My dear, I have enjoyed your family's presence in my home. But we have a call upon us, Bella. Not by accident did you and Johan and Abel come into my life. Your sojourn with me has been a time where my thoughts became clarified and the path of my journey opened before me. Each of us will take something from our friendship that God will use for the extension and purification of his Kingdom. I see the call on all our lives, but I shrink from it for I fear following this call means the end of our fellowship."

As the days shortened into winter, Menno pondered on the horror of the Münster rebellion and the carnage of Bloemkamp. His musings led him to preach against the revolutionaries' use of violence to achieve their ends. His sermons spoke of the true nature of a believers' church. He preached pure doctrine, scriptural sacraments, obedience, love for neighbors, an open witness of one's faith, and a willingness to suffer persecution without striking back.

The lessons learned from the fall of Münster enabled him to help those who clung to the violent ways of Rothmann and Bockelson. He moved further and further away from the Catholic Church's dogma, which he considered misguided and rigid. In January 1536, he asked Johan to come to his study and the two of them sat before the fire, neither speaking for a long time.

Menno stared at the flames. At last he sighed and looked up. "This will not surprise you, Johan. I am leaving the Catholic

Church. I can no longer live a life that betrays the Word of God and the truth of the Gospel."

Johan picked up a poker and stirred the fire. "What will that mean for you?"

"I must leave this place and go into hiding, for I will accept the believers' baptism and the authorities will want to arrest me. My talks with you and Bella have convinced me that God is building a flock that needs a leader, and I believe God is calling me to be that leader."

"What will that mean for my family and Magda?"

Menno sighed again. "I know I should not place this burden on you. You and your family have become more than dear. Your strength and wisdom have helped me find my way, and I want to ask you to come with me into hiding."

Menno watched as Johan rose and looked around the room.

"This place has become a refuge for me and my family, Menno. I had hoped to live out my days here but now... If it were only me, I would not hesitate. But I must speak with Bella. I do not wish her to be in danger."

"This request is something I ask after much prayer, Johan. I need friends around me who will keep me focused. Since you came here, my preaching and teaching have changed. But my position has become known, and I will not find safety here any longer. I leave the decision to you. I will resign in three days. When I do, I must leave immediately."

"Where will you go, Menno?"

"I will cross the border to Gröningen to shepherd a small congregation of individuals who maintain the truth. I will start there. The believers there need someone to help the unsaved, reclaim them from the snares of damnation and bring them to Christ, and a group of them have asked me to come. I would have you with me, but you must choose for yourself and your family." He paused. "If you come, I think Magda will have to return to Pingjum, for she is too old to make this journey."

Johan found Isabella in their bedroom. She was reading from a manuscript, one of many Menno had penned in the months they had shared with him. When Johan entered, she said, "Listen to this, Johan. *And this is the voice of Christ. Ye have heard it hath been said, an eye for an eye, and a tooth for a tooth: But I say unto you, that ye resist not evil. But whosoever shall smite thee on thy right cheek, turn to him the other.* Menno has written Pieter's message. Isn't that wonderful?"

"Menno is leaving, Bella."

"What?"

"He is leaving the Catholic Church, and he must go into hiding, for he can no longer hide his teaching behind the facade of the church. The Catholic authorities will not tolerate such a challenge."

"But what will we do?"

"He has asked us to go with him, but I said I must speak with you first. It will mean..."

"I know what it means, Johan. We will leave this beautiful place and once again live the life of wanderers."

"If it were only me, Bella..."

"I know, Johan. But God calls you to be Menno's friend and helper and that is clear. And if God calls you, I am also called. We will go with Menno."

"Isabella, Magda cannot come with us."

Johan saw the look of pain cross his wife's face. "But Johan, she is... she has become the mother I never had."

"I know, dearest. But she is too old for the journey. If you cannot bear the parting..."

Johan saw a tear trickle down Bella's cheek. "Alas, Johan. All my forebodings are bearing fruit."

CHAPTER 30: THE WAY OF PEACE

*I*sabella stood beside the cart, watching Magda's brother arrange the old woman's few worldly possessions in the back. The day was so cold that her breath seemed to crystallize in the air. Johan was busy packing their own cart as Menno carried his precious books from the house. When Maarten finished, he slapped his gloved hands together. "Are you ready, Magda?"

The horse snorted.

Maarten laughed. "Sofie here is as eager to return to a warm stable as I am to hurry home to a warm fire."

"Give us a moment, please." Magna wrapped her arms around Isabella, and they embraced for a long time, Isabella crying into the older woman's shoulder.

At last Magda stepped back and held her by the shoulders.

Isabella looked at her beloved mentor one last time, burning every line and wrinkle into her memory. "You have been like a mother Magda—the one my mother could never be. I will miss you as I miss Frederich."

"Ah, my little one…" Magda opened her coat and lifted her apron to dab at her cheeks. "You have been the daughter I never had. When you and Johan wandered into Michael's camp that day, I knew you were special, but I didn't realize God would entwine our lives in such a wonderful way."

Isabella wiped her tears away with the back of her hand. "Will you be all right?"

"Maarten and Annika will take good care of me. We belong together, the de Jonges of Pingjum, three old buzzards who will live out our years croaking at each other."

She smiled, but then she grew serious. "I fear for you, Isabella. Frederich recognized who you were the first time he saw your horse. And I saw you were no common girl, but a lady of quality, a princess. You need to be very careful. I know your father is still looking for you. God has hidden us here. By going across the border you will be closer to Poland. Be careful when you travel, stay close to Menno—don't strike up easy acquaintances. Do nothing to draw attention to yourself."

"We will be careful, Magda. And we will take care of Menno. The Lord knows he needs it."

"His head is in the clouds," Magda whispered. "But his heart is always pure."

"His friendship has changed my Johan. My husband has always been gentle and kind, but tucked away in his heart was rage against those who hurt his loved ones. In Münster, he was eager to kill Catholics and Lutherans. He wanted to pay them back for all they had done. But when he killed that boy in the battle, he saw how wrong the hate was—and now that he has met Menno he is shedding that hate a little at a time. I don't like this uprooting." Isabella looked around at the beloved place, the house, the fields, and a tear trickled from her eye. She brushed it away. "I know the Lord has something for us all to discover—a message from heaven that will change our lives once again."

Johan called. "Come, Isabella, we are ready." He brought Abel to Magda. The old woman took the toddler in her arms. She kissed his face many times and wept. Then she gave him to

Johan and took Isabella into one more embrace and whispered to her, "You are right, Isabella, and somehow that message will reach out to touch our world. The peace of God go with you, my darling."

~

ONCE THEY ARRIVED IN GRÖNINGEN, a day's journey across the border into Germany, they moved into a cottage with two bedrooms behind the house of an Anabaptist believer named Adelbert Beenhouwer. Johan continued as Menno's helper, driver and confidant, while Isabella took over the cooking and cleaning. Menno worked ceaselessly on the writings he had started in Witmarsum, titled *The Spiritual Resurrection, The New Birth,* and *Meditations on the Twenty-Fifth Psalm.*

Johan marveled at the times when Menno spent days in prayer, seeking to find precisely the right words. "My work must be perfect, Johan," he would say. "If I lead just one of these little ones astray, I will suffer for it." When he was not writing, Johan would take him to seek those who maintained the truth. Often people came to them for help—the erring and the misguided—and together Johan and Menno reclaimed them from the snares of damnation and brought them to Christ.

Johan especially loved the times during the following months when they crossed back into Friesland, taking with them the pamphlets that Menno had produced. Johan had grown to love the sea and when their travels took them to Zurich or other coastal towns, he would take time to walk along the shore, listening to the cries of the gulls and watching the endless waves. Once, when they walked together by the sea, Johan turned to his friend.

"Julius once told me something that Pieter said—that the people of the world are like this ocean, tossing and turning in their unrest because they do not know the kindness and love of our great Savior. It is a sad picture."

Menno smiled. "Ah, Johan remember the scripture that says, 'Cast thy bread upon the waters: for thou shalt find it after many days.' God has sent us to cast his bread on the troubled waters of the world."

Johan looked at the kindly face of Menno Simons and nodded. "To be with you is to see things with clarity, and I thank you for it."

With Johan's help, Menno soon became known among the Anabaptists as a capable and devoted leader. One night, as they were visiting with Adelbert, someone knocked on the front door. Adelbert left the room to answer it, and when he returned, a man followed him in.

Johan started up from his chair, but Adelbert waved him back.

"It's all right, Johan. This man and his companions are here to see Menno, but do not fear, for I know him and he is a true believer." He nodded to Menno. "They all wish to speak with you."

Menno stood and held out his hand to greet the stranger. "By all means, Adelbert, bring the rest in."

Adelbert left and returned with seven men who appeared by their clothing to be farmers and craftsmen. Holding their hats in their hands, they waited while their leader spoke.

"I am Herbert Braam," the man said. "These are my brothers in Christ. We are of one heart and one soul in our desire to follow Christ. We try to live our lives beyond reproach as far as a man can judge in doctrine and life, but we cannot do it alone."

Johan approached the man. "Where do you stand on the Münster rebellion?"

"We…" Herbert glanced at the others. "We abhor the errors of Münster. God does not bring his kingdom at the point of a sword as do the Moslems."

"And why do you come?" Menno rose from his chair. "What is it you wish of me?"

Herbert held out a hand. "We have read your writings and believe God has given you a clear message for all true believers. Please use the talents you have received from God—put them to work in his vineyard. We, like many others, need an able pastor. Our hunger is so great but faithful stewards so few."

Menno put his head in his hands. "Your request troubles me. I have limited talents, a weak nature and a timid spirit, and the wickedness and tyranny of the world are great. Like the apostle Paul, I struggle to keep my life in line with God's Word. How can you ask this of one such as I?"

Herbert took Menno's hand. "There is great hunger and need among the God-fearing, but we are sheep who have no shepherd. I beg of you; please come."

Menno looked over at Johan. "What do you think, my son?"

Johan was silent for a long time, head bowed. Then he spoke. "For many years, I wondered what my destiny was to be. When I met you, I found the answer. When I heard your vision for a world where each man and woman displays the love of Christ, revealing God in words and deeds, I knew it was right. These teachings soothe me. The hatred I harbored in my heart is giving place to a desire to see Christ glorified. I believe these men are God's messengers to you. I think you should consider their request."

Menno looked at Herbert. "I will pray about this matter for a season, as I hope you will also do."

The visitors nodded their assent. "We will."

"Come again in one week, and I will give you my answer. Now, before you go, break bread with us."

ONE WEEK LATER, they met again. Johan ushered them into the

room where Menno sat. He stood and greeted the men, who stood silently, awaiting Menno's words. "Johan and I have prayed over this matter and discussed the need. And God has answered. From this time forward, I surrender my soul to the Lord and my body to his work. I will teach and baptize, until the vineyard of the Lord, build up his holy city and temple and repair the tumbled-down walls."

"And I will be your right hand," Johan said.

The faces of the men broke wide in smiles of quiet joy. One man raised his hands in praise while another wept.

NOW BEGAN the days of toil in the vineyard. Isabella marveled as God opened doors and led Johan and Menno by his Spirit. Often they returned to Gröningen exhausted for, though the fields were white for harvest, the workers were few. At these times, Isabella exercised a newfound gift of nurture and care and the two men thrived under it.

For Isabella, the times were not without worry, for the knowledge of Menno's work had come before the leaders of the Catholic and Lutheran churches. The churches worked with the secular authorities to find Menno and bring him to them for examination and punishment. When they were away, Isabella spent many hours in prayer for their safety. During this time she learned to place her trust in her God and as the work and influence of the two men spread, Isabella's faith grew strong.

So for Isabella, the season in Germany was the most unsettled time of her life and yet the most rewarding. Often, as she cooked or cared for the mundane chores, Menno would call her to him. "Isabella, you work at many things, but as our Lord said to Martha, 'You need only one thing.'" He would open his Bible and motion for her to sit next to him. "Choose as Mary chose—that which is better, and no one can take it away from you."

Like Mary, Isabella pondered these things and took great comfort in remembering those times sitting with Menno Simons and listening as he broke the bread of God's Word and then taught her the meaning. Often, he would say, "For man can lay only Christ Jesus as the foundation for all things." She listened in awestruck silence as he spoke to her of the Trinity of God, the incarnation, the work of the Holy Ghost, faith, and so much more.

Once as he was speaking to her and Johan, he stopped in the middle of what he was teaching and a great light came into his eyes. "Our weapons are not swords and spears, but patience, silence, hope and the Word of God. With these, we must maintain and defend our cause. Paul says, 'The weapons of our warfare are not carnal, but mighty through God.' With these, we resist the kingdom of the devil, not with swords, spears, cannons and coats of mail."

"If, in the rest of my life I only remember one thing," Johan whispered, tears in his eyes, "it will be these words. I thank you, for as you spoke, I felt the Holy Spirit lift the last of the burden of my anger and hate and set me free."

Isabella rose and went to her husband's side. "Now we know why God sent us to you. In the years to come, we will always have tonight to look back on, and we will remember our friend and how he taught us of the only God and Savior, the Lord Jesus Christ, and his way of peace."

CHAPTER 31: THE OATH

*F*ranz von Waldek, the now-restored Prince Bishop of Münster, stared at the man standing in front of him. "What did you say your name is?"

"Jügen Fromme, Your Holiness."

"And you say you know where the Polish princess is?"

Von Waldek watched as Fromme tried to smile but the smile, added to the jagged scar running down the side of his face, created a rather unpleasant effect. "Yes, Your Holiness, I know where she is."

Von Waldek stared at the thickset man for a moment. "How is it you know what the princess looks like? Are you Polish?"

"No, Your Holiness, but I had dealings with her in Münster."

Von Waldek stood up, walked around his table and came face to face with Fromme. "Münster? You were one of the thrice-damned Anabaptists who stole my city?"

"I was never an Anabaptist, Your Holiness. They hired me to guard the king, er... Jan Bockelson."

"Why did you not die with the rest of the vermin?"

"I almost did. A swordsman wounded me in the battle, and I fell among the piles of dead in the square. Your troops overlooked me. When I came to, I had enough life left in me to crawl out of the city. Some of my old comrades found me—those I fought beside in the Landsknecht at Frankenhausen. They thought I was still one of them and nursed me back to health."

"So one rat from Münster escaped my wrath. Why should I not kill you now? Do you understand what I did to Bockelson and his cohorts?"

Fromme squirmed before von Waldek's icy stare. "I know it did not go well with them."

Von Waldek walked to the window. "Come here! I will show you how it went with them."

Fromme limped hesitantly to von Waldek's side. The prince bishop pointed out the window to St. Lambert's Church across the square. "Do you see what is hanging on the spire?"

Fromme peered out the window. "Three cages."

"What do they contain?"

Fromme shuddered. "I can't tell."

Now it was von Waldek's turn to smile. "When we broke into the city, my men searched everywhere for Bockelson and found him hiding in his bedroom. His foolish wives, all fourteen, tried to defend him, but their fingernails were no match for my troops' swords. They captured Jan Bockelson, Bernard Knipperdolling and Bernard Kretchtinck. We looked for Rothmann but never found his body so I assume he died in the fighting.

"On January 22 of this year, I called the remaining Catholic citizens of Münster to the square to witness the torture and execution of Bockelson, Knipperdolling, and Kretchtinck. My executioners ripped the flesh from their bodies with hot tongs for an hour before stabbing them each in the heart."

Jügen Fromme's face paled.

Von Waldek pointed out the window. "Then they shoved their bodies into those iron cages and hoisted them up the tower. The white you see is their bones, which will remain high on the wall of the cathedral forever as a warning to any heretics who would ever again try to bring down the mother church."

Von Waldek took Fromme by the arm. His eyes narrowed. "Why should I not do the same to you?"

"The princess escaped, did she not?"

Von Waldek turned back to the window. "Yes, she escaped." His eyes narrowed as he looked at Fromme. "But Gresbeck and I were the only ones who knew that."

Fromme shrugged. "Not the only ones, for I have seen her."

Von Waldek slumped into a chair. "I would have had her but for a great swordsman who kept us at bay while she fled."

Fromme's face twitched. "That would be Frederich Weisbach."

"Who it was is of no matter. All I know is that the swordsman thwarted me. But he paid the price."

Von Waldek looked up at Fromme, "You say you saw the princess... since Münster?"

Fromme nodded. "Yes, Your Highness."

"Tell me where she is. If you do not, I will have you tortured and then put up in the cage with your king."

"He was not my king. And yes, you could torture me, Your Holiness, but I have been on the rack before. I might tell you the truth before I died, and I might not. Perhaps you would find the princess, but you might not. Wouldn't it be simpler if you rewarded me for my service and I led you to where she is hiding?"

Von Waldek laughed out loud. "Perhaps you are right, Fromme. I have grown weary of the bloodshed. A simple business transaction might be easier. Although I assure you that if you give me the wrong information..."

"And why would I risk doing that, Your Holiness?"

Von Waldek nodded to a servant who stood by a table filled with different bottles of spirits. He motioned Fromme into a chair. "A glass of wine, perhaps, while you give me the details? How did you find Isabella?"

Fromme nodded his acceptance and settled into his seat. "I was in a town not far to the north in Germany. The Anabaptists, led by a man named Menno Simons, held a meeting there that night. Knowing that authorities in Holland and Friesland want to arrest him for preaching abominations, I thought perhaps if I alerted them as to Simons's whereabouts, they might reward me. When he left the meeting, I followed him."

The servant brought the wine and Fromme took a long draught. "To my surprise, that fellow Johan, who used to work in Bockelson's stable, was with him. He is the husband of the princess. I followed from a distance, and when they came to the house where Simons was staying, who should greet them at the door but the princess herself."

Fromme finished his wine in one gulp and stood. "We have little time, Your Highness, for Simons does not stay in one place long. If we are to capture them, we must leave soon."

Von Waldek clapped his hands. A door opened, and a servant entered. "Tell my troop commander to prepare his men. He will ride north today." He motioned at Fromme. "Our friend, Jügen, will lead."

JOHAN AWOKE FROM A DEEP SLUMBER. The room was pitch black and he could not see his hand in front of his face. Outside he heard noises, horses, and the low sound of voices.

Isabella came into the room with a candle. "Johan, what is it? I hear someone outside."

Johan threw back the covers and went to the window. Outside in the half-light from the moon he could see mounted men had surrounded the house. He turned to Isabella. "Menno, where is Menno?"

"He is not here. He has gone to the house of a sick woman to pray for her."

Just then they heard a crash downstairs and heavy footsteps came into the house. After a moment someone yelled, "They must be upstairs," and then Johan heard them tramping up the stairs. Abel cried out in fear. Isabella hurried to his bed to take him in her arms. The door burst open and a familiar-looking man with a scar running down the side of his face was leering at them.

"What do you want?"

The man sneered. "Don't worry. We are not here for Simons. We come for you and your wife, Princess Isabella of Poland." More men crowded into the room.

Johan grabbed a walking staff leaning against the wall and raised it. "Run, Isabella!"

Their son in her arms, Isabella moved to Johan's side. "I have nowhere to run, my husband." She placed her hand on the staff. "Our weapons are not swords and spears, but patience, silence, hope and the Word of God. With these we must uphold the cause of Christ."

Johan lowered the staff.

Fromme smirked. "Gather your belongings and bring your son. We leave at once for Krakow."

Seated between his wife and King John Zápolya, Sigismund leaned forward, listening as a messenger told of the capture of his daughter and Johan Hirschberg.

He leaned back and clapped his hands. "This is good news, good news."

"Wonderful!" Bona beamed at Zápolya. "Now we can complete the negotiations for your marriage to our daughter."

"But... she is no longer a virgin." The old man grunted.

"She's married to a stable boy, and she has a son. She's been living the life of a peasant. Why would I wish to marry her?"

Sigismund scowled. "I am the Catholic king of Catholic Poland. A Protestant marriage such as theirs has no legal binding in my country. Getting an annulment will be no challenge." He lifted an eyebrow. "As for my daughter, you will marry her because I am the only person who can keep your miserable little country from being annexed by the Hapsburgs."

"You think too highly of your influence, Sigismund," Zápolya whined.

Sigismund slammed his fist on the table. "For fifteen years, the treacherous Hapsburg family has promised to help you withstand the Ottomans, but to my knowledge, they have never sent a gulden or a soldier to your doorstep."

He leaned close. "You must be weary of holding out all alone against Suleiman. With your marriage to my daughter, I will guarantee financial support and troops to prop up your faltering throne. In return, you will act as a buffer between my country and the voracious Turks. This marriage will solve both our problems."

Zápolya frowned. "I'm told your nobles do not support such a marriage."

"My nobles do not understand." Sigismund waved his hand as if flicking them away. "The wedding will proceed as soon as Isabella returns."

Zápolya nodded his assent. Bona grinned a wide victorious smile. "Yes, the wedding will proceed. I will begin the preparations today."

Eyeing her over the old man's stooped head, Sigismund winked. "Now, shall we talk about dinner?"

ISABELLA, Princess of Poland, stood holding Abel's hand in front of Sigismund who sat on a raised platform in the Envoy's Room in Wawel Palace. Bona and John Zápolya, King of Hungary, sat in chairs on either side of him. A massive tapestry of God Speaking to Noah hung on the wall. Bright sunlight streamed through the many-paned window on the back wall and Isabella had to hold one hand over her eyes to see. This room had been one of her favorites as a child, but today those memories had faded into a grim reality.

Sigismund's bishop and several clerics stood against the wall to the left. Two guards held Johan between them a few feet away from Isabella. Several servants stayed close behind Isabella. Despite the sunlight pouring in, the mood in the room was far from bright. Isabella could see the dark anger in her father's eyes.

"And who is this?" Bona pointed to Abel.

"This is my son, Abel. He's your grandson, Mama."

"Grandson?" She spat the word. "I have no grandson. Perhaps when you are in John Zápolya's bed, you will do your duty, and I may then have a grandson. As for this bastard, I will send him to an orphanage and if he dies there, so be it."

Johan broke free from his guards and grabbed Abel. "You will not harm my son!" he shouted, backing away.

Sigismund jumped to his feet, leaped down to Johan and with a powerful backhand, knocked him and Abel to the floor.

Abel cried, "Mama!" and shrieked. Isabella ran between her father and Johan. "Please, Papa. Do not hit him again. He will not fight you."

Sigismund backed away, trembling with rage—his neck and his face were as red as his robe. Johan got slowly to his feet, still holding his crying son.

Hands clenched, Isabella stepped close to her father, who towered over her like a giant. "And now I will have my say." She glared at him though he was still seething. "You cannot give me to this old man. It is a sin, for I am married, Papa."

"Married by some backwoods German Protestant? Ha! You have no marriage. My papal representative..." He nodded to the Bishop who bowed... "has already drawn up the terms of the annulment."

"No, Papa!" Isabella stamped her foot. "You can annul my marriage, but I will never marry this man."

John Zápolya nodded to one man guarding Johan. The man snatched Abel from Johan and put a knife to the boy's throat.

Johan lunged for his son, but the other guard grabbed his arms.

Zápolya rose slowly from his chair. "I thought things might go this way." He spoke softly to Johan. "If you value your son's life, don't move!" Johan stopped struggling, but the anguish on his face broke Isabella's heart.

The old man stepped down from the platform and walked to Isabella. "Isabella," Zápolya said, "perhaps it is not a matter of what your father does to you, but what I do to your son." He glanced at the guard, who drew the knife across the child's neck, raising a thin line of blood. Abel screamed again and struggled.

"Don't move, Abel," Johan shouted. The boy stopped and looked at his father with terrified eyes.

Isabella ran to her son, but the guard threatened to cut the boy again and she stopped. "Please, don't." Isabella cried. She turned to her father. "Stop him, father."

Zápolya took Isabella's arm and turned her until she was face to face with him. She could smell garlic on his breath and his rheumy eyes disgusted her.

"Here is my suggestion, Isabella. Either you agree to the marriage, or I will have my guard kill your son this instant. I will also imprison your husband in Hungary where he will suffer the tortures of the damned before I have him executed." He studied her for a moment. "Is that what you want?"

Isabella felt a rush of blood go to her head and she almost fainted. Zápolya held her up, his grip hurting her arm cruelly.

He turned her to face Abel. "Look at him, Isabella. He is alive, but he might be dead in the next instant. I mean exactly what I say. I will kill your son and your husband will die in my dungeon."

He smiled a ghastly smile. Isabella felt as though she would vomit.

This can't be happening...

"That is what will happen if you refuse. But, if you agree to the marriage, after the wedding I will deliver them together to Poland's border and release them, but only if your husband gives me his solemn oath he will never return to Poland or ever enter Hungary. If you want me to show them mercy, then you will swear before God that you will marry me and when they leave, you will never see them again. Otherwise, they will both die." He paused. "Those are my terms."

"Papa, please." Isabella clung to his arm. "Abel is my son, your grandson. Johan is my husband. Please, Papa, please."

Sigismund shook her away, and she fell to her hands and knees, weeping. Sigismund stood over her. "You will do as Zápolya demands. There is much more at stake here than your feelings, Isabella." He scowled at her. "Agree to his terms, or I will allow him to kill your son."

Isabella looked up at Johan, tears streaming down her face. "Johan, oh, Johan. What am I to do?"

His deep love for her blazed from his eyes. "I do not care about my life, Isabella, but this is our son. I would not have him harmed, nor would you." His voice broke. "We must do as they say." She'd never seen him look so sad.

The greatest despair she had ever known welled up in Isabella's heart. "But to never see either of you again... Oh, Johan, I cannot bear this." She put her face in her hands and whispered, "It is too deep a river for me to cross."

"You must, my love, for Abel."

And in that moment, Isabella, Princess of Poland, remembered her own words, spoken to her husband in promise as she sat before the gates of Münster. "If anyone ever tries to harm you or our child, I will give my life before I will let that happen."

She looked from Johan to Abel and then to her father. Sobbing, she nodded her assent.

Zápolya motioned to the bishop who stepped forward and held a crucifix before her lips. "Swear it now, Isabella, Zápolya commanded.

Isabella lowered her head.

"Swear it!"

"I swear it...," she whispered.

"Kiss the cross and repeat it—louder this time so that we can hear your oath and God can hear it also!"

Tears streaming down her face, Isabella kissed the cross. "I..." Her voice faltered. "I swear."

Zápolya nodded to the guard, who lowered the knife and handed Abel to Johan.

Sigismund waved his hand. "Take them out!"

As the guards led her loved ones from the room, Abel's heartrending pleas rang in her ears. "Mama, Mama..."

CHAPTER 32: JOURNEY'S END

*A*ll of Krakow was humming with excitement. This was the day Princess Isabella of Poland was to wed John Zápolya, King of Hungary. Hundreds of people filled the streets of Krakow—dignitaries, scholars, rulers from all over Europe, soldiers and peasants. Five hundred knights had traveled from Hungary at the command of their king.

They came to see a young princess marry an aging king. Many were old enough to remember Bona Sforza's wedding to Emperor Sigismund twenty-odd years before. Theirs had been the most lavish wedding in European history, highlighted by the Italian food Bona introduced to Poland. Now the citizens of Krakow looked forward to yet another extravagant event—one resplendent with balls and feasts for the rich, and wine and bread for the poor.

The streets were also alive with rumors. After dropping out of sight for three years, Isabella had only reappeared the previous April. The official story was that she had spent that time at the royal castle in Lithuania.

But others had it her parents had sent her to a convent to purify her rebellious behavior. One rumor suggested a Turkish general had captured Isabella while she was traveling and spirited her away to a castle near Istanbul. Hungarian and Polish knights working together had saved her in a bold foray.

For most citizens of Poland, however, none of that mattered. All they cared about was that their princess was home and she was to become a queen.

FROM HIS LOCKED room on the upper floor of Wawel Castle, Johan Hirschberg looked out the barred window at the festivities below. Even though it was still day, torches lit the courtyard while rich tapestries draped the frescoed walls. Servants and workers scurried about, setting up long tables and loading them with food and drink for the feast to come. On the hill just behind the castle rose the cathedral where the wedding would take place. Johan felt a deep grief, so profound it was almost a physical pain. He remembered feeling this way when they martyred his aunt and then again when his mother died.

He turned from the window to the stark, shadowed room behind him. Abel sat on a narrow cot against the wall, staring at Johan with sad eyes. "Where is Mama?"

Johan picked up the boy and held him close. "Your mother is doing something magnificent tonight. She is giving her life, so you and I might live."

"When will we be with her again, Papa?"

"She is traveling a different road now, Abel. But we will always remember her, won't we?"

Abel threw his arms around Johan's neck and clung to him. "Mama." He cried. "I want my mama."

"Do not cry for your mama, Abel." Johan patted his back. "She is living the way our Lord would have her live. Jesus said, 'Greater love hath no man than this, that a man lay down his life for his friends.' You must always remember your mother as someone who followed the words of Christ and gave herself... for you... and for me. So don't cry... my son."

Johan's voice broke, and he wept. Abel clung to him as Johan sat on the bed, his body shaking with sobs.

∼

ACROSS THE COURTYARD, in much more elaborate chambers, Isabella stood on a small dais. Her maid, Maria, was fastening the back of the Florentine wedding gown. Bona's favorite Italian designer had designed it. From a white bodice, long magenta sleeves flowed to her wrists, and a dark, magenta-trimmed skirt swept the floor. Isabella's face was ashen in hue—fixed and hard. But she could not keep the tears from running down her cheeks. She put her hands to her face. "Oh Maria, I cannot bear this," she whispered.

Maria handed her a handkerchief. "I am sorry for you, my princess. To lose the man you love is a terrible tragedy. But it's done. If you want Johan and Abel to live you must go through with this; you must look to the future. As the priest says, *Sic fata Volunt.*"

"What does that mean, Maria?"

"It means, 'it is the will of fate.' Whatever has happened to you is the will of God, and now he has something else for you to do. But you and I know the truth. Johan will always be your only love and you his." She adjusted the gown and stepped back to view it. Then she brought a veil and attached it to Isabella's headpiece. "I know your heart is breaking, but if you weep today, you will show John Zápolya that he has defeated you. You have done the only thing you could do. You saved the lives of your husband and your son and Johan will not fail you. He will raise Abel to be a real man, like his father. Do not weep today."

"Am I to make merry then, Maria—when my heart feels as though someone has stabbed a lance through it?"

"No, my princess. Show Zápolya that though he may have forced you into marriage, he will *never* have you. Every man wishes the woman they marry to worship them, to adore them. Zápolya may have your body, but he does not have your heart, nor will he ever. Now, dry your eyes. When Zápolya sees you walk into the church, he must not find the warmth of summer in your eyes but the cold of winter."

AT THE FAR end of her father's ornate cathedral, the orchestra played the first notes of Isabella's favorite praise hymn, the *Te Deum*. Isabella began the long walk up the wide center aisle; head high, mouth grim, eyes focused straight ahead as the choir sang...

We praise thee, O God: we acknowledge thee to be the Lord.

All the earth doth worship thee: the Father everlasting.

I do not feel praise in my heart today, Father.

To thee all Angels cry aloud: the Heavens and all the Powers within.

To thee Cherubim and Seraphim cry,

Holy, Holy, Holy: Lord God of Hosts;

This is breaking my heart, God. Why did you allow this to happen?

Heaven and earth are full of the Majesty: of thy glory.

I do not see your glory today, Lord.

A glorious company of the Apostles: praise thee.

The goodly fellowship of the Prophets: praise thee.

A noble army of Martyrs: praise thee.

Our holy Church throughout all the world: doth acknowledge thee;

My life is no longer worth living...

The Father: of an infinite Majesty;

Thine honorable, true: and only Son;

Also the Holy Ghost: the Comforter.

Thou art the King of Glory: O Christ.

Thou art the everlasting Son of the Father

I too have a son, Jesus. Did you forget that?

When she came to Zápolya's side, he blinked his rheumy eyes in amazement at her, for Isabella was beautiful. But she did not show him the radiant joy of an expectant bride, not with her face, her posture or the way she carried her hands. She looked at him with contempt and her heart was dark but then, as she stepped before the altar, a single ray of light from the setting sun shone through one window above and fell on her face, and in that moment, she, at last, heard the voice of her God.

Fear not, Isabella. Be strong, for I am with thee.

ISABELLA SAT between her new husband and her father at the feast table. Her mother sat on the other side of Zápolya. Sigismund leaned over. "Well, my daughter, all is well that ends well. You are now Queen of Hungary, a participant in a great moment in European history."

Isabella whispered in his ear. "You do not fool me, Father. You and mother only wish to have a Jagiellon on the throne. If you can use me to destroy the scheming Hapsburgs by raising up a Jagiellon who might one day take the thrones of Europe from them, you will do it." She took a drink of her wine and turned to face him.

"You do not care for me or my happiness and I have no interest in your political manipulations. When I become the ruling Queen of Hungary, and I will, for the old fool beside me is not long for this world…," she nodded at Zápolya with her head and narrowed her eyes, "then I assure you, I will *never* consult you about the destiny of my new country." Isabella rose from the table and looked down at her father. "From this day forward, I am John Zápolya's wife, but I am *not* your daughter. After this day, I will never speak to you again."

Sigismund's mouth opened in shock as Isabella walked away.

ISABELLA STEPPED from the dressing room into the bedchamber where John Zápolya was waiting in a red silk robe, wide-eyed and eager to claim his prize. He started up from his chair and lifted his arms to embrace her, but Isabella stiffened and pushed him away. "I am now your wife, yes, but you must perform one service for me before you bed me."

Zápolya frowned. "I am your king." He stared into her eyes, his own watery eyes hard as flint. "*You* are my subject. You do *not* negotiate with me." He pointed a gnarled finger at the rose-petal sprinkled bed. "That bed is my husbandly prerogative."

Isabella folded her arms over her dressing gown and returned his stare without blinking.

He broke the gaze first, walked away and came back. "What service?"

"I wish to see Johan and Abel once more before they leave."

"No!" He shook his head, his thin gray locks moving with the motion. "It is not possible. You swore an oath you would never see them again."

Isabella lowered her hands to her waist and stood taller. "I swore that once they left Poland, I would never see them again. They have not left Poland. If you grant my request, then I will come to your bed. If you do not, I promise you, King John, you will *never* have me. Grant this one request, and we will consummate our marriage."

He dropped into the chair. "You may go to him one last time." He waved the back of his hand at her as if sending her away. "But only for a few minutes. I do not want you planning anything."

"And my son?"

"Yes, yes." He tapped the chair arm, again and again. "Hurry and do what you must. Take a chaperone but do not embrace or kiss the peasant. I will be waiting."

She bowed her head and curtsied. "As you wish."

∿

AT THE SOUND of a key turning in the lock, Johan turned. The guard stepped into the small room, followed by Maria, Isabella's servant. "Come, Johan." She motioned to him. "And bring the boy and your things. You are leaving tonight. We have one thing to do before you go and we have little time."

Johan picked up Abel and the three of them hurried down the hall and into a room, followed by the guard. Like an angel, Isabella stood in the room's center dressed in a flowing white dressing gown and wrapped in a fur-trimmed robe, more lovely than Johan had ever seen her. Despite the great sadness that enveloped her like a shroud, she had a resolute hardness to her chin. He knew her well enough to know she did not come bearing good news.

She stepped to Johan and took Abel into her arms, holding him close.

Their son wrapped his arms around his mother as though he would never let go. "Mama, Mama. I love you, Mama."

Tears coursing down her cheeks, she kissed his hair and cheeks and whispered, "I love you, too, son. Now be a good boy and don't cry for I must speak to your father." She handed the boy to Maria and took Johan's hands in hers. She looked into his eyes. "I must not embrace you, dear one, for Zápolya demanded that of me before he agreed to let me see you this one last time."

"Bella, oh, Bella. I..."

"Please listen, my darling. I want you to know I will not

regret the choice I made if you raise our son as Menno taught us. Keep the faith that the Lord delivered to you and make sure Abel lives the way of peace. Let our son know the truth always."

She touched his cheek. "And know this—I will always love you and Abel. Like the apostle, I am persuaded, that neither death, nor life, nor angels, nor principalities, nor powers, nor things present, nor things to come, nor height, nor depth, nor any other creature, shall be able to separate us from the love of God, which is in Christ Jesus our Lord. Neither can those things separate you from my love. I am yours forever, Johan Hirschberg."

Johan lifted her soft hands to his lips as he'd done so many times before and looked into her deep blue eyes. "Likewise, I am yours forever. I will gladly keep the true faith and pass it on to our son, my dearest. And yes, *nothing* can ever separate me from you in my heart, neither in this life nor in the next."

Isabella's face paled.

Reluctantly lowering her hands, Johan went to the few bags he and Abel had packed and pulled out a small bundle. Taking it to Isabella, he unwrapped the golden crucifix and handed it to her. "Take this to remember us by."

Isabella shook her head. "Johan, no, it is your treasure…"

"Take it, Bella." He settled the cross on her palms, wrapped her fingers around it and his own around hers. "When you look upon it, remember that in your heart you are a Hirschberg and that we will love you, forever. Thank you for these blessed years you have given me, for the joy and love we've shared. They are my true treasure, that which neither moth nor rust doth corrupt, and which thieves cannot steal."

Isabella took his hand. "For where your treasure is, there will your heart be."

"I love you, Isabella, for all eternity."

"And I you."

He looked into her eyes, at her cheeks, her chin, her lips, searing every detail of her face into his memory.

The guard opened the door. "Your Majesty, your husband awaits."

She drew the cross and his hands to her heart. "Johan... Johan!"

Against every fiber in his being, he whispered, "Goodbye, my love. Until eternity..."

He released her hands. Tears coursed down his face, but he smiled at her once more.

Isabella gave the cross to Maria and then took Abel and held him in a long embrace. She kissed his face and hair and then whispered in his ear. Then she handed him to Johan.

"Go with your father, my son, and do not cry. I love you with all my heart."

"Mama, Mama!"

Isabella lifted her head, her face pale. She reached out toward Johan once more and then pulled her hand back. "Goodbye, my beloved," she whispered, and then turned and walked away.

PART VI
THE MENNONITE QUEEN

ISABELLA WAS RIGHT, *for the old man she married did not outlast the
wedding day by ten months. When John Zápolya died, Isabella had
just given birth to a son, John Sigismund Zápolya. The king had
signed a treaty with the Hapsburgs before his death, making Archduke
Ferdinand of Austria heir to the throne of Hungary. However, the
Hungarian nobles did not wish to see their homeland fall into the
Hapsburgs' greedy hands and refused to abide by the treaty. Instead,
they elected Isabella's infant son as King of Hungary and Isabella as
his regent. Ferdinand responded by sending an army against Buda,
Hungary's capital, precipitating a struggle that lasted for the next
twenty years. With the onset of that conflict and the nobles' decision,
Isabella began a new journey as a ruler, a journey that would change
the face of Europe forever.*

"The Mennonite Queen"
From The Journals of Jenny Hershberger

CHAPTER 33: A QUEEN FOR ALL PEOPLE

*I*sabella bent over her infant son's cradle and lifted him to her breast. "Ah, my little John Sigismund, so like your father—always complaining, although you do not have gout or ill health, just a contrary nature."

The newborn quieted in her arms. "The king has gone to quell a revolt by some of his unhappy subjects. But he will be home soon to meet you, the one great accomplishment of his life, a handsome heir who will one day be King of Hungary." Smiling down at her small son, her thoughts returned, as they often did, to a tiny room in Münster, Germany, and another baby with a much different temperament.

"And you, my dear Abel," she whispered. "What will you become?"

At the sound of a knock, she turned toward the door. "Come in."

The door opened, and a servant showed Bishop George Martinuzzi in.

Isabella steeled herself. She could not stand the man, but he was deep in her husband's counsel, and so she did her best to tolerate him. Martinuzzi was a schemer, always working in the background to manipulate John Zápolya and Hungary's future. Being a devout Catholic, he often encouraged the king to persecute those of other faiths. Today, however, he did not wear his usual ingratiating smile.

"What is it, Bishop?"

"It is the king, Your Majesty."

Isabella tilted her head, studying his grim features. "What about the king, Bishop?"

"I am sorry to say…" The bishop folded his hands. "He suffered a brain hemorrhage following a battle near the town of Szászsebes." Looking down, he took a prolonged breath and then looked up again. "… He died two days ago."

Isabella stared at him. His words had a strange effect. John Zápolya was dead. She examined her feelings, but she did not find sorrow, only gladness and relief, followed by a small twinge of guilt for feeling that way. She stared at the priest wanting to put into words what she was feeling but realizing she should keep her thoughts to herself.

I do not rejoice in any death, but John Zápolya was a hateful, lustful old man. He used me for his own pleasure but never showed me any kindness or love.

"I am sorry for this news, Your Majesty, and I can see your sorrow has left you speechless." He ducked his head and backed away. "I will withdraw. But as soon as you are able, we must talk. This changes everything."

How she loathed this man. Isabella drew herself to her full height and dismissed him with a wave. "You may go, Bishop. I will inform you when I am ready to speak with you. I need time to mourn in peace."

"Yes, Your Majesty, but do not tarry long. Suleiman and Ferdinand will soon hear the news. Hungary's fate hangs in the balance. What you do next could change the history of Europe."

She nodded. "Good day, Bishop."

Martinuzzi bowed and left. Isabella picked up a small hand

bell and rang for her maid and confidante, who came at once. "Yes, Isabella?"

"King John is dead."

Maria's face paled, and she put her hand to her mouth. "The king? Dead?"

"The Bishop informed me he died of a hemorrhage after a battle. I once warned him he would not live to enjoy the fruit of the bargain he struck with me. And now he is dead."

"And you have a son to care for, Isabella; a son without a father." Tears welled in her eyes.

"I am saddened, not because John Zápolya is dead, God forgive me, but because I am here in Hungary and not in Friesland or Holland, or wherever Johan is."

"Can you not go to him?"

"I would not know where to find him." The baby stirred. She looked down at him. "Even if I knew, John Sigismund is too young for such a journey, and I feel God put me here for a reason. Martinuzzi is right. He said the fate of Hungary is now in my hands. The country will plunge into anarchy if I leave."

She sighed. "Ferdinand wishes to annex us to his Austrian empire. Suleiman desires to make us all followers of the Prophet Mohammed. Martinuzzi wishes to take Hungary for his own and place it under the Catholic Church's rule. I cannot leave the Hungarian people to the destruction that would follow my departure. Some might even take this baby boy from me to preserve the kingly line. The only way I can solve this dilemma is to remain as Hungary's queen. Of that, I am sure. But Martinuzzi may have other plans. I will need to be very careful."

Maria sniffed. "That horrible man. He is always looking at me in that lustful way. He would bed me if he could. For a priest to do that... Oh..." Maria shuddered.

"Yes, he is horrible, and that is why I cannot leave our country to him. For now I will entrust Johan and Abel into

God's hands." She looked out the window, tears falling onto her cheeks. "Perhaps a time will come..."

Maria took her queen into her arms. "For one so young, one born into privilege, fate has filled your life with much hardship and many difficult decisions. I am glad I can be with you."

Isabella held Maria. "You have always been like an older sister Maria. I do not know what I would do without you."

TWO DAYS LATER, dressed in black, Isabella had tea with Bishop Martinuzzi in a small drawing room at Buda Castle. Outside the windows, Isabella could see the city of Buda sprawling below castle hill. After offering his condolences again, Martinuzzi wasted no time addressing their country's lack of leadership. "As you know, King John signed a treaty with Ferdinand of Austria making Ferdinand his heir. As soon as Ferdinand hears of the king's death, he will come with his army to assume the Hungarian throne."

Isabella took a sip of tea. "John Zápolya did not have an heir when he signed that treaty. Now he does."

"Exactly, Your Majesty, and that is why our country's nobles, myself included, have agreed that we will not abide by it."

Martinuzzi folded his hands and gave her that smug smile that so infuriated her.

This little man has something in mind, something that will ultimately give him the power in Hungary.

"What do you and the nobles plan to do, Bishop?" She put her cup down and looked directly at the bishop.

"We will put Ferdinand off until we can gather enough electors to make John Sigismund the king."

"But, he is just a baby. How can he be the king?"

"Yes, just a baby, Your Majesty, and that is where you come

in. The nobles will elect you as regent. You will be the nominal ruler of Hungary until John Sigismund comes of age."

"But that will be twenty years from now, Bishop." She waited, for she knew there was more.

"Yes, Your Majesty." He rose from his chair and went to the window. He was silent, so Isabella pressed him.

"And what of Ferdinand? He will not take your... our presumption without response."

"No, he will not, but we do not fear him." He pointed out the window. "The walls of Buda are strong and our army is fierce. For all his bluster, Ferdinand is a pussycat. Incompetents run his army."

"But what if he invades, Bishop? Our army may be loyal, but the Hapsburg army outnumbers us ten to one. What will you do when he encircles our city and puts us to siege?" A memory came to her mind of the army of von Waldek entrenched in their siege lines outside Münster. She shuddered. "A siege would be a horrible thing for my subjects."

"I have considered that. If the worst comes we will ask Suleiman for help."

"Suleiman? Suleiman?" She rose to her feet and drew herself to her full height. "You would call upon an infidel who denies the truth of Jesus Christ to defend a Christian country against a Christian ruler?"

"When your country's fate is at stake," he shrugged, "you do what you must."

"Your country's fate?" Isabella stabbed a finger at Martinuzzi. Don't you mean *your* fate, Bishop? You sit here in Buda gnawing at your plots and hatching your schemes. But we both know if Ferdinand assumes the throne, you will hang.

"I know that, Your Majesty."

"But are you also aware that if Suleiman conquers us, he will cut off your head, for he knows as I do, that you wish the rule of Hungary for yourself?"

"Perhaps, Your Majesty, perhaps." He shrugged. "In the meantime, I am the guardian of your child, and I am the power here, as you well know."

"And if I do not do as you wish?"

"I will have you arrested."

"At last you make yourself clear. No more veils, eh, Bishop," Isabella sank back into her chair. There was a long silence and then she looked up at him, her eyes narrowed. "Since there are no more veils between us, Bishop, I will tell you what I think. I have despised you since the day I met you. You are a wicked man. I will stay, but only to protect my country and my son from your schemes."

The priest bowed and smirked. "A wise choice, Your Majesty. A wise choice."

TURMOIL FILLED the next few months. In September 1540, Ferdinand of Austria invaded Hungary to claim the throne as accorded in his treaty with King John. Isabella watched from her castle windows as the Austrian army surrounded Buda and placed it under siege, but as Martinuzzi had predicted, the incompetence of his commanders turned the siege into a fiasco. Ferdinand withdrew.

But in May 1541, the armies of Austria again surrounded Buda. Isabella was at breakfast in her private chambers one morning during the second week of the siege. Outside, the trees were bursting into bloom and birds sang at her windows, but her mood was dark for she was contemplating the fate of her city and her people. There was a knock at her door and a servant announced that Martinuzzi was outside seeking an audience.

Isabella summoned him and the bishop entered the room. He seemed in good spirits.

Isabella looked at her breakfast with disgust for the man soured her stomach. "What is it, Bishop? Since you have interrupted my breakfast, it must be important."

The priest flushed but kept his face calm. "I bring good news, Your Majesty. Suleiman's armies are coming to lift the siege."

Isabella sighed. "Suleiman does not do us such a great favor for nothing, Bishop. What is the price?"

The priest twisted his hands. "Hungary will become a vassal state to the Ottoman Empire and Suleiman will convert most of Hungary to *pashaliks*, provinces governed by Turkish pashas."

Isabella rose from her seat as anger filled her heart. "You traitorous dog. May God strike you down where you stand."

Martinuzzi paled at the curse but continued. "It was that or surrender to Ferdinand. It is a steep price to pay, but there is good news. Suleiman has given Transylvania and the provinces east of the Tisza River to John Sigismund and you. From there you can govern free Hungary in your son's name, awaiting the day when he will be old enough to challenge Ferdinand and Suleiman in his own right—"

"—And challenge you and your schemes. Get out of my sight."

The Bishop bowed and beat a hasty retreat.

It was a cold winter's night in 1548 in the royal residence in Cluj, Transylvania, seven years later. Isabella and her son had left Buda when the Turks conquered Buda and now reigned at the whim of Suleiman in Transylvania. Isabella sat by the fire in the study with John, teaching her son about diplomacy.

"What is diplomacy, Mama?" John Sigismund asked.

Isabella smiled at her eight-year-old son's serious expression. "Diplomacy is the art of keeping the dogs away until you can find a big enough stick."

His brown eyes widened. "Keep the dogs away?"

"Just a silly way of explaining it." She chuckled. "All over the world, large countries like Austria and the Ottoman Empire surround smaller countries like Hungary. The large countries are the dogs—they want to gobble up the small countries. So, the leader of a small country, the king—"

"Like me, Mama?"

"Yes, John, like you." She patted his head. "The king of the small country must learn to say and do things that make the large country think it is not such a good idea to gobble him up. He must learn to make the large country think he is a friend that needs support. In the meantime, the king of the small country is looking for a big stick to drive the dog, the big country, away. That stick might be a large army or another country with a large army."

"You mean, like the way Suleiman helps us keep Ferdinand from taking our country away from us."

"Yes, my brilliant son, like that. The king must also help all the different people inside his country get along, including those with different religions. That is also diplomacy."

"That must be hard, Mama."

"It is one of the hardest things to learn, John."

Isabella watched her son's face grow serious as John thought about what his mother had said. Then he looked up at her. "One day I was walking with Maria, and I saw two boys yelling at each other. I think one was a Catholic and one was a Protestant." John knit his brows and frowned.

"They were calling each other names. I told them to stop. One of them told me to shut up and leave them alone. I told them I was the king, and I commanded it. They did not believe me until I showed them my signet." He held up his hand to display his royal signet ring. "And Maria told them I was telling the truth, so they both bowed and stopped fighting. Then I told them to shake hands. They did not like it, but they did what I asked. I continued on my walk, and when I looked back, they were sitting on a wall, talking."

"I am so proud of you, John." She took his hands. "You used your God-given kingly influence, your power to help those boys do the right thing. A king can use his power to make good happen in his country, or bad. You must always use your power for the good of your people. That's what I try to do as Queen."

"How do you decide what is for the good?"

"When you told those two boys to shake hands, they decided that maybe it was better to talk instead of fight. As Queen, I've found that convincing people to talk, to negotiate, to discuss their differences is a good thing. Most people desire peace. A strong king has the power to bring and maintain peace by protecting his people from harm and helping them to do the right thing. People feel safe when they know someone is protecting them."

Isabella caught her breath and looked away. Then she lowered her head.

John Sigismund came around and took her hand. "Mama? You are crying. Why?"

Isabella looked at her beautiful son.

So alike and yet so different...

She wiped the tears from her face. "Our talk reminded me of a young man I once knew who was very strong. He protected me, and when I was with him, I always felt safe."

"Who was he, Mama?"

Isabella lifted her son up on her lap and held him close. She closed her eyes and saw a little cottage in the woods of Germany, a gentle old pastor beaming as she pronounced her vows, the face of old Magda holding a dark-haired infant up for her to see and the handsome face of her beloved...

"Just a friend from a long time ago," she whispered.

CHAPTER 34: THE EDICT

1557

"*O*h, that man!" Isabella crumpled the letter, threw it on the floor, and walked to the window. She muttered a Hungarian swear word. There was a sound behind her and she turned as Maria came into the room. "What man, my queen?"

"Martinuzzi. As if I don't have enough to worry about. The nobles have never sent enough money and our castle is in a ruinous state. People war with each other over religion. And because of Martinuzzi's constant scheming, I have to appease the Ottomans to keep Suleiman from taking over the rest of Hungary, including Transylvania. One day Suleiman will have that traitor's head." She threw up her hands.

"So what has the bishop done now?" Maria asked.

"Suleiman's war against Persia occupies him, and so Martinuzzi has entered secret negotiations with Ferdinand to unite Hungary and defend it against the Turks. If he succeeds and Ferdinand can defeat Suleiman, that means Martinuzzi will control all of Hungary, Transylvania included, as Ferdinand's puppet. Oh, the unbridled ambition of that man."

"What does it mean for us, Your Majesty?"

"If they conclude a treaty, it means we must leave Transylvania. Martinuzzi offers me some small provinces in Silesia and promises my son will marry one of Ferdinand's daughters. Hungary will suffer if he does. It also means a cardinal's hat for Martinuzzi." She bent and picked up the letter and smoothed it on the desk. "It seems I am Queen in name only."

Isabella read the letter again and then slammed her fist on her desk. "No! We will not surrender to Ferdinand after all these years of fighting him off. I will defend my rights and take up arms and I will ask my brother, Sigismund, for help. Bring me a pen and paper, Maria."

～

AFTER DAYS of traveling across Transylvania, Isabella's procession stopped near Meszes, on Silesia's border. She and John climbed out of their carriage to stretch their legs beneath the shade of magnificent oak trees while their retinue prepared the midday meal. It was spring in Transylvania, and the trees were turning green with new growth. The air was fresh, and the horses were sleek and fat from the new grass along the way. She turned to look at the road they'd just traveled. They were leaving Transylvania, forever, she thought.

Georg Keglevic, her army commander, came alongside her. He patted John's shoulder. "How's our little soldier faring on this long trip?"

John smiled up at him. "I like it when we get out and I can run." With that, he took off, zigzagging through the trees.

"I've said it before…" Isabella touched Georg's shoulder. "I so appreciate you taking John under your wing. He idolizes you."

"It is my honor." He bowed. "John Sigismund is a wonderful boy, Your Majesty."

Georg turned serious. "I regret you must make this difficult journey."

"I should never have counted on my brother." Isabella sighed.

"He is as deceptive as my father was. All the while I was waiting for his help against Martinuzzi and Ferdinand, he was negotiating his own secret treaty with Ferdinand. The only good thing is that Ferdinand had Martinuzzi assassinated after he tried to cheat the Hapsburgs by betraying them and negotiating behind their backs with Suleiman. And now, my beloved Transylvania has fallen to Suleiman."

The commander bowed. "I am sorry, Your Majesty. The Ottomans outnumbered us. If Sigismund had sent help…"

"Do not trouble yourself, Georg." She lifted her palms to the heavens. "*Sic fata Volunt*—it is the will of fate." Extending a hand, she said, "Give me your knife."

His brow furrowed. "Your Majesty?"

She laughed. "Do not worry; I will not kill myself."

He pulled the knife from its case and gave it to her.

With a few deft strokes, she carved *Sic fata Volunt* into the nearest oak tree. "Maybe someone who is wondering why God is giving them troubles will read this, accept their circumstances, and get on with their life."

"Interesting concept, Your Majesty."

John darted around a tree and ran to them. "Mama, the food is ready. Time to eat!"

She laughed. "Come, Georg, let's enjoy a good meal, forget the past and move ahead. The seat of our banishment, the magnificent town of Opole awaits us."

To Isabella's deep disappointment, the house where they were to live in Opole was unsuitable for habitation, and her brother, Sigismund, neglected to send the promised finances to repair it. After a few months in rented quarters, her only option for herself, her son and her entourage was to seek refuge with her brother, who, upon the death of her father, was now King of Poland.

Thanks to early rains, the road to Krakow was a slippery, muddy, morass. The horses labored hard and made slow progress. Staring through the rain-streaked window of the carriage, she couldn't help questioning God's providence. Would she live the rest of her days in Krakow? Did God have something for her, or had he abandoned her to a monotonous fate as an unwelcome guest in her brother's castle.

John, who'd been napping on her lap, sat up and rubbed his eyes. "Where are we going, Mama?"

"To Krakow, where we will live with your uncle, the King of Poland."

He looked past her at the rain-drizzled window. "I wish we were back in Transylvania, Mama."

"Me, too, John."

"What will we do in Krakow?"

"We will live in the castle where I grew up." She smiled and tried her best to sound cheerful. "I will show you the best hiding places for when you play hide-and-seek, and the beautiful chapel my father built. We will do all the fun things I did when I was a girl."

When I was a girl. Oh, Johan...

ISABELLA SPENT the next five years in Krakow. John Sigismund grew into a handsome sixteen-year-old, but the enforced idleness galled Isabella. Returning to Wawel Castle was a mixed blessing for Isabella. Her father was dead, so she did not have to deal with him, but her mother was still alive and as self-centered as ever. They seldom talked, but when they did, Bona's discourse was a litany of complaints. She did not exhibit interest in Isabella's life or John's and was even less inclined to act as a grandmother than she was to mothering.

One day, in early spring, as Isabella sat at tea with her mother, Bona surprised her with an announcement. "Isabella, I have decided something." She paused... "I will return to Italy soon."

Isabella tilted her head. "Mother?"

"Your brother's wife has made it clear she considers me excess baggage." Bona lowered her voice. "The worst part is she has not given my son an heir. I fear Sigismund will be the last of our dynasty. When he dies, who knows what will happen to Poland. I think she is also afraid that if her husband dies, your son will become King in his place." She leaned close. "I know the danger, but if I were you, I would return to Hungary, where your son may one day take the throne." Displaying a rare hint of concern, she added, "Knowing the ambition of your sister-in-law I think you will be more welcome there than here."

Later that day, Isabella wandered to the stables. The smell of the pace—the liniment, the sweet grain, and the fresh hay— filled her senses as it had in days past and filled her heart with memories of Johan... She came to the stall that once held Al-Buraq but it was empty and disused.

We sat here and talked... this is where you rejected me... and this is where you first kissed me. Oh, Johan...

She smiled at the memory of a young princess running through these hallways and crashing into a filthy stable boy who splattered her dress with manure. "You were so proud, Johan," she whispered. "I was a princess, and you were a commoner, but you carried yourself like a conqueror." She chuckled. "And conquer you did, for from that moment on, I was your prisoner."

She sank down on the bench where the two of them had once passed the time in sweet communion. "Now my world is full of uncertainty," she murmured. "When you loved me, even though we faced danger every day, life had no uncertainties, for your love and my faith held me safe. Now I have nothing to hold to. Even my faith seems like a distant memory. How I need your counsel."

As she sat in the silence of the empty stable, she remembered the words Johan spoke the day they sat before the gates of Münster and decided what they would make of their lives.

You and I must decide who we are, Isabella. We can slink off into the woods and find a place where no one will know us. There we could live out our lives pretending we believe nothing. We could watch while the authorities murder true believers in front of us and never say a word. Or we can take a stand for what we believe and stop here. No more running, no more fear. And when the day comes, we will stand before our Lord and hear him say, 'Well done, good and faithful servant.' What good is our faith if we do not stand for it?

"Yes, Johan, I remember. And I agree. What good is our faith if we do not stand for it?"

More words came slipping out of the past.

You are an amazement, Bella. When I first met you, I thought you were a spoiled young girl with not one practical thought in your head. But I was wrong. You are deep, Bella, as deep as the ocean. A simple man like me could never hope to win the love of a girl... of a woman such as you, and yet you have given me your heart. I am blessed...

That was the same day she'd spoken those words she now knew were prophetic. *If anyone ever tries to harm you or our child, I will give my life before I would let that happen.* She had given herself to save her loved ones, but what now? "Oh, Johan, what am I to do?"

A picture came to her—Menno Simons sitting at his desk and looking up at her with his gentle smile.

We have a call upon us, Bella. Not by accident did you and Johan and Abel come into my life. Your sojourn with me has been a time where my thoughts became clarified and the path of my journey opened before me. Each of us will take something from our friendship

*that God will use for the extension and purification of his kingdom. I
see the call on all our lives, but I shrink from it for I fear following this
call means the end of our fellowship...*

"You were right, Menno," she ran her finger along the rough
wood of the bench. "Our fellowship ended, but have I been true
to the call? What can I do to glorify God and extend his kingdom? I may be the sister of a king, but inside I am just Bella, a
simple girl lacking wisdom or piety. Show me what I can do,
God, for your kingdom."

As though Menno was sitting beside her, his words came
to her.

*And this is the voice of Christ, ye have heard it hath been said, an
eye for an eye, and a tooth for a tooth. But I say unto you, that ye
resist not evil, but whosoever shall smite thee on thy right cheek, turn
to him the other.*

She thought of the years behind her, the death and tragedy
stemming from people's intolerance toward one another. The
streets of Münster had run with the blood of Anabaptists and
Catholics alike as they fought over the simple issue of child
baptism. She remembered the blackened ruins of Bloemkamp
and the dying words of Pieter Simons.

*But I say unto you, love your enemies, bless them that curse you,
do good to them that hate you, and pray for them which persecute
you.*

"Oh, God," she whispered. "The hearts of people who love
their own ideas more than they love your Word are the source
of unrest in this world. A strong ruler could use the power of
the throne to change the way people treat each other."

She stood and paced. "In Poland, I am not a ruler. I live in
Wawel Palace as a guest, at the whim of my brother. I must
return to Hungary, where I might regain the authority to help
this wicked world, to make people stop fighting over religion."
A great clarity came into Isabella's mind and she saw what she
must do. She raised her hands to God. "I have not heard your

voice for many years. Are you speaking now? If you are, then please open a door for me, for I must go home."

When she returned to her rooms, there was a letter from Transylvania waiting. She tore it open. Melchior Balassa, a leader in the Transylvania Diet, had signed it.

To Her Sublime Majesty, *Isabella of Hungary,*

Emperor Suleiman has urged the members of the Diet to request that John Sigismund Zápolya and you, Isabella, return to Transylvania to rule Free Hungary. If you do so, the Diet will grant you full regency as Queen Mother until John Sigismund Zápolya comes of age.

Melchior Balassa

When Isabella read the message, she looked to heaven and spoke her thanks. "Oh my Father, you have opened the way. I know now what I am to do."

A few days later, Isabella returned to Hungary with her mother. As she traveled, her thoughts about tolerance and destroying the divisions between the different faiths crystallized in her mind. She sent a messenger ahead of her to Suleiman and in response, the Turk sent Ottoman troops to escort her into Cluj where they restored her to her castle. Suleiman also proclaimed that Isabella would have free rein to rule until John became King if she would continue Hungary's alliance with the Ottomans and reject Ferdinand's scheming.

When Isabella arrived in Cluj, she called all her servants about her. "The nobles of Transylvania have given me a five-year regency on behalf of John Sigismund, but he will be King long before that. In the meantime, God has given me a great work—a work I believe will glorify him and help extend his Kingdom. I will need the help and patience of every one of you. Religious differences divide our country and I believe God is leading me to help change that. Will you help me in this?" Each of her servants came to her, kissed her ring and knelt. "I will help." "I will help." "I will help."

ISABELLA PUT down her pen just as her servant, Angyalka, entered her study with a pot of tea. "Your Majesty," Angyalka said, "you must drink this. It will help you sleep. The midnight bell just tolled."

"In a bit, Angyalka. Right now I need you to please call Maria. I have something important to tell her."

"Yes, Your Majesty."

In a few moments, Maria came in, rubbing the sleep from her eyes.

"Yes, Your Majesty?"

Isabella held up the document. "I finished it, Maria."

Maria came to Isabella. "The edict, Your Majesty?"

"Yes." Isabella sighed and stretched. "I am not a great writer, but perhaps in this I communicated my desire for tolerance."

"You have worked on that document for months. It has taken its toll on you. You are exhausted and you are not well."

"Yes, Maria, but God has given me the strength to complete the work. With this edict, I declare religious freedom for the largest denominations in Free Hungary—Catholics, Lutherans, Calvinists and Unitarians. It is not all-encompassing, but it is a beginning."

"An edict of toleration guaranteeing religious freedom— Hungary has never had such a thing before, Your Majesty. I offer my congratulations, for your wise words will prevent many wars."

"If the people accept my decree without too much resistance…" Isabella sat back, pushing her hair behind her ears away from her face. "Then I will strive to make Hungary a place where *all* religions, including Anabaptists, Jews and Muslims, are free from persecution." She smiled. "I hope that this edict glorifies God and that I can continue to glorify him in all I do for the rest of my time as Queen of this country. John will be King in a few months and then I can rest."

She stood, rubbing her neck and then dismissed Maria and Angyalka. "Leave me now. I need to pray over the edict before it is complete."

Angyalka protested. "But, Your Majesty, you are not well. I fear for you. You must take better care of yourself, Your Majesty."

"I will go to bed soon. Now leave me."

As Angyalka left, Maria turned and came back to the Queen.

"Menno Simons would be proud of you, Your Majesty," she whispered.

"Menno is a great man," Isabella replied. "The time Johan and I spent with him in Witmarsum, helping him transition from Catholic priest to Anabaptist pastor, were some of the most wonderful days of my life. This edict is just my little part of the great work he is doing. My contribution may end up on the back pages of history, but Menno's influence will live on through the centuries."

Maria kissed the Queen and withdrew, leaving Isabella alone, reading the edict.

ISABELLA GROANED and turned on the couch, awakened by a patter of rain rattling the windows. Outside, dark heralds of the unseasonal storm hid the moon. Distant lightning illuminated the room. An unearthly light touched her face and then faded as the gray predawn took victory over the indigo night. A long roll of thunder shook the window again, and she pulled her shawl tighter, a frown furrowing her brow.

The fire in the small stone fireplace had burned down, and the still-flickering coals cast dancing shadows. The mantle's lone occupant, a golden crucifix, glowed in the flickering light from the embers—like the flames on Münster's tower the night they escaped...

She sighed and turned away. The edict lay on the floor where it had fallen when she fell asleep. She reached down to retrieve it and a sharp pain shot through her arm. She groaned and picked up the document.

I must tell John... before I go...

CHAPTER 35: FAREWELL

1559

$\mathcal{K}$ing John Sigismund Zápolya sat next to his mother, holding her hand. He looked down at Isabella.

Isabella took her son's hand. "Are you shocked, my son?"

"No, Mother." John shook his head. "Yours is a wonderful story. I am just sorry you didn't tell me earlier. Why did you never see Johan again?"

Isabella sighed. "When your father made me swear, he made me swear before God. I held the oath as sacred even though he forced the marriage upon me and I had no choice."

"But after Father died, couldn't you have seen Johan again? Wasn't the oath completed? I would like to meet the man you loved."

"I swore I would never see him again for the rest of my life. And when you came, my world changed. Once I was part of a calling to help Menno Simons establish his work. When you were born and your father died a week later that calling changed. I was the mother of a future king, and the fate of Hungary was in my hands. I couldn't leave you, or my country. And so the years just seemed to slip away. And Johan and Abel were far away. At some point it seemed more like it had been just a dream." She lifted off the bed and violent coughing shook her body.

John stood and looked for Maria. "Mother, should I get someone?"

"Help me sit up, please." She coughed again. "And hand me my water."

John poured her a cup of water from a pitcher on the night-stand. She drank it and began again.

"As mother and guardian of the future King of Hungary, I could never reveal I married a commoner. The Hungarian Diet would not have voted to make you their king. Martinuzzi would have made a treaty with Ferdinand, and our country would now be part of Austria. I kept my life with Johan and Abel a secret to protect your future. But I always remained a follower of Menno, and Johan and Abel never left my heart."

John gripped his mother's hand. "What wonderful adventures you had, Mother. I'm jealous of Abel. I wish I knew my brother."

Isabella pointed to the golden crucifix that now stood near her bedside. "This crucifix has been with me all these years. Johan gave it to me. It was a family treasure, and Johan left it with me when we parted. He said he wanted me to remember that I was once a Hirschberg. He said his treasure would be the memory of the days we spent together. Like in heaven where neither moth nor rust doth corrupt, he would keep his memories in his heart and live for the day we would be together in the next life…"

John nodded. "For where your treasure is, there will your heart be."

"Yes, my son."

~

THAT AFTERNOON KING JOHN SUMMONED Dr. Biandrata. "Please, Doctor, have a seat." John motioned to the seat across from him in front of the wide hearth. "Can I call for a cup of tea for you?"

"No, thank you, Your Majesty." The doctor sat and folded his hands in his lap.

"I'll get right to the point, then. How long has my mother to live?"

"Since your return from Istanbul, she has rallied." Dr. Biandrata smiled. "I see a marked improvement. However, the long-term prognosis is not good." He paused. "I would like to give you better news, but I believe Queen Isabella has two months remaining."

John sighed and sat in silence for a moment. "Only two months?"

"Maybe a little more, I cannot be certain."

John thanked the doctor and walked him to the door. He instructed a servant to accompany him out of the castle and then returned to his desk. He sat for a long while thinking of the things his mother had shared with him. Then he took up a pen and paper and wrote a short letter.

After affixing his seal on the letter, he sent for Pastor Santa, a Protestant Reformist known to hold considerable influence throughout Hungary. The next morning Pastor Santa arrived at the castle and a servant ushered him into King John's sitting room.

When the servant had finished pouring the tea, John said, "Thank you for allowing me to interrupt your work." He took a sip of the tea. "Please, drink."

The pastor lifted his cup. "I am honored to do the king's bidding."

"I have an unusual request."

Santa drank the tea and then set the cup down. "What does Your Majesty wish of me?"

"I wish to discover the whereabouts of a man named Menno Simons."

"Simons!" Santa stiffened. "Your Majesty does not think I would know such a man…"

"Do not worry." The king smiled at the pastor's discomfort. "I wish to find him for personal reasons only. I've heard you have connections throughout the European Protestant movement. Surely you can tell me where to find him."

Santa eyed him warily for a moment. Then he spoke. "A German clergyman told me some time ago the authorities granted Simons safe conduct to Wüstenfelde. As far as I know that is where he is now living and teaching."

"Good." John smiled. "Thank you, Pastor. You have been of great service to me. That is all I require of you at this moment."

After Santa left, John rolled a map of Europe out on a long table beneath a big window and studied it for several minutes before calling for his most trusted messenger. When the man came, John handed him the letter. "Take ten soldiers from my personal guard plus two extra horses and ride to this city." He traced the route from Cluj to Wüstenfelde on the map. "Go to the authorities in this town. Ask if Menno Simons or Johan or Abel Hirschberg live there. If Simons is there and Hirschberg is not with him, then ask Simons if he knows where Hirschberg is. You must find Johan Hirschberg. It is imperative you get this letter to him.

"When you do, wait until you receive an answer. If they are in Wüstenfelde, I expect Johan Hirschberg and his son to return to Cluj with you. Make all haste, for this is a matter of life and death. Leave as soon as preparations are complete."

The messenger looked at the map and checked the distance. "I can leave at daylight and we will make it there in ten days of hard riding. If the men you are sending for can ride…"

"I understand that Hirschberg is a master of horses and assume his son can ride."

"Good, Your Majesty. If I find him, we should return before the month is out."

"Go, and Godspeed."

~

In a small house in Wüstenfelde, Germany, Johan Hirschberg sat before a small fire, listening to Menno and catching up on the day's events as Menno's wife put food on the table. She called them, and they rose and went to the table. Johan smiled at the simple but hearty meal spread before them. "It looks wonderful, as usual, Gertrude."

Gertrude beamed. "Thank you, Johan. I do my best to please you men." The three sat together as Johan blessed the food. As they ate, Johan looked over at the happy couple.

"Gertrude has been a blessing to you."

Johan paused, remembering the days when his young wife brought the fresh bread and cheese, worked in the garden, milked the cow...

"You are thinking of Isabella, my friend."

Johan blinked and then smiled at Menno. "Yes, Menno. I was thinking of Isabella. But now I am also thinking of Abel for he is late to supper."

Just then they heard horses coming up the lane to the house. The door opened and a young man came into the room. He was tall and handsome, with long dark hair and large piercing blue eyes. Johan smiled at his son. "Hello, Abel, who is here?"

"I am sorry to be late, Papa, but I have just come from the Mayor." Abel handed his father an envelope. "There is a messenger outside who says he is on an urgent mission. He had this for you."

Johan looked at the envelope. It had the seal of the Royal House of Hungary. He looked at Menno. "It is from Hungary, Menno."

Menno rose. "Isabella?"

Johan tore the envelope open. Inside was a brief letter written in Polish. Before reading it, Johan looked at the bottom. The signature was that of John Sigismund Zápolya, King of Hungary. He stared at it, his heart pounding.

To JOHAN HIRSCHBERG,

My mother, Queen Isabella of Hungary, is ill. The doctors say she has only two months to live. She recently told me about you, about her undying love for you, and my brother, Abel. She did not ask to see you, for she is keeping the vow she made before God when my father separated you, but if you receive this letter, I urge you to come at once to Cluj, in Transylvania. I have sent members of my bodyguard to escort you. I wish for you to see her before she dies, and I want to meet my brother.

John Sigismund Zápolya

ABEL CAME and stood behind his father looking at the letter. "Who is it from, Papa?"

"Your brother."

Abel gasped. "My brother?"

"Yes, your brother, the King of Hungary." Johan handed the letter to Menno, who showed it to his wife.

"My brother is a king?"

"Yes."

"Why did you not tell me?"

"I did not know it myself, for I had no contact with your mother in all these years. But that is not important."

He took the letter back from Menno.

"Your mother is dying. Your brother has requested, no

—*beseeched*, that we come to Hungary to see her before she passes."

Abel smiled. "When do we leave?"

～

KING JOHN LOOKED down at his mother as she lay in her bed. Her breathing was shallow and irregular. Dr. Biandrata sat by the bed. "How much time, Doctor?"

"A day, a few days…" he shrugged, "but soon."

John rose and went out. He found his servant. "Any word from Germany?"

"Not yet, Your Majesty.

"I hope they come soon."

～

ISABELLA WAS SITTING on a Witmarsum knoll on a cool spring morning just before dawn, facing the east. The first golden edge of the sun was rising over the hills, spreading a golden glow that touched the clouds. Above the gold, pale rose faded into deep blue and then into the indigo of the night sky. A songbird in a nearby birch began its morning praise. She felt a light touch on her shoulder. Without turning, she spoke. "Johan."

"Yes, my beloved?"

"Am I in heaven?"

"No, my dearest, you are still here with us."

"It seems like heaven," she whispered, "for everything I love is about me—you, Abel, the fields of Witmarsum, Menno… And the sun's golden rays warm me, for I have been cold of late and frightened."

"It is spring, my dearest, and life is returning to the fields. You are safe now, for I am with you and God is with you."

Isabella opened her eyes. A face was close to hers, a familiar handsome face with piercing blue eyes and a kind smile.

"Johan? Is it you?" Her lips trembled.

"Yes, my beloved, we are here."

"We?" She glanced around.

"Abel and I."

Another face came before her clouded sight—a young, strong face and a hand touched hers. She gasped. "Oh, Abel, my son, my son." She reached out her hands.

Her son encircled her with his arms and held her. "Yes, Mama, I am here."

She felt another hand touch her face and heard John Sigismund's voice. "I am here, too, Mother."

Abel whispered in her ear. "John sent for us. We came as soon as we could."

She looked up from her sons into the face of her beloved, who stood by the bed. "Johan, I was dreaming you were with me and we were in Witmarsum. We were peaceful once again, and the cares of the world were no longer on my shoulders. Oh, Johan." Her sons stood and John nodded to Johan, who knelt by the bed.

Her arms slipped around his shoulders and then he was holding her. She could feel the strength and love in his embrace and she hid her head in his shoulder. Her heart pounded, and she felt tears running down her cheeks.

"All this time, I have been with Menno, Bella." He brushed her hair from her forehead. "He has been teaching and preaching all over Holland and Germany. Many, many people know Christ because of Menno."

"Oh, my faithful one." She tried to blink the tears away, but they filled her eyes.. "Have you, did you… ever marry again?"

"No, little one." He chuckled. "You were more wife than I ever needed." Then he whispered in her ear. "There never has been nor ever will be anyone else for me, Bella. You are my only true love. You are my treasure."

She spoke to John, who was standing beside Abel. "John, in my drawer... the small box, please."

John went to the drawer, retrieved the jeweled box and gave it to his mother, who handed it to Johan.

"Open it, my love."

Johan opened the small box. Inside were two round objects covered with a cracked candy coating.

Johan's mouth dropped open in amazement. "The comfits! The candy-covered cherries I found for you in Münster. You kept them all these years?"

Isabella touched his cheek. "To remind me how God blessed me with a husband like you. I have never forgotten."

She opened her eyes wide and smiled at the three men at her bedside. "How much God loves me—to send those I love most to be with me as I go." She reached up and took John's hand. "John, you will be a great king. You are a Zápolya but you are also a Jagiellon—the son of two great houses. It has honored me to rule in your stead, but now Hungary's reins are in your capable hands. Rule well and use what I taught you."

Then she drew Abel down and kissed his cheek. "Abel, my firstborn... without a doubt, your father has raised you to be a good man. Become acquainted with your brother, for in your old age, you will need one another." She released him, and he stood.

"Johan..."

John touched Abel's arm, and the two brothers left the room.

Johan sat next to her on the bed.

Isabella touched his face. She could feel the tears.

"Take me to the window, Johan, so I can see the sun."

His strong arms about her, he lifted her and carried her to the window.

"Isabella..." His voice broke.

She held him tight, her cheek on his shoulder. The sun was just coming over the horizon. She could see its golden rays reaching up and touching the purple clouds of dawn, burnishing them with golden and rose hues, and then she was going toward the light, his voice in her ear.

"This way, Isabella. Lift your feet, run like the wind. I am with you, I am always with you…"

The End.

EPILOGUE

$\mathcal{I}$n an Amish cemetery outside Apple Creek, Ohio, the writer walked along the row of graves. The names were like a litany, a roll call of these plain people who had entered his life long ago and now seemed like family—Hannah Hershberger, Jerusha Springer, Reuben Springer, Jonathan Hershberger, and now, at last, Jenny Hershberger.

Hearing a light step behind him, he turned. A lovely Amish woman stood there, dark auburn hair tight beneath her kappe, but with a stray lock escaping to challenge the world, so like her mother. Beside the woman stood a tall, handsome, blonde man who reached out to take his hand.

"Daniel, Rachel," the writer exclaimed. "So good to see you again. I came as soon as I heard."

Daniel nodded and Rachel patted his arm. "And it is good to see you, my friend."

"She passed a few weeks ago." Rachel nodded at the grave. "Her last words were of Jonathan, but she mentioned you, for she read the final book. When she finished, she said, 'Now, at last, I have completed my work. With the help of my friend, I have told my family's history through the eyes of the Hershberger women. Now, I can go.'"

Rachel brushed away a tear. "She so appreciated your help. When she knew she could not publish her books on her own, she wondered how she would tell the stories that burned inside her. Then *du Lieber Gott* sent you to her. As she saw the books unfold under your care, she knew you were the perfect one to write them. Now her journey is over. I thank you on behalf of my family for recording our chronicles with such a skillful hand."

His looked down at Jenny's grave, remembering his visits to her through the years. He remembered the way she smiled, how her kappe was always slightly askew, and her rebellious curls that fought to escape at the slightest breeze.

Rachel reached into her pocket and pulled out an envelope. "She asked me to give this to you."

He thanked her and opened it. Inside was a letter written in Jenny's beautiful script.

My Friend,

I may not see you again, and so I write to you this last time. Thank you for being part of my life and sharing all that has made me who I am. Thank you for telling the story of Isabella. The story would not be complete without me adding that seven years after she died, her son, King John Sigismund, passed the Edict of Torda, which granted religious freedom to every faith in Hungary.

And with the telling of Isabella's story, my story ends, too. As I write this, my memories of Apple Creek and Paradise are like early morning dreams—bits and pieces that emerge into sharp focus for just a moment and then fade to the dark edges of sleep. I see my mother, sitting at her quilting frame, her lovely brow knit in concentration as she works the magic of her gift. I feel her strong heart beating close to mine, reminding me once again that she was my place of safety and strength.

And there is my father, Reuben, sitting in his chair before the fire, the Bible in his strong hands, his face stern as he reads. Then he looks up at me and I see a smile behind his beautiful blue eyes. I remember Grossmüdder Rachel and my Englischer Grandfather Robert, snapshots in an album, yet always a part of me and who I am.

And Jonathan—I see my Jonathan as he was the day I met him— strong, handsome, but so lost. Yet, somehow, the hand of the Lord was guiding him even then, and he brought me Jonathan as the most precious gift I have ever received. From Jonathan came my Rachel, my daughter, a bright ray of sunshine amid the trials of this life.

Before me in my mind's eye is the land, the land of my youth, the land of my marriage, the land of my old age, rolling away to the horizon, fertile and verdant. My people walk upon this land, their labor and love wrenching life from the soil. The land and the plain people, my family and my faith become one stream in my dreams—flowing from the distant past into a future yet unseen. These are my Apple Creek Dreams and my Paradise Chronicles.

Now it is time for you to tell your stories, the ones in your heart. When you do, keep spreading God's message of hope. And if you find a place for me in those stories, remember me well.

Goodbye,

Jenny

THE RAYS of the setting sun reached out to him in a golden embrace. The writer stood by the grave, head bowed. Feeling something run down his cheeks, he reached to wipe it away. Tears? For a moment, they surprised him—but then... He smiled and shook his head. No, not at all surprised...

ABOUT THE AUTHOR

Patrick E. Craig is both a Traditionally Published and Indie author. In 2013, Harvest House Publishers published his *Apple Creek Dreams* series—*A Quilt For Jenna, The Road Home* and *Jenny's Choice*. His current series is *The Paradise Chronicles* and the first book, *The Amish Heiress* remained on the Amazon Top 100 best sellers list for seven months. *The Amish Princess* was followed by *The Mennonite Queen*. In 2017 Harlequin purchased the Amish Heiress for their Walmart Amish series. In 2019 Elk Lake Publishing contracted to publish Patrick's *The Adventures of Punkin an Boo* series and the first book, *The Mystery of Ghost Dancer Ranch* was published in September, 2019. The second book, *The Lost Coast,* will come out in February 2020. Patrick also signed with Elk Lake to publish and anthology of Amish stories by the men who write Amish fiction—*The Amish Menorah and Other Stories—coming in 2020.* Patrick and Murray Pura will also publish their new book, *Far On The Ringing Plains,*

in 2020. Patrick and his wife, Judy, make their home in Idaho. His website can be found at https://www.patrickecraig.com

facebook.com/PatrickECraig

twitter.com/PatrickECraig

instagram.com/patricke.craig

P&J PUBLISHING

BOOKS BY PATRICK E. CRAIG

PUBLISHING

~

Apple Creek Dreams
A Quilt for Jenna
The Road Home
Jenny's Choice

~

The Paradise Chronicles
The Amish Heiress

The Amish Princess
The Mennonite Queen

~

The Adventures of Punkin & Boo
The Mystery of Ghost Dancer Ranch
The Lost Coast

~

The Islands Series by Murray Pura and
Patrick E. Craig
Far on The Ringing Plains
The Scepter and the Isle
Men Who Strove With Gods

MORE BOOKS BY PATRICK E. CRAIG

THE ADVENTURES OF PUNKIN AND BOO SERIES

**Mysteries for kids and young adults
in the tradition of the Hardy Boys and Nancy Drew**

Book 1—The Mystery of Ghost Dancer Ranch

The Mystery of Ghost Dancer Ranch is the gripping story of two teenage cousins who are thrown together for the summer at their grandparents' ranch in California. While exploring the old ranch, the girls stumble upon a mystery that involves desperate crooks, the ghost of a long-dead Sioux war chief, a young American Indian man on a mission to save his tribe, and secret tunnels and caves left over from an old Spanish mission. Throw in a guardian angel who protects the girls from some evil spirits that want to bring the story to a bad end, and you have **The Mystery of Ghost Dancer Ranch**, the first in a series of faith-filled mystery adventures for kids, featuring Punkin and Boo. Published by Elk lake Publishing.

The Mystery of Ghost Dancer Ranch Amazon

Book 2—The Lost Coast —Coming February 2020!
A family trip turns into a deadly adventure when Punkin and Boo uncover the operations of a ruthless gang of marijuana smugglers. When the gang discovers that Boo's dad is there to buy land for a resort, they kidnap the girls' families to keep them from discovering the gang's secret pot gardens. With the help of an undercover DEA agent, the girls escape into the untamed Sinkyone Wilderness on the wild Lost Coast of northern California. They face much danger as they seek to elude the gang, find their parents, and bring the criminals to justice. Pursued by a desperate gangster known only as "El

Fuente", and some very evil fallen angels, the girls discover anew the reality of God's protecting hand over them, and the wonder of lost souls coming to know their Savior. They also receive unexpected help from some mysterious treasure hunters and their old friend Jack Wilson, as they solve the mystery of **The Lost Coast**.

FAR ON THE RINGING PLAINS

MURRAY PURA &
PATRICK E. CRAIG

NEW FROM MURRAY PURA AND PATRICK E. CRAIG

A great new WW II adventure from the pens of Murray Pura and Patrick E. Craig. Coming in 2020

Far On The Ringing Plains—Book 1 in the Islands Series

Three men of the Mennonite faith: Two who swore to save their country and another who swore to save lives—facing the horrors of war on tropical islands in the Pacific, dealing with demands upon their courage unimaginable back home, never forgetting those they loved, never forgetting their duty, never forgetting they had each other's backs, never forgetting the meaning of sacrifice—never forgetting that love was still possible in a world torn by conflict and suffering, that men and women who had feelings for each other could always find one another again, that the possibility of true love between a man and a woman was one of the reasons they faced death every day.

A great war story with a Christian view—this book is not for the faint of heart. Desperate men facing desperate battles, hand to hand combat, bombardment, death and disease in the jungles of Guadalcanal.

COMING IN 2020—LOOK FOR IT!
The Islands Series
Far On The Ringing Plains
The Scepter and the Isle
Men Who Strove With Gods

THE AMISH PLUS BOOK CLUB

Made in the USA
Middletown, DE
24 March 2024

52003441R00197